SIX SWEETS UNDER

SIX SWEETS UNDER

Sarah Fox

BERKLEY PRIME CRIME
New York

BERKLEY PRIME CRIME
Published by Berkley
An imprint of Penguin Random House LLC
penguinrandomhouse.com

ISBN: 9780593546611

First Edition: February 2023

Printed in the United States of America
1 3 5 7 9 10 8 6 4 2

Book design by George Towne

For Nazzy, Fergus, and Orion

Chapter One

"BINX, I HAVE A FEELING WE'RE NOT IN HOLLYWOOD anymore."

I stood on the front step of my adorable stone cottage, cradling a mug of chai tea in my hands as I took in the sight before me. Just beyond the path that wound its way past my cottage, the morning sunshine glinted off the water of the canal.

"Of course, you were never actually in Hollywood," I added, glancing down at Binx, my black cat. "But I was, and this place is about as different as it gets."

If I'd seen this view while I was living in Los Angeles, I would have pegged it as a film set. The grass was a vivid green and my two-story stone cottage, like those of my neighbors, looked as though it had been plucked from the pages of a fairy tale. Many of the bridges that spanned the network of canals were also made of stone, and not a car's engine could be heard. Aside from emergency vehicles and a few golf carts, the closest land vehicles could get to Larch Haven, Vermont, was the parking lot on the outskirts of town, and any motorized boats on the canals had to be what we called whisper boats, powered by a quiet, electric motor. That meant that here in the heart of the picturesque village, there was just the sweet twittering of birds in the trees and the gentle lapping of the water against the banks of the canal.

This was no set constructed for a movie, though. This was my beloved hometown. After graduating from college, I'd lived in Hollywood for seven years, but a few months ago I'd returned to Larch Haven, and during moments like this I didn't question that decision in the least.

As I stood there on my doorstep, soaking in the idyllic view, a gondola glided by, steered by its lone occupant, Oliver Nieminen, the owner of a local café. Oliver raised a hand in greeting as he passed by, and I waved back as I breathed in the scent of the summer flowers blooming in my window boxes, mingled together with the aroma rising from my mug of tea.

Smiling, I glanced down at Binx. His tail switched back and forth as he kept an eye out for any birds or squirrels that might dare set foot in his yard.

"Time for me to get to work. Come on, Binx."

After scanning the front lawn with his green eyes one last time, Binx preceded me into the cottage, heading straight for the kitchen at the back. I followed and found my gray tabby, Truffles, sprawled in a patch of sunlight on the floor. She raised her head and watched me as I headed into the small laundry room off of the kitchen. There, I unlocked the kitty door that gave Truffles and Binx access to their catio, an outdoor enclosure I'd built for them with the help of my grandfather, Pops. The cats recognized the sound of the door being unlatched and zoomed into the laundry room. Binx came around the corner so fast he skidded across the tiles, making me laugh.

I scooped both cats into my arms before they could slip outside to their catio, giving each one a cuddle and a kiss on the head before releasing them. After moving back to Larch

Haven, I'd adopted the cats from the local animal shelter, and now I couldn't imagine my life without them. They were so sweet and loving, and they made me laugh on a daily basis.

"See you later!" I called to Binx and Truffles as they disappeared through the flap.

I made sure that the cats' water dishes were full, and then I left through the front door, locking it behind me. Some residents of Larch Haven didn't bother with locking their doors, but after spending seven years in Los Angeles, it was something I did automatically.

Since I wasn't carrying anything that didn't fit in my pockets, I bypassed the small boathouse where I kept my flat-bottom Jon boat moored and struck off along the paved walkway that followed the edge of the canal. The summer sun was already warm on my face and arms, despite the early hour, and I spotted a few other early risers out and about. A middle-aged couple walked a golden retriever on the other side of the canal and a young woman jogged past me with a cheery, "Good morning!"

My cottage was nestled on a small island in a residential part of town, where emerald-green lawns and colorful flower gardens surrounded the charming homes, all of which were either stone or timber-frame cottages. More than once I'd overheard tourists say how Larch Haven looked like a cross between Venice, Italy, and a quaint English village. I'd described it that way myself when telling my friends in Los Angeles about my hometown.

By the time I crossed a couple of bridges, I was drawing closer to the main part of town at the southern edge of the network of canals. Things weren't quite so sleepy here. Several gondolas glided past me, moving more swiftly than their usual unhurried pace. The gondoliers kept their eyes straight ahead, focused on propelling their boats, which currently had no passengers.

Later in the day, the professional gondoliers would take tourists around for leisurely rides, but for now they were practicing for the upcoming gondola races, a popular annual event. I wouldn't be taking part, but I planned to be on the sidelines, cheering on the racers.

At the moment, however, I needed to get to work.

Crossing one more bridge took me to the town's main street, Venice Avenue, a wide cobblestone walkway lined with colorful timber-frame shops and restaurants that faced the canals. Amsterdam Avenue ran perpendicular to Venice Avenue and was dominated by the stately Larch Haven Hotel, which resembled an English manor house. I doubted there were many vacancies at the moment. Tourists always flocked to Larch Haven in the summer, and the gondola races had attracted even more visitors. Some intended to take part in the races, while others planned to simply watch and enjoy all that our town had to offer.

I hoped all the tourists would stop in at my family's chocolate shop, True Confections, which was my current destination.

I waved to Mr. Henderson, who was sweeping the front step of his souvenir store, two doors down from the chocolate shop. Then I dug out my keys and let myself in through the front door of True Confections. Pausing just inside, I drew in a deep, appreciative breath as I did every morning, enjoying the enticing aroma of chocolate. After switching on the lights in the kitchen, I tied back my dark hair, donned my apron, and washed up. It was time to make some bonbons.

Most of the people I knew in Hollywood didn't understand why I'd chosen to leave behind my acting career to make chocolates in a small New England town. After a couple of years of struggling to get good jobs and having to wait tables to keep a roof over my head, I'd landed a role in the pilot episode of *Twilight Hills*, a television drama with an ensemble cast.

The show had quickly gathered a dedicated following, and partway into the second season, with my character appearing on every episode by that time, I'd been able to quit my waitressing job. Then, after four seasons, the network canceled the show. Initially, I'd planned to pursue more acting jobs, but then I ended up in the hospital with a ruptured appendix. If not for my roommate calling an ambulance for me when I collapsed, I probably would have died.

While lying in my hospital bed, recovering from surgery, I realized how homesick I was. Once I was well enough, I packed up my belongings and boarded a plane to come home.

I'd been making chocolates with my grandparents, Lolly and Pops, since I was ten years old, but after returning home I'd qualified as a chocolatier. Lolly and Pops had mostly retired now, leaving the shop in my hands and those of my cousin Angie. She looked after the business part of the shop and I made the chocolates. So far, it was a perfect arrangement.

To start, I got busy making mango jelly, which I would pair with dark chocolate ganache to make mango tango bonbons. The ganache would sit atop the jelly, and the two-layered center would be encased in a dark chocolate shell painted with speckles of orange and white cocoa butter.

While the mango jelly was setting, I moved on to making the filling for one of the newest truffles on offer at the shop—peanut butter pretzel. I loved the contrast of smooth peanut butter with the crunch of chopped pretzels. The pretzels also added a nice saltiness, and I mixed in tiny bits of toffee for more crunch and sweetness.

I was in the midst of rolling the filling into balls when the bell above the front door jingled. I figured it was my cousin Angie, but then I heard my grandmother's voice call out.

"Good morning, Rebecca!"

Quickly, I washed my hands and hurried out of the kitchen.

"Lolly!" I exclaimed happily. I spotted my grandfather too. "And Pops!" I gave my grandmother a hug. "I wasn't expecting you two so early."

My grandparents often stopped by the shop to say hello or lend a hand, but usually not until after we'd opened for the day.

I gave my Pops a hug next.

"Good morning, my Hollywood star," he said as he gave me a good squeeze.

"Hardly a star," I said as I stepped back.

"You are to me."

My smile brightened and my heart nearly burst. I was so happy to be back home, where I could see my Lolly and Pops on a daily basis.

Lolly checked out the display cases, and I knew she was making a mental list of which chocolates needed to be brought out from the back. "I'm holding down the fort for a couple of hours while Angela goes to a dental appointment."

"Right." That had temporarily slipped my mind. "What about you, Pops? Should I be putting you to work?"

"Not this morning, I'm afraid. I'm on my way to help with the final day of registration for the gondola races."

"It seems like the event is as popular as always," I said.

"Maybe even more so." Pops settled his favorite gray flat cap on his head. "Duty calls."

I gave him a kiss on the cheek and saw him to the door. More people were out and about now than when I'd arrived at the shop. Hopefully we'd get plenty of shoppers coming into True Confections, eager to buy some tasty chocolates.

Lolly and I got the shop ready to open and then I retreated to the kitchen again to spend a few more hours making bonbons and truffles. Angie showed up partway through the morning, but since we had such a steady stream of customers, Lolly stayed on to help out until my teenage cousin, Milo, arrived for his afternoon shift. Angie was my aunt Elizabeth's daughter and Milo was the son of my aunt Kathleen. I had many relatives in Larch Haven, and the chocolate shop was definitely a family affair.

By the time Lolly left, my stomach was rumbling with hunger—despite having sampled one of my peanut butter pretzel truffles—so I texted my best friend, Dizzy Bautista, to see if she wanted to meet up for lunch. She soon responded in the affirmative, although she wouldn't be able to get away from work for another half hour. I did some tidying up and said goodbye to my cousins before heading out into the summer sunshine.

Tourists strolled along Venice Avenue, pausing to snap photos and pose for selfies here and there. Some had their sights set on the shops, while others climbed into gondolas to cruise along the canals, and maybe out onto Shadow Lake. I pulled the elastic out of my hair, letting it tumble down my back, and immediately wondered if that was a good move. The outdoor temperature had climbed while I was in the air-conditioned kitchen and the sun was beating down from the gorgeous blue sky.

Leaving my hair loose for the moment, I hurried home so I could trade my jeans for shorts and check in on Truffles and Binx. Within minutes, I was on my way back toward Venice Avenue. I bypassed the row of shops facing the canal and followed the cobblestone walkway to the public library on the next street over.

Desiree Bautista—Dizzy for short—had been my best friend since we were three years old. We attended preschool together, and on the first day she gave me her purple crayon when mine broke. After that, we'd been practically inseparable. Dizzy now worked as a librarian here in Larch Haven, having returned home after getting her master's degree. We always stayed in touch while living in different parts of the country, but I loved being back in the same town as her again. There was nothing quite like pizza night or a lunch date with my bestie.

I enjoyed the feel of the sun heating my skin, but by the time I reached the front steps of the library, I was looking forward to having an ice-cold drink with my lunch. When I stepped into the air-conditioned library, the sudden change in temperature sent goose bumps down my arms.

Off to my left in the children's section, one of the teenage volunteers read a book to a group of young kids, all of whom appeared to be enthralled by the story. An elderly gentleman sat in the reading area, perusing a newspaper, and several people of various ages browsed the shelves. I was tempted to check out a few books myself, but I already had a stack at home that I hadn't yet finished.

I spotted Dizzy at the circulation desk, where three people stood in line, waiting to check out their books. I waved at Dizzy and she smiled and held up her hand to signal that she needed another five minutes. I nodded and drifted off toward the mystery section. The shelf of new releases caught my eye so I stopped there first. I was about to pick up the latest book by Louise Penny when a man's angry voice caught my attention.

The voice was coming from the back meeting room, not far from the mystery section. Curious, I moved closer to the open door and saw that about a dozen people had gathered in the room. Oliver Nieminen—owner of the Rialto Café and president of the local hiking club—stood at the front, facing the others. He didn't look happy, but he wasn't the one talking.

I almost rolled my eyes when I realized that the angry voice belonged to Archie Smith. The sixty-something man was known as the town curmudgeon, and I'd never seen him with anything other than a scowl on his face. He was always complaining. I felt sorry for the other people in the room with him.

Trying to tune Archie out, I turned back to the new mystery releases.

But I couldn't ignore his next words.

He drew everyone's attention when he shouted, "Over my dead body!"

Chapter Two

DIZZY CAME RUSHING OVER. SHE CHARGED PAST ME into the meeting room.

"I'm afraid I have to ask you to *keep it down*," she said sternly to everyone in the room.

Even though she had her back to me, I could imagine the chilly glare she was aiming at Archie and the others. Although Dizzy was barely five foot two, she could be a force to be reckoned with, especially when she was in librarian mode.

"I wouldn't have to shout if these imbeciles weren't bent on destroying this town!" Archie fumed.

I edged closer to the open door, unable to ignore the show.

Estelle Granger, a local woman in her fifties, stood up from her chair and put her hands on her hips. "You weren't even invited to this meeting, Archie. We're talking about hiking club matters."

"I thought you agreed with me," Archie groused. "Don't tell me you've let these idiots brainwash you."

"Enough!" Oliver bellowed from the front of the room. His normally pale face was a startling shade of red.

"And you!" Archie jabbed a finger in Oliver's direction before looking to everyone else. "He's a member of MUFON! And you think he's worth listening to? You're a bunch of morons!"

"All right. That's it." Dizzy pointed to the door. "Archie, you need to leave. And if I hear another raised voice, I'll have to ban the club from using this space."

Oliver opened his mouth to protest, but wisely shut it again after one look at Dizzy.

"Hooligans," Archie muttered.

He crammed his dirty green baseball cap on his head and stormed out of the room. I had to jump aside to avoid getting trampled.

"Sorry, Ms. Bautista," I heard Oliver say. "We'll keep it down from here on out."

Dizzy marched out of the room and tugged the door shut behind her.

"Sorry about that," she whispered to me. "Who knew a hiking club could have so much drama?"

"It could have been a scene from *Passion City*," I said, referring to a soap opera I'd appeared on.

"Seriously. And Archie made it sound like MUFON is a bad thing. What's up with that?"

Dizzy had a love for all things paranormal. It wouldn't have surprised me if she joined the Mutual UFO Network herself.

Dizzy blew out a breath, her shoulders relaxing. "Give me two more minutes?"

"No worries. I'll be browsing."

As I waited, I read the back covers of a couple of the new mystery releases. They both tempted me, but I decided to hold off and read the books I already had at home first. I didn't want the stack of books on my bedside table growing so precariously tall that it posed a danger to me or my cats.

When Dizzy waved at me a couple of minutes later, I set down the book I was holding and met her as she came out from behind the circulation desk. Patrons still stood in line to check out books, but one of Dizzy's colleagues had everything under control.

"Looks like you've been having a busy day," I commented as we pushed out the front door into the bright sunshine.

"It's been crazy, but I love it. Except for dealing with the unruly adults in the meeting room."

"Causing more trouble than the kids, I'm guessing."

Dizzy smiled. "As is almost always the case."

We made our way down the steps and paused to wait for a group of tourists to amble past.

"So, where to?" I asked.

"The Rialto Café?" Dizzy suggested.

My mouth watered. "I can hear a Mediterranean wrap calling my name."

We struck off along Venice Avenue, heading for the café. Although Oliver was busy with his meeting at the library, he had employees to keep the restaurant open in his absence.

If we'd showed up at the café at noon, there likely wouldn't have been a table to spare. Even now, well after the typical lunch rush, most of the tables were occupied. Dizzy and I managed to snag an outdoor one shaded by its blue and white umbrella.

"So," Dizzy said once we were seated. "How many more days until Justin arrives?"

Justin was my boyfriend. He still lived and worked in Los Angeles, where we'd met, but he'd finally managed to clear his schedule enough to come visit me in my hometown.

"Six." I took a quick look at my phone before tucking it away in my pocket. I'd exchanged texts with Justin that morning, but I hadn't received any messages from him since then.

Dizzy studied me carefully from across the table. "And are you excited or nervous? Because I'm getting mixed vibes here."

"Your radar is spot-on."

Dizzy smiled. "As usual." Her expression grew more serious. "But why the mixed feelings?"

I was about to answer when a waitress appeared by our table. We came to the café often enough that we didn't need menus, so we placed our orders right away. As the waitress hurried off, we returned to our conversation.

"I'm excited to see him," I said, "and to show him Larch Haven, but I guess I'm nervous because it's a big step."

Dizzy nodded. "He's going to meet your grandparents. And your brother. Are you worried they won't like him?"

Aside from my parents, who were living in Florida, none of my family members had met my boyfriend yet. Dizzy hadn't either, aside from a brief introduction during one of my video calls with Justin. Our relationship had been a long-distance one ever since I left California.

"It's not that," I said. "It's just . . . I want things to go well."

"Hopefully that's exactly what will happen. I for one can't wait to grill—I mean meet—him." Dizzy tried and failed to hide her mischievous smile.

"Hey, no grilling, please," I protested. "I don't want you scaring him off."

"As your best friend, it's my job to make sure he has honorable intentions."

I rolled my eyes. "Now you sound like Gareth."

My older brother had a tendency to be overprotective, and I was nervous about how he'd react to Justin when he met him.

"I can be far more subtle than Gareth," Dizzy assured me.

"Not exactly difficult."

She laughed. "Don't worry. I promise I won't scare him. But if he's thinking of moving all the way across the country to be with you, I'm sure he wouldn't be easy to scare off anyway."

The waitress arrived with our drinks at that moment, so I didn't say anything further on the subject. I did, however, hope Dizzy was right. I just needed to make sure that my LA-born-and-raised boyfriend would fall in love with Larch Haven. But really, who wouldn't?

AFTER EATING LUNCH WITH DIZZY, I RETURNED TO True Confections to spend another couple of hours in the kitchen. By the time I'd finished for the day, I had completed batches of mango tango bonbons, peanut butter pretzel truffles, and two of the shop's classic favorites, chocolate-hazelnut and mint melty. I sorted out the less-than-perfect ones—which we affectionately called misfits—and set those aside to be sold at a lower price. There weren't many that didn't make the cut for the display cases, so I considered it a good day's work.

When I had the kitchen sparkling clean, I decided to head home. There was still enough time left in the day for me to sprawl out on my lawn with a good book or to take my kayak out on the lake. Maybe I could even manage to do both.

Angie and Milo were busy serving customers when I emerged from the kitchen, so I simply waved at them on my way out the door. The shop would stay open for another couple of hours, and it didn't look as though the steady stream of customers would slow down much before then. That brought a smile to my face. The business had flourished for years, but I was glad that my decision to move home meant that Lolly and Pops could now work only when they wanted to. Since they were both eighty, I figured it was high time they enjoyed retirement.

I made my way along Venice Avenue, heading for the nearest bridge that would take me across the first canal. A folding table sat near the bridge, with a woman stationed in a chair behind it. A banner hanging from the table proclaimed it to be where people could register for the gondola races. Pops's shift at the table had ended hours ago, but it appeared as though potential entrants were still wandering up to the table now and then to secure spots.

As I got closer, I recognized the woman stationed behind the table—Estelle Granger. She had been at the hiking club meeting at the library earlier, and she was also a friend of my mom's. When I passed by the table, no one was waiting to register, so I stopped to say hi.

"I hear a lot of people are interested in racing this year," I said once we'd exchanged greetings.

"Not many spots left," Estelle confirmed. "Even the junior races filled up quickly. Are you wanting to register?"

"Oh, no," I said quickly. "I'll just be watching, but I'm looking forward to it."

"Hopefully it'll be good, clean fun without any unnecessary drama."

Her comment surprised me. "Is there likely to be drama?"

"There will be if Archie Smith has anything to do with it. He came by earlier and ripped down our banner. He would have torn up the registration forms if I hadn't grabbed them away in the nick of time."

"Does that man hate everything?" I asked.

Estelle shrugged. "Sometimes I wonder. The races attract tourists, and he claims tourists are the bane of his existence."

I had trouble understanding that. "The tourism industry is the lifeblood of this town."

"Try telling that to Archie. He's obsessed with his privacy. He says that hikers and tourists are always trespassing on his land. I doubt it happens anywhere near as much as he claims, but there's no arguing with the man."

"What was his problem at the hiking club meeting?"

"You heard about that?"

"I was in the library at the time," I said.

"Then I guess it was hard to miss." Estelle sighed. "You know the old hiking trail that led up to the top of Whisper Mountain?"

"Sure." I hiked that trail many times in my teens. "Didn't it get washed out by a landslide years ago?"

"That's exactly the issue. Oliver and many other members of the hiking club want to clear the trail so it's usable again. The trail runs right past Archie's property, so he thinks clearing it will attract so-called hooligans to his land."

I recalled what Archie had said to her at the meeting. "But he thought you were on the same side as him, right?"

"I am. Sort of. But for different reasons. And I'm not vehemently opposed to the idea. I'm just concerned about the cost and the potential environmental impact of clearing the trail. There's a lot of debris, and in some places the trail was completely wiped away."

Two young men who were probably in their early twenties approached the table, wanting to register, so I said a quick goodbye to Estelle and continued on my way. When I let myself in through the front door of my cottage, Binx and Truffles came to greet me, rubbing up against my legs as I kicked off my shoes and dropped my keys on the table in the foyer.

I gave each of them a cuddle, set out fresh water, and sprinkled a few treats into their food dishes—salmon-flavored treats for Binx and tuna for Truffles. Binx liked to have a varied diet with the flavors of his food changing from time to time. His sister, however, was far pickier. If I gave Truffles her favorite brand of treats in any flavor other than tuna, she'd take one sniff and turn away in disgust.

While my cats were happily munching on their snack, I decided to go kayaking first and enjoy some reading time later. I tied my hair back in a ponytail and lathered on some sunscreen. Then I grabbed my sunglasses and crossed my small front lawn to my boathouse. I had a whisper boat—a flat-bottom Jon boat with an electric motor—and a kayak stored inside. I mostly used the whisper boat for transporting groceries home. The kayak, on the other hand, I used for recreation.

I carefully climbed into the kayak, holding my breath until I was seated. As much as I loved going out on the water, I didn't want to end up *in* the water. That was why my kayak had outriggers to help with stability. I wouldn't have used the craft without them.

Safely settled, I pushed off and glided out of the boathouse. Going at a leisurely pace, I paddled along the canal, exchanging smiles and greetings with the occupants of the gondolas and whisper boats heading in the opposite direction. I passed by picturesque cottages and beneath bridges, often in the sunshine but occasionally shaded by weeping willows and other trees that reached their branches out over the bank of the canal.

It didn't take me long to reach Shadow Lake. It wasn't quite as busy as the canals, but there was still plenty of activity. I spotted a canoe heading back toward shore from Mad Hatter Island, which sat in the middle of the lake. There were also a couple of speedboats off in the distance, and two teenage boys zoomed around on Jet-Skis.

My plan was to paddle along the shore for a while before turning around and heading back home, but I didn't make it far before angry voices caught my attention. I recognized Pops standing outside the Boat Barn, which rented out canoes, kayaks, gondolas, and other types of watercraft. Pops was facing off with another man, who sounded angrier than he did. A few others, including the owner of the Boat Barn, Mike Kwan, stood in a loose semicircle around Pops.

Concerned, I paddled closer and soon recognized the man Pops was arguing with.

Archie Smith.

I wasn't surprised that he was making a scene, but I was

taken aback by the fact that Pops was involved. He didn't make a habit of shouting or getting into public arguments.

"If you try to interfere with the races again, I won't hesitate to call the cops," Pops warned Archie.

"Go ahead!" Archie yelled. "I'll have them arrest the lot of you for interfering with my right to live peacefully!"

"The only person interfering with anything here is you!" Pops shouted. "And we've had enough of your attempts to sabotage the races. Not to mention the other things you've been up to."

"What other things?" Mike asked.

"Remember my vintage scooter that went missing?" Pops said. "Archie stole it. I'm sure of it."

"Liar!" Archie bellowed. "You can't prove a thing!"

"Hey, what's going on?" I called as I quickly paddled closer.

Nobody paid any attention to me. I climbed out of my kayak and tugged it up the beach. I left it there and hurried closer to Pops.

Archie tore the green cap from his head and crumpled it in his fist. "You can't be falsely accusing me. I'm a taxpaying citizen of this town and I have rights!"

"You don't have the right to vandalize my property," Mike Kwan spoke up.

"Who says I was?" Archie challenged.

"I caught you in the act," Pops said.

"Like I said, you're a liar." Archie stepped toward Pops. "And this is what I do to liars."

He raised his fist and took a swing at my grandfather.

Chapter Three

"STOP IT!" I YELLED.

Pops ducked. Archie's fist missed his head by mere inches.

I jumped in front of Archie as he was about to take another swing. My eyes widened when his fist came flying at my face.

A split second before impact, Archie let out a grunt and stumbled to the side. Officer Sawyer Maguire had intervened just in time, grabbing Archie and hauling him away from me and Pops.

Keeping a hold on Archie, Sawyer's dark eyes met mine. "You okay, Becca?" he asked.

"Yes," I said, still dazed by the fact that I nearly got punched in the face.

Sawyer addressed Pops next. "Mr. Ransom?"

"I'm fine," Pops said, glaring at Archie with disgust.

I couldn't believe that Archie had taken a swing at my grandfather. The two men were similar in size, but Archie was nearly twenty years younger than Pops.

One of Sawyer's fellow officers jogged over our way. I wondered if someone had called the police, or if Sawyer had simply happened to notice the confrontation, as I had.

I'd known Sawyer since kindergarten, but I'd never seen him in action as a police officer until I'd moved home a few months ago. And up until today, I'd only ever seen him patrolling the town. He had an air of command about him that was calming and reassuring, especially considering the tension of the current situation.

The other officer stayed with Archie, who was grumbling nonstop, while Sawyer walked closer to the Boat Barn with me and Pops.

"Are you sure you're okay?" he asked me, concern showing in his brown eyes.

"He didn't hurt me," I said. "But he meant to hurt Pops."

"You shouldn't have jumped between us," Pops chided me. "You almost got hit!"

"So did you! I wasn't going to let that happen."

Pops put an arm around me and kissed the top of my head.

"Are you going to arrest Archie?" Mike asked.

"I'd like to know what happened first," Sawyer replied.

"I can't tell you much," I said. "I got here just as Archie started swinging his fists."

"He was planning to vandalize my boats." Mike hooked a thumb over his shoulder at the Boat Barn. "Ernie caught him in the act."

"Or just about," Pops amended. "I saw him sneaking in there with a sledgehammer. He was about to take it to one of the gondolas when I yelled at him."

"Is he seriously that determined to derail the races and our tourism industry?" I asked. It astounded me that he was willing to go to such extreme lengths.

"He's been a problem for years," Mike said. "His behavior has been escalating, and now this."

Pops put a hand on my shoulder. "You don't need to

trouble yourself with this, Rebecca. Go enjoy what's left of the afternoon."

I wasn't eager to leave, but the other officer had Archie under control and well away from my Pops now. I glanced to Sawyer.

"Go ahead," he said.

I made my way down the beach to my kayak. I pushed it out onto the water and looked back to make sure everything was still okay. As I watched, Sawyer left Pops and Mike to join his colleague and Archie.

I glanced up the shore again once I was in my kayak, but I couldn't tell if Archie had been placed under arrest or not. If his fist had connected with my face, he would have been, but I was glad that hadn't happened. I was even more relieved that he hadn't managed to strike my grandfather.

I tried to enjoy the rest of my paddle along the lakeshore, but the incident had left me unsettled. Now that the police were involved, I hoped Archie would dial down his antagonistic behavior, but something told me that wasn't likely to happen.

TO MY RELIEF, THE NEXT FEW DAYS PASSED WITHOUT any further drama caused by Archie Smith. I heard that he hadn't been arrested after the incident at the Boat Barn, and judging by the gossip flying around town, that wasn't a popular decision. So far Archie hadn't attempted to vandalize the gondolas again, and I hoped that would hold true. The races were only two days away now, and everyone aside from Archie was hoping they'd go smoothly.

On another gorgeous summer day, I set out on my walk to work, enjoying the peace and quiet of the early morning. There were signs of life on Venice Avenue, but aside from the local coffee shop, the stores and restaurants wouldn't open for another hour or two. I liked starting my workday early, at least in the summer, when I could make the short trip to the shop in daylight. My morning walk gave me a chance to soak up the charm of my hometown and to appreciate the change of pace from my former life in LA.

As I crossed the final bridge that would take me to Venice Avenue, I noticed a poster tacked to a tree. Signs and posters weren't supposed to be placed on trees, buildings, or any of the old-fashioned lampposts around Larch Haven. They were thought to detract from the aesthetic of the town. There were a couple of community noticeboards where people could advertise various events, and any rogue signs that made it onto trees or lampposts were typically swiftly removed.

Apparently, none of the official or self-proclaimed enforcers of the rule had spotted this poster. Or maybe no one had the heart to remove it even if they had seen it. That possibility occurred to me when I drew close enough to read the sign.

The poster stated that a candlelight vigil would be held to mark the tenth anniversary since local teen Lexi Derendorf had gone missing. Lexi had disappeared while I was away at college. I hadn't known her personally, other than by sight. She was a few years younger than me and our paths hadn't really crossed, but I remembered hearing about her disappearance.

She was seventeen at the time and had stormed out of her house after having a fight with her parents, Karl and Susan Derendorf. Initially, it was thought that she'd run away and would return before long, but no one ever heard from her again. Half the town had gone out searching for her, to no avail. No one knew what had happened to her. Or if they did, they weren't saying.

The poster featured a picture of Lexi—probably a school portrait. Her dark hair cascaded over her shoulder as she smiled at the camera. She wore a Viking rune pendant on a leather cord. I recalled from reading about the story online that she always wore that necklace. The police had mentioned it in their pleas for information. It was hoped that the necklace would help to identify Lexi.

I felt terrible for her parents. Ten years later and still no closure.

I certainly wasn't going to take down the poster, so I kept on walking.

On my way along the avenue, I took in the sight of the new town house development up on a hill overlooking the lake. I hadn't been past the site recently, but from what I could see from my current vantage point, it appeared as though the development was almost complete. The homes were built in the timber and frame style, so they matched the character of the rest of Larch Haven. The project wouldn't have been given the green light if that hadn't been the case.

I wondered what Archie Smith thought about the new homes, which would likely attract new residents. Then I decided not to think about Archie any longer.

"On your way to the shop?"

I turned toward the voice, already knowing it belonged to Sawyer. He was in uniform, with sunglasses shading his eyes. The summer sunshine had bronzed his usually light brown skin, and his hair, which was such a dark shade of brown that it was almost black, ruffled slightly in the gentle morning breeze.

"Lots of chocolates to make," I said in response to his question.

"I hear you've got a new peanut butter truffle."

"You heard right. You should come by and try one sometime."

Sawyer had always loved peanut butter.

"I might just do that," he said as we watched a gondola cruise past. "Are you racing this year?"

"Me? No way."

He seemed amused by my answer. "Don't tell me you still don't know how to row a gondola."

"I've been busy since I moved back."

Sawyer was shaking his head before I finished speaking. "You visited a few times over the years. And you should have learned long before that, anyway. You were born and raised here. It's practically sacrilege that you've never learned."

"That may be, but I'm not about to risk falling in the water." I pointed at a gondolier as he guided his craft past us. "Look how precariously he's perched there!"

"Seriously, Becks? Have you ever seen a gondolier fall in?"

"Tanner Gibson did," I reminded him.

Even though I couldn't see Sawyer's eyes through his sunglasses, I knew he was rolling them.

"He was three sheets to the wind at the time," he pointed out. "Besides, you're a strong swimmer, so what's the problem?"

I bit down on my lower lip, not keen to answer his question.

Unfortunately, he knew me well enough to interpret my hesitation.

"Hold on," he said. "Don't tell me this is about the fictional lake monster you were scared of as a kid."

"The fictional part is up for debate."

"You know your brother told you that story to scare you, right?"

"That doesn't mean the story isn't true," I countered. "As I got older, I thought it was just a story too, but then I distinctly felt something brush against my leg one time when I was swimming back from Mad Hatter Island."

"A fish," Sawyer said. "Or a plant."

"That's not what it felt like." The mere memory nearly made me shiver.

Sawyer shook his head again. "I've been swimming in that lake every summer of my life, and I've never seen any sign of a monster."

"That's because it's good at hiding."

"You can't be serious."

I really was. Whatever had brushed up against me had been bigger than a typical fish. I was certain of that. I didn't mind swimming in pools or other clear water, but anywhere I couldn't see what might be lurking beneath the surface was a no-go for me. That included the canals and any parts of the lake deeper than a few feet.

"Ask Dizzy," I said. "She'll tell you that the possibility of some large, prehistoric creature living in the lake really isn't that out there."

"Ask Dizzy?" Sawyer echoed. "She's always 'out there.'"

I crossed my arms, glaring at him.

"Monday is my day off," he said.

"What's that got to do with anything?"

"That's when I'm teaching you how to be a gondolier." He took a step backward. "Six a.m. at the main dock. Don't be late."

He walked off.

"What if I'm busy?" I called.

He kept walking.

I jogged after him.

A woman's scream stopped us both in our tracks.

By the time I turned in the direction of the sound, Sawyer was already sprinting past me. I broke into a run and followed him down Venice Avenue and across a stone bridge. I didn't catch up to him until he stopped at the edge of the canal, not far from where it connected to the lake.

A blond woman stood on the bank, her hands over her mouth as she stared at the water.

As soon as I reached Sawyer's side, I saw why the woman had screamed.

A body floated facedown in the canal.

Chapter Four

I RETREATED TO A NEARBY BENCH, ONE THAT OFfered a view of Shadow Lake rather than the canal. Two other police officers had joined Sawyer on the scene, and I didn't want to watch when they retrieved the body. If it had been in the water for more than a short time, it likely wouldn't be a pretty sight. It was bad enough that I'd seen the gruesome gash on the back of the head.

The owners of the closest cottage had come running at the sound of the scream, just as Sawyer and I had. The middle-aged couple had since taken the sobbing blond woman into their home to calm her down. I hoped she'd be all right.

As much as I didn't want to recall what I'd seen in vivid detail, I focused on the memory of the body bobbing gently in the canal. All I'd seen was that he had short gray hair and was wearing jeans and a dark green shirt. There were plenty of tourists in town at the moment, and since I'd been living across the country for the past seven years there were many local residents I didn't know. Still, I couldn't shake the feeling that I knew the drowned man's identity. The size and build of the body and the thinning gray hair matched what I remembered about Archie Smith.

If Archie *was* the dead man, that would explain why he hadn't caused any more problems in town since the incident at the Boat Barn. Having grown up next to a lake, I knew that drowning victims often stayed beneath the water for a few days before floating to the surface. That meant Archie could have died soon after I'd last seen him.

I tried my best to push all those thoughts away from the center of my mind, but I didn't have much success. My gaze drifted off to my left, toward where Sawyer and his colleagues stood on the bank of the canal. Another officer appeared, putting along in a small motor boat, likely there to retrieve the body.

I resolutely turned away again, not wanting to see what would happen next. Closing my eyes, I breathed in the fresh summer air and imagined myself lying in the sun on the top of the rocks on Mad Hatter Island. It was a trick I'd used often in Los Angeles whenever I felt nervous about an audition or when my anxiety became overwhelming.

I tried to tune out the sounds around me, but the splashes from the canal were hard to ignore, and a new murmur of voices had joined that of the police. My eyes popped open when I heard footsteps heading my way.

"You okay, Becca?" Sawyer asked as he stopped next to the bench where I was seated.

"Better than Archie. It is Archie, isn't it?"

"He hasn't been formally identified yet." Sawyer's expression gave nothing away.

I rubbed my arms, even though the morning sunlight had warmed my skin.

Sawyer rested a hand on my shoulder. "Seriously, Becca. Are you all right?"

I stood up and his hand fell away from my shoulder. "I'm good. How about you? Have you come across a lot of dead bodies as a police officer?"

"A few, unfortunately."

That didn't surprise me. No doubt he'd seen other drownings as well as accidents on the highway that led out of town, not to mention the natural deaths that must happen now and then.

"You don't need to stick around," he said. "Were you on your way to the shop?"

I nodded. It seemed like ages ago that I'd set off from home, even though it probably hadn't even been a full hour yet.

"Can I go back the way we came?" I asked.

More police officers had arrived and were preventing boats and people from getting close to the location where the body was found.

"Go ahead," Sawyer said with a nod.

I averted my eyes from the canal as I hurried along the pathway to the nearest bridge.

"What happened?"

"Did someone die?"

"What's going on?"

The questions pelted me like hail as I threaded my way through the crowd of onlookers on the other side of the bridge.

"Someone drowned, I think," I said without stopping. All I wanted to do was to get away from the questions and reach the familiar haven of the chocolate shop.

"Who?" several people asked.

"I'm not sure." That was the truth. I *thought* Archie was the dead man, but I didn't know for certain.

I broke free of the crowd and hurried away, not wanting to have to face any more questions. When I reached Venice Avenue, I jogged the rest of the way to the shop. I locked the door behind me and leaned against it, taking in a deep breath and allowing the familiar and delicious scent of chocolate to calm me.

My cousin Angie emerged from the back hallway while

I was still leaning against the door. She had her curly dark hair tied back and wore a cardigan over her yellow sundress.

"There you are," she said. "I was about to text you. You're always here before me. Did you oversleep?"

"I wish that was what had happened."

I quickly told her about the body floating in the canal.

"Oh my gosh." Angie rested a hand over her heart. "I'm sorry you had to see that. I probably would have fainted."

"I might have done that if I'd watched when they turned the body over." I shuddered. "I'd better get to work."

I checked the kitchen thermostat three times before the temperature reading registered in my mind. My brain felt scattered, my thoughts constantly trying to stray back to the canal. Forcing myself to focus, I got ready to work, satisfied that the kitchen was at the right temperature for making chocolates.

As I'd hoped, working helped to calm me down. I started out by making the fillings for piña colada bonbons and coffee creams. The piña colada bonbons were made of pineapple jelly and coconut rum ganache, encased in white chocolate. I painted the molds so the chocolate shells would be bright blue and yellow, like the sunshine and water of a tropical beach. I didn't paint the coffee creams, which were encased in milk chocolate, but I used molds with a fancy swirl pattern that would imprint the top of the bonbons.

Once I had all the fillings prepared, I moved to the tempering machine, holding the molds beneath the waterfall of tempered chocolate. I scraped off the excess and set the molds aside so the chocolate could set before I added the fillings. I always found the process of making bonbons and truffles soothing and satisfying, and today it helped to ease the tension that had tightened my muscles ever since seeing the body in the canal. The delicious aroma of chocolate helped too.

I was in the midst of piping ganache into the molds for the piña colada bonbons when I heard my grandmother's voice. I set aside the piping bag and hurried out into the shop. Angie had opened the store while I was working, and I now found several townsfolk gathered around Lolly.

"No one knows how Archie ended up drowning," she was saying to the small crowd. "Maybe he simply lost his footing and fell in, hitting his head on the way down."

"It was probably his paralysis that caused him to fall," Delphi Snodgrass spoke up. She was a tall, thin woman with large glasses and gray hair that fell to her shoulder blades in frizzy waves. Her grayish-blue eyes gleamed, as they often did when gossip was flying around town. Delphi and her lifelong best friend, Luella Plank, loved nothing more than gossip, and they weren't above starting wildly untrue rumors. It almost seemed to be a sport to them. They were known around Larch Haven as the Gossip Grannies. I didn't know if Delphi and Luella were aware of the nickname or not.

"He wasn't paralyzed," Lolly said, shooting a stern look at Delphi. "He had some loss of feeling in his left hand, that's all."

Delphi didn't seem bothered by the correction. "He had a terrible disease," she whispered to the woman standing next to her.

I doubted that was true, simply because of the source of the information.

Several of the people in the shop peppered my grandmother with questions, but when she caught sight of me, she made her way through the crowd and pulled me into a hug.

"Rebecca, I heard you were there when the body was found."

Everyone who overheard her now aimed their barrage of questions at me.

For a second, I felt completely overwhelmed, but then Lolly tucked her arm through mine and led me into the back, firmly shutting the door to the kitchen behind us.

"Thanks for getting me out of there," I said with relief. "I thought they were about to eat me for lunch."

"You know how curious people get when something out of the ordinary happens here in Larch Haven. Forget about them." She put her hands to my cheeks. "Are you okay?"

"I'm fine. Really." My mind circled back to what I'd heard her say earlier. "Are you sure it was Archie Smith? I thought it was him, but Sawyer wouldn't confirm or deny that."

"There hasn't been any formal identification," Lolly said, "but I've heard that the dead man matched Archie's description and was wearing the clothes he was last seen in. Plus, Archie's wallet was in his pocket."

That was confirmation enough for me.

"Will you be okay here?" Lolly asked. "I'm meeting Joan for a game of table tennis at the rec center."

"Of course. Have fun."

After Lolly left, I stayed in the kitchen, focusing on my work. I didn't stop again until my stomach gave a loud rumble of hunger. I glanced at the clock on the wall and realized that it was well past noon. Sometimes I got so far into the chocolate-making zone that I lost track of time and the world around me, just like I did when reading a really good book.

I finished up my latest batch of chocolates and then stretched my arms over my head. My stomach gave another rumble. It was time to wrap up for the day and get myself some food.

Before heading out, I checked in with Angie and transferred some bonbons from the back to the display case. Fortunately, the only customers at the time were tourists who had no idea that I'd seen Archie's body floating in the canal. Not a single question got thrown my way, and for that I was grateful.

I'd only made it a few steps out the front door of the shop when I noticed Estelle Granger power walking toward me, her frizzy fair hair coming loose from her short ponytail. I wished I could avoid her, but there was no way of doing that without being obvious about it. I was worried she wanted to ask me about what I'd seen that morning, but it turned out that wasn't what was on her mind.

Estelle held a sheaf of papers in her hands and she thrust one toward me. "There's a candlelight vigil for Lexi Derendorf tomorrow night, Becca. I hope you'll be able to make it."

I glanced down at the paper in my hands. It was a copy of the poster I'd seen that morning. I was about to tell Estelle that I would do my best to be there, but I didn't have the chance. She'd already hurried off, handing out more flyers to other locals.

I noted the time of the vigil before folding the paper and tucking it in my pocket. I planned to attend as a show of support for the missing girl's parents.

What a sad time. Archie had died and the somber anniversary of Lexi's disappearance was nearly upon us. Melancholy weighed upon me as I walked along the canal, heading home. Then I reminded myself that I had plenty of good things to look forward to: Justin would be arriving in a few days, and the gondola races would soon be starting. All around me, all I saw was beauty. The sun glinted off the water, flowers bloomed in window boxes, and the sky overhead was a gorgeous shade of blue.

Once I reached my cottage, I spent a few minutes playing with Binx and Truffles, and that helped to lift my spirits. I filled a whole wheat pita with hummus and plenty of vegetables, and then took my lunch out to my back patio, enjoying the gentle summer breeze as I sat in the shade, eating. After I'd finished my meal, I nearly dozed off in my chair. Shaking myself awake, I decided I needed some exercise to fend off the sluggishness threatening to take over my body.

I set off in my kayak, sticking close to the shore where I could see what was—or wasn't—lurking in the water beneath me. Feeling ambitious and enjoying the beautiful weather, I decided to kayak around the entire lake. As I passed the Boat Barn, I recalled the unpleasant scene I'd witnessed a few days earlier. Archie had been such an unpleasant man. Would anyone miss him now that he was gone? The real possibility that no one would threatened to send my spirits crashing again, so I resolutely focused on the world around me, determined to enjoy my outing.

As I paddled along, my gaze drifted over toward Mad Hatter Island, the source of many great memories. Before I'd become too scared to swim in the deeper waters, I'd often raced my brother and our friends from the shore to the island. We'd spent hours exploring the island, playing games, and picnicking. There was a wooded area at the eastern end, and at the western point was the rock formation that had given the island its name. It rose nearly forty feet into the air and resembled a tall and somewhat crooked top hat. I'd climbed those rocks hundreds of times, although it had been several years since I'd done so.

All the good memories put a smile on my face. I really was glad to be home. I missed my acting career—sometimes quite a lot—but Hollywood couldn't hold a candle to Larch Haven, Vermont.

I was about three-quarters of the way around the lake when I slowed my pace. Sawyer was up ahead, standing on the shore with three other police officers. They appeared to be searching for something on the wooded lakefront property, and that sparked my curiosity.

Through the trees, an old log cabin was partially visible. I knew that Archie lived somewhere over this way. I figured it was a good guess that it was his property the police were searching. Maybe they were trying to figure out how he ended up in the water.

As I drew closer in my kayak, one of the officers waved the others over her way. She pointed to something in a cluster of bushes near the shoreline. Another officer raised a camera and snapped some photos. Sawyer parted the branches and crouched down for a closer look at whatever had grabbed their interest. When he stood up again, I thought about calling out to him, but I kept quiet. He was working, and clearly busy.

His gaze shifted my way as I paddled past. I lifted a hand in greeting but then picked up my pace again. I tried to see whatever it was that had Sawyer and his colleagues so interested, but I wasn't close enough.

An uneasy feeling threaded its way through me. By the time I reached home and climbed out of my kayak, I'd managed to leave some of my apprehension behind, and whatever remained of it disappeared when Dizzy showed up at my cottage a couple of hours later. She found me out on my back patio, where I was reading a mystery while Truffles and Binx relaxed on the perches in their catio.

I set aside my book and stood up when I saw Dizzy hurrying across the lawn toward me.

"Oh my gosh!" She practically launched herself at me, hugging me tightly. "I heard you saw Archie's body when he was in the canal. Are you okay?"

"I'm fine," I assured her, returning her hug.

"I can't believe this happened in Larch Haven!"

"What do you mean?" I asked as she released me. There had, unfortunately, been a few drowning deaths in Larch Haven in our lifetime.

"You haven't heard the latest?"

"I'm not sure," I said, the uneasiness I'd felt out on the lake making a sudden comeback. "What are you talking about?"

Dizzy lowered her voice, despite the fact that we were alone. "It turns out Archie didn't drown by accident. He was murdered."

Chapter Five

EVEN THOUGH THE SUN STILL SHONE BRIGHTLY FROM the bold blue sky, I had to fight off a shiver. I sank down into my seat, and Dizzy dropped into the other chair on my patio.

"Are you sure?" I asked.

"I don't think the police have said anything officially, but Amanda Ng was out on her boat and saw the police searching Archie's property. She looked with her binoculars and swears they found a branch with blood on it. Amanda says they took it away as evidence. It was tucked in a bush, not in a place where Archie could have knocked his head on it if he fell."

"So someone hit him with it? That would explain his head wound."

Dizzy cringed. "I'm glad I didn't see that, and I'm sorry you did. But, yes, that's the theory flying around town. Someone gave Archie a good smack to the head and dumped his body in the lake."

"Then he drifted into the canal," I finished. "I thought I

was leaving violent crime behind me when I moved away from Los Angeles."

"I guess these things can happen anywhere."

I thought back over the years. "What is this, the second murder in Larch Haven in our lifetime?"

"Probably. There was that deadly domestic dispute back when we were teenagers." She frowned at the memory. "So sad. I know there was a stabbing up at Snowflake Canyon a couple of years ago, but that's not here."

Snowflake Canyon was a ski resort town located fifteen minutes higher up the mountain. It was Larch Haven's closest neighbor.

"I hope the police find out who did it, and soon." I didn't like the thought of a killer living among us.

"I bet the cops have a long list of suspects already," Dizzy said. "Archie wasn't exactly well-liked."

"That's an understatement, I think. I hope the killer isn't anyone we know."

"I don't know that a tourist would have any reason to kill him," Dizzy pointed out. "So the murderer could well be one of our own."

"Ugh. Let's not think about that. Are you going to the vigil tonight?"

"I'll be there." Dizzy leaned back in her chair and looked out over the canal. "I didn't know Lexi well, but I remember her."

"Same," I said. "I feel terrible for her parents."

"They've been having trouble with Archie lately. I guess they won't be any longer."

"What kind of trouble?" I asked.

"He was their next-door neighbor."

"That couldn't have been easy."

"Right? Apparently, Archie had a fit when Mr. Derendorf built a shed a few weeks ago. Archie claimed it encroached on his property, but Mr. Derendorf swore that every inch of it was on his land. Mrs. Derendorf even caught Archie trying to tear the shed down one day. She had to call the police to get him to stop."

"I remember hearing something about that," I said. "I don't recall the details, though. What happened in the end?"

"You know, I'm not sure. Archie was threatening to take the Derendorfs to court over it, but I don't think he actually made good on that threat."

"Maybe he knew he'd lose in court."

Dizzy shrugged. "Could be." She got to her feet. "Anyway, I need to go grab some groceries before the vigil. See you there?"

"Definitely."

She took a moment to talk to Binx and Truffles through the wire of their catio. Then she set off along the canal, sending a wave in my direction.

I tried to go back to focusing on my book. As much as I was enjoying the story, I couldn't concentrate. My mind kept circling back to the fact that Archie had been murdered. Or at least had possibly been murdered. Maybe I should wait for official confirmation of that before I got too worried. I considered Amanda Ng a reliable source of information, though. She was two years younger than me and Dizzy, but we'd been on the high school swim team together for a year and I knew she wasn't prone to exaggeration or to making up rumors, unlike Delphi Snodgrass and Luella Plank.

After reading the same page several times, I gave up and decided to clean my cottage instead. By the time I'd finished scrubbing, dusting, and vacuuming, I'd worked up an appetite again. I ate a light dinner while Binx and Truffles munched away at their own meals, and then I read out on the patio until the sun began to sink toward the mountaintops.

My cats were in their catio watching a small bird with intense fascination when I set off for the candlelight vigil.

Everyone was meeting on Venice Avenue, and then proceeding to Cherry Park, located at the edge of town.

I spotted Dizzy as I crossed the last bridge before Venice Avenue. She waved and hurried over to join me. Together, we got in line to receive candles. Estelle Granger was handing them out and a young woman named Maria Vasquez was using a lighter to ignite the wicks. Maria was a few years younger than me, but she'd been living here in town for a long time, if not for her whole life, and she now owned a shop where she sold soap and skincare products that she made herself.

As Maria held the lighter to the wick of my candle, I thought she was about to say something to me, but then another woman called her name and hurried over to speak with her. I thanked her for lighting my candle and moved on.

The crowd of vigil attendees quickly grew so large that we nearly clogged Venice Avenue. We drew some curious looks from tourists who were out for an evening stroll, but once they decided they weren't missing out on something exciting, they moved on. I waved at Lolly and my cousin Angela, who were on the far side of the crowd, but I didn't bother trying to reach them. I would have had to squeeze around too many people.

"I feel so terrible for the Derendorfs," Dizzy said.

Lexi's parents stood together at the head of the crowd. Estelle, now finished passing out candles, joined them and put an arm around Susan Derendorf's shoulders. I thought my mom had mentioned at one time that Estelle and Susan were best friends.

"I can't even imagine what it must be like for them, not knowing what happened to their daughter." I averted my gaze from Lexi's parents and took a steadying breath, which helped me banish the prickle of tears in my eyes.

Estelle seemed to be the spokesperson for the Derendorfs and the leader of the vigil. Once she had the crowd's attention, she thanked everyone for coming and then led the slow procession to the park, with Karl and Susan at her side.

The crowd slowly filed along the cobblestone street, which wound past shops, restaurants, cottages, and the town hall before leading to Cherry Park. At the entrance to the park was an avenue lined with ornamental cherry trees. In the spring, when pink blossoms adorned the trees, the effect was breathtaking. It was one of the many things I'd missed terribly while living in Los Angeles.

Everyone gathered around a large oak tree, where Estelle said a few words about Lexi and how much she was missed. Then she invited Maria up to the front to sing a song.

"This was one of Lexi's favorite songs," Maria said to the crowd before singing the opening lyrics to Sarah McLachlan's "I Will Remember You."

She had a beautiful voice.

"I didn't realize Maria was friends with Lexi," I whispered to Dizzy as we stood at the edge of the crowd.

"Best friends, I think."

After Maria finished singing, a few other people who'd been close to Lexi each said a few words, and then Estelle thanked everyone for coming. Some people formed a loose line so they could speak with Susan and Karl, but Dizzy and I, and several others, blew out our candles and meandered back to the heart of town. As we passed beneath the cherry trees, someone hurried up next to me.

"It's Becca, right?" Maria Vasquez said as she flipped her dark hair over her shoulder. "Rebecca Ransom?" I didn't have time to confirm or deny that before she added in a rush, "I saw you on *Passion City*. It's my favorite show. I loved your character. I just wish you could have stayed on the show longer. I cried so hard when you died."

"Thank you," I said. "That's so nice of you to say so."

Passion City had been running for a couple of decades now. The soap opera's storylines were silly, sometimes bordering on absolutely ridiculous, but it remained popular after all these years. And if my performance on the show had elicited an emotional reaction from Maria as a viewer, I figured I'd done my job.

"I have to ask," Maria said. "What's Chase Goodwin like in real life? He's so good-looking he takes my breath away."

That was a question I'd been asked several times before. Chase Goodwin had joined the regular cast of *Passion City* a few years ago and was now one of the fan favorites.

"If you can believe it, he's actually even better-looking in person," I told her. "And he's a nice guy, too."

Maria looked like she was about to swoon. "You're so lucky you got to work with him."

I wasn't too sure what to say next. Thankfully, Dizzy came to my rescue.

"That was a nice song you sang, Maria," she said. "You have a lovely voice."

Maria beamed. "Thank you." Her smile faded. "Lexi loved Sarah McLachlan's music. Whenever I sing that song, I feel closer to her."

"I'm so sorry you lost a friend," I said. "It must be especially hard, not knowing what happened."

Maria nodded, her face somber now. "I stayed hopeful for so long, thinking that surely one day she'd reappear, that maybe she'd just run away to start a new life somewhere else. But no matter how upset Lexi was with her parents that night, she wouldn't have done that, not without telling anyone where she was going and if she was all right. I'd never say this in front of her parents, but I know she's not coming back. I don't know how it happened, but I know she's dead."

"Do Karl and Susan still think she might be alive?" I asked, my heart aching for them.

Maria shrugged. "I'm not sure." She shook her head sadly. "They've aged so much since Lexi disappeared."

Sadness settled over us like a dark cloud.

"It's nice that so many people showed up tonight," I said, trying to dispel some of the sorrow.

A sad smile made a fleeting appearance on Maria's face. "It was a good turnout. I think that will be of some comfort to Karl and Susan."

"I wonder if there will be a memorial or funeral for Archie."

Maria let out a sharp, derisive laugh that took me by surprise. "Who would show up?"

Her words sounded so cruel, but I realized she might well have a point. Archie hadn't exactly endeared himself to people when he was alive. Still, it was sad to think that he wouldn't be missed. At least, not by anyone I knew.

I recalled something I'd heard a long time ago. "Doesn't Archie have a daughter?"

"Jolene Doyle-Brodsky," Dizzy said with a nod.

Maria huffed. "Not that Archie ever admitted it."

"What do you mean?" I asked.

"He never acknowledged that Jolene was his daughter," Dizzy explained. "Even though a DNA test proved it."

"Tammy Doyle—Jolene's mother—took him to court and everything," Maria added. "Archie was ordered to pay child support, but he claimed he had no money. I'm pretty sure he spent some time in jail because he refused to pay."

"I think I remember hearing something about that." The story had triggered a vague memory. "Jolene is older than us, right?" I directed the question to Dizzy.

"Yes, by a couple of years."

"She married Alex Brodsky," Maria said. "She doesn't need any money from Archie now, that's for sure."

Alex Brodsky was a property developer, the one behind the new town houses overlooking Shadow Lake. He'd also developed several properties in the nearby ski resort town of Snowflake Canyon. I didn't know exactly how much money he had, but I did know that he was a millionaire. Everyone in these parts knew that.

"Do you think Jolene's connection to the new town

house development had anything to do with Archie trying to stop it from going ahead?" Dizzy asked Maria.

"Archie tried to stop the development?" I hadn't heard that before.

"Last year," Dizzy said. "Before you moved back."

"That horrible, horrible man." The bitterness in Maria's voice took me by surprise. "Karma finally caught up with him."

She stormed off, disappearing into the darkness.

"Whoa," I said as Dizzy and I turned onto Venice Avenue, lit by its old-fashioned streetlamps. "She sounds like she really hated Archie."

"He wasn't exactly popular," Dizzy reminded me.

"I know, but Maria's anger sounded personal."

I shook off the shadow of bitterness that her words had left behind, and by morning the conversation had drifted to the back of my mind. I spent several hours whipping up a variety of chocolates at True Confections. At this time of year, the shop was open seven days a week because of all the tourists in town. I only worked six days, but I was hoping to take some extra time away from the shop while Justin was in Larch Haven. Lolly had offered to come in for a day or two to take over for me in the kitchen, but I wanted to leave as little work for her as possible, so I made more chocolates than I normally would.

Finally, in the middle of the afternoon, I called it a day and cleaned up the kitchen. My stomach grumbled as I tidied and scrubbed. I'd barely stopped for lunch, eating only an apple before getting back to work. Now my stomach was demanding that I make up for it. I was thinking about stopping by my brother's restaurant to see what he was cooking, but when I got out to the front of the shop, I realized that would have to wait.

My cousins Angie and Milo had a store full of customers to deal with. They each stood at one of the cash registers

ters, ringing up purchases. Lines had gathered at each register, with some people wanting to pay and others wanting to select chocolates from the display case. I'd just let my hair loose, but I tied it back again and jumped into the fray to help out, boxing up chocolates for those customers who wanted to mix and match from the displays.

Half an hour later, the crowd had finally thinned.

The only customers left in the shop were two teenage girls who were doing an awful lot of giggling as they got Milo to tell them about all the different products on the shelves. I had a feeling the girls were far more interested in Milo than they were in the chocolates.

My teenage cousin had an impressive collection of waistcoats that he wore with jeans and button-up shirts with the sleeves rolled up. With his dark, tousled hair slightly long at the front and swooped backward, he looked like he could be a member of a boy band. I didn't know how he managed to be so cool at age fifteen. Hopefully he wouldn't break too many hearts before he graduated high school.

The girls eventually left, each with a small purchase in hand, just as Pops came in the door. Sawyer followed, almost on his heels, dressed in his police uniform.

"Got a craving for chocolate?" I asked Sawyer as I let my hair loose again.

My smile faded when I took in his serious expression.

"Actually, I'm here to speak with your grandfather."

"What can I help you with?" Pops asked.

A wave of apprehension hit me, triggered by the solemnity in Sawyer's dark eyes.

"Mr. Ransom," he said to my grandfather, "I'm afraid I have to ask you to come with me to the police station."

Chapter Six

"WHAT? WHY?" I SAID BEFORE POPS HAD A CHANCE to respond.

"Is this about Archie's murder?" Pops asked.

"It is," Sawyer confirmed.

"So he really was murdered?" I hadn't heard anything about an official statement to that effect yet, but I'd been in my own little world of chocolate-making for most of the day.

Pops rested a hand on my shoulder. "It was in the paper this morning."

"But Pops didn't have anything to do with Archie's death," I said to Sawyer. "Why do you need to question him?"

"Archie and I had that disagreement," Pops reminded me, although I hadn't forgotten. I just thought it ridiculous that anyone could think that Pops knew anything about the murder.

"It's standard procedure," Sawyer said to me. "He's not the only person we're talking to."

That reassured me. Slightly, anyway.

Pops squeezed my shoulder. "It'll be fine, Rebecca. Don't worry."

I stood rooted to the spot in the middle of the shop as Pops preceded Sawyer out the door. Angela and Milo appeared next to me.

"He'll be fine," Angie said, echoing Pops's own prediction.

"Of course he will," Milo added without an ounce of worry. "It's Pops. The cops just want to know if he has any useful information. No one would ever suspect him of hurting anyone."

Angie nudged me with her elbow. "Shouldn't you get a move on, Becca?"

I tugged my phone out of my pocket and checked the time. "Shoot. You're right." I was supposed to meet Justin in less than an hour. "I hope I'm not going to be late."

Angie smiled. "We're all looking forward to meeting Justin."

"As long as he's not stuffy," Milo said.

"Milo!" Angie admonished.

He shrugged and grinned. "He's a lawyer, right? Aren't lawyers stuffy?"

I narrowed my eyes at him, even though I wasn't really mad. "Way to judge a guy before you've even met him. How many lawyers have you met in your lifetime, anyway?"

"None?"

I gave him a playful shove that sent him back a step. "Exactly. You'll like him."

"Is that an order?"

This time Angela gave him a gentle shove. "Leave her alone." To me she added, "Go on. You don't want to keep him waiting."

With nerves dancing around in my stomach, I jogged to the parking lot at the edge of town, glad I'd decided to wear shorts that morning. Once again, the sun was beating down from a clear blue sky, and the temperature was more suited to swimming than jogging. I made a quick stop at a coffee shop to get myself a frozen lemonade to help cool me down, and then I continued on my way. When I reached my car, I cranked up the air-conditioning and set off for the airport in Burlington.

The drive took me about an hour, and when I finally found a parking spot, I knew I was running late. Sure enough, Justin had already retrieved his luggage and stood waiting for me inside the building, his suitcase resting on the ground next to him. My nerves had danced more and more vigorously the closer I got to my destination, but when Justin caught sight of me and a grin appeared on his face, I relaxed.

"I'm so glad you're finally here!" I greeted him with a hug and a kiss.

"So am I. I've missed you."

I was already smiling, but that made my smile even brighter. "Same." I nodded at the suitcase sitting next to him. "Is that all your luggage?"

He reached behind the suitcase and picked up a messenger bag I hadn't noticed before. "And my laptop."

"You're not going to be working while you're here, are you?"

Justin swung the bag's strap over his shoulder and pulled out the handle of his suitcase. "I didn't want to waste the time spent on the plane."

I didn't miss the fact that he hadn't really answered my question. I tried to ignore the ping of disappointment in my chest. At least he was here in Vermont. If he had to keep in touch with the office now and then, that wasn't such a big deal.

"Have you been doing a lot of surfing?" I asked as we made our way out of the building.

He was more tanned than when I'd last seen him, and there were golden highlights in his light brown hair.

"Whenever I get the chance." He grinned at me. "I'm guessing there's no surfing in Larch Haven."

"No, but there are plenty of other great things."

"I'm looking forward to checking them out, but I know for certain that the best part of Larch Haven is right beside me."

"Smooth," I said, unable to keep myself from smiling.

"I try."

We packed his luggage into my car and began the drive back to Larch Haven. We chatted the whole way, catching up on each other's lives. Even though we texted regularly and talked via video calls at least once a week, we still had plenty to share. Somehow remote communication wasn't quite the same as seeing each other in person.

By the time we reached the edge of town, the afternoon had slipped into early evening. The sun had yet to set, but most of the shops were closed, and tourists were flocking to restaurants for dinner. I regretted not leaving my Jon boat at the main dock before heading to the airport. Without it there, we'd have to walk to my cottage. At least Justin's suitcase was on wheels. I offered to carry his laptop, but he refused.

I stopped when we reached Venice Avenue, wanting to give him a chance to take in the sight of the canals and the colorful timber-frame shops.

"What do you think?" I asked.

"It's like we're suddenly in Europe. Or on a movie set."

I beamed. "Isn't it great?"

I led him over the bridge and along the canals, pointing out some of my favorite cottages on the way.

"And this is home sweet home," I said when we reached my cottage.

Justin stopped to admire it. "Are you sure we're not on a movie set?"

"Positive. It's the best of real life."

By the time we dropped off Justin's luggage and I'd introduced him to Binx and Truffles, we were in danger of running late for the welcome dinner my family had planned. My nerves resurfaced as we set off along the winding path that would take us to the northern end of town. It was like butterflies had decided to dance a jitterbug in my stomach. I felt confident that most of my family would like Justin. It was more what he would think of life in Larch Haven that had me feeling less certain. Justin was born and raised in Los Angeles, and my hometown was about as different from LA as you could get.

I did my best to push my worries aside, determined to enjoy the evening. Things would work out in the end. Or so I hoped.

As we crossed the final bridge before reaching the restaurant, I pointed down the canal. "That's where we're headed."

The Gondolier—which was owned and operated by my brother, Gareth, and his husband, Blake—faced the canal where it opened out to Shadow Lake. Situated at the end of a line of businesses, the restaurant's patio extended out over the cobblestones, from the front of the building to the edge of the canal, allowing diners to enjoy their food while overlooking the water. Pots and barrels around the patio's edge practically overflowed with brilliantly colored flowers. Soon, when the daylight began to fade from the sky, lanterns and twinkle lights would light up the area.

The patio was nearly full when we arrived at the restaurant, with only a couple of tables free. I noticed a few familiar faces, but the rest of the diners were likely tourists. Inside, there were more free tables, but the place was still busy. I felt the familiar sense of pride that always welled up inside of me when I visited the restaurant. Gareth and Blake had made a huge success of the place. It had taken a lot of time and hard work to get to this point, but now they had the most successful restaurant in Larch Haven, and the Gondolier had been featured on a foodie television show and in a couple of magazines over the past two years.

I waved at the hostess, Natasha, but bypassed her, heading for the banquet room at the back of the restaurant that was used for private parties. The butterflies picked up their frantic dancing in my chest. I took a deep breath, trying to calm down. I definitely didn't want my brother knowing I was nervous. He'd probably misinterpret my anxiety and count it as a strike against Justin before he'd even had a chance to get to know the guy. As for the rest of my family, they'd accept Justin more easily.

Before we reached the back room, my brother-in-law emerged from the kitchen. Over six feet tall with a muscular build and blond hair and blue eyes, Blake resembled a stereotypical California surfer dude. He'd never actually lived in California, but he did enjoy going on surfing trips to the West Coast, Hawaii, and wherever else he could catch a good wave.

Blake grinned when he saw me. He came over our way and gathered me into one of his bear hugs.

"You must be Justin," he said to my boyfriend once he released me.

"This is my brother-in-law, Blake," I told Justin as the two men shook hands.

"Good to meet you," Blake said. "I hope you won't be overwhelmed by the number of people at dinner."

"I'm looking forward to meeting everyone," Justin said.

"Is anyone else here yet?" I asked Blake.

"Everyone."

"Then we'd better not keep them waiting." I took Justin's hand and walked with him into the banquet room.

It took close to ten minutes before we sat down at the big table. Introducing everyone took time, especially since each of the adults wanted a chance to exchange a few words with Justin. Milo, the youngest family member present, contented himself with lifting a hand in a wave when I introduced him.

"See," I whispered to Milo when I found myself at his side. "Not stuffy at all."

We watched as Lolly and Pops chatted with Justin a few feet away.

"Hey, the jury's still out," Milo said.

"Seriously?"

He shrugged, but he had a grin on his face.

I figured I didn't need to worry about Milo. He'd come around. Gareth concerned me more. His overprotective streak could be annoying at times. I'd introduced him to Justin when we first came into the banquet room, and that had gone well enough, but now he was watching Justin from across the room and looked suspiciously like he was sizing him up.

He must have sensed my gaze on him because he glanced my way. I shot him a look of warning. He raised one eyebrow and then returned his attention to my boyfriend, his eyes as focused as lasers.

I sighed and once again tried not to worry. If Justin moved to Larch Haven, Gareth would learn to accept him.

If, or when?

That thought stirred up my nervous butterflies again. They eventually settled, once everyone was seated at the table with food in front of them. The conversation flowed easily, and Justin even had Lolly laughing when he told her about funny encounters with celebrities he'd met at industry parties.

That was how I'd met Justin. Hollywood parties weren't exactly my favorite way to spend time, but I'd attended them now and then for networking purposes. Justin was an entertainment lawyer, and he worked for one of the most prestigious firms in LA. I'd found him down-to-earth for a Hollywood lawyer.

We stayed late at the Gondolier, the gathering only breaking up once Angie and her husband, Marco, declared that they needed to get home to relieve the babysitter who was looking after their two kids.

It took another twenty minutes for all of us to say our

goodbyes, even though most of my family members would probably see more of Justin over the coming week.

Eventually, Lolly, Pops, Justin, and I were the only ones left in the banquet room. Gareth and Blake were still at the restaurant, but my brother had retreated to the kitchen, his domain, while Blake was checking in with the front of the house.

While Lolly chatted with Justin, I pulled Pops aside.

"How did things go at the police station earlier? Was it what you thought? Just some standard questions?"

"Pretty much."

My heart dropped like a stone.

There was something Pops wasn't telling me. I could tell from the way he avoided my gaze and clutched his cap in one hand.

"Pops . . ."

He patted my shoulder. "You don't need to worry about it, Rebecca."

"I don't need to worry about what?"

"It's getting late. I should get your grandmother home."

"Lolly stays up later than you." I crossed my arms over my chest. "Pops?"

"I didn't kill Archie."

"Of course you didn't." I interpreted what he hadn't said. "Do the police think you did?"

"Hm." Once again, he wouldn't look me in the eye.

"Pops, please. Just tell me what you're not saying."

"All right," he said, relenting. "But don't go worrying about it, sweetheart."

"Worrying about what?"

Pops cleared his throat. "I guess you could say I'm a murder suspect."

Chapter Seven

ALTHOUGH POPS TRIED TO ASSURE ME THAT THERE was no need to be concerned, I couldn't help but worry. My grandfather was a murder suspect. As absurd as that might sound to me, the police obviously didn't think it ridiculous.

I didn't want my worries to distract me from Justin during his visit, so I did my best to convince myself that everything would work out fine for Pops. After all, he wasn't the killer, so there wouldn't be enough evidence for the police to arrest him. I should have asked him if he had an alibi for the murder, but he'd cut off our conversation as soon as Lolly and Justin had wandered over our way.

I was awake earlier than Justin the next morning. He was usually an early riser, but with the three-hour time difference between Vermont and California, I wasn't surprised that he was still asleep. I ate some fruit salad for breakfast, and then took Binx and Truffles out for a walk. It wasn't always easy to take them out on their leashes together. More often than not, Binx decided to go one way and Truffles wanted to go in the opposite direction. I usually ended up having to carry one for half the walk and then the other for the second half. Today, however, they both seemed content to wander along the same path. We never strayed too far from home on our outings, but Binx liked to cross the nearest bridge and stare down the Lhasa apso that often sat in the front window of the cottage across the canal.

By the time we wandered back home, Justin was awake and ready to go. The gondola races would be starting that morning with the preliminary rounds for each category. The following day would be the semifinals, with the finals the day after that. Justin and I would take in at least some of the races that morning. It was such a tradition in Larch Haven that it would have been practically sacrilege for us not to attend. Plus, my brother would be competing. I didn't know if I'd catch his preliminary race, but I didn't doubt that he'd advance to the semifinals, and I planned to watch that round for sure.

First, however, we took a leisurely walk to Gathering Grounds, the local coffee shop, which was tucked around the corner from Venice Avenue. Dizzy had the day off and we'd arranged to meet her there so the three of us could go watch the races together. She lived in an apartment above the local bookshop, and I spotted her walking from that direction as Justin and I approached the coffee shop.

When Dizzy caught sight of us, she broke into a jog. She greeted me with a hug, and then hugged Justin too.

"I'm so glad to finally meet you in person!" she enthused.

"Same here," he said.

They'd seen each other briefly and had exchanged a few words during one of my video calls with Justin, but otherwise all they knew about the other was what I'd told them. I was glad they were finally getting a chance to meet properly.

"We'd better get in line," Dizzy said as she opened the door to Gathering Grounds. "Otherwise we'll have no chance of getting a table. It looks like everybody's trying to power up with caffeine before the races."

"Why don't you two grab a table while I get drinks for all of us?" Justin suggested.

"Good idea," I said as we entered the coffee shop.

The delightful smells of coffee and baked goods greeted us. I took in a deep breath, enjoying the scents as I glanced around the shop. Dizzy was right. There were only a couple of free tables left inside, and four people stood in line at the counter.

"What would you like?" Justin asked Dizzy.

"An iced caramel mocha, please." She pulled out her wallet, but Justin waved her off.

"My treat," he said.

Dizzy smiled. "That's so nice of you. Thank you."

"How about you, Becca?"

"Orange pekoe tea, please."

"Black, right?" he checked.

"One cream, one sugar."

He smacked a hand to his forehead. "Of course. I'll be right back."

Dizzy and I claimed one of the free tables and sat down across from each other.

She leaned closer to me over the tabletop. "So . . . how's the visit going so far?"

A ridiculous surge of panic shot through me. I grabbed Dizzy's wrist. "He didn't remember how I like my tea. I always get it the same way. That's not a bad sign, right? I mean, we've been long-distance for months now. It's totally normal not to remember, right?"

Dizzy peeled my fingers off her wrist and patted my hand. "Let's just give him points for getting the drinks for us."

I sat back. "You're right. I shouldn't be freaking out. There's no reason to freak out."

Dizzy raised an eyebrow. "Why are you so worried? What aren't you telling me?"

I drummed my fingers against my leg. "I think my anxiety about the whole murder thing is just encroaching on everything."

Dizzy lowered her voice. "Because there's a killer running loose among us?"

"That . . . and other things." I glanced around, noting that we couldn't have a very private conversation at the coffee shop. "I'll fill you in later."

"Okay, so how does Justin like Larch Haven?"

"So far so good, I think. He hasn't had much of a chance to take it in yet. We're planning to go hiking tomorrow. I want him to see that he can do some of the things he enjoys here just as well as he can in California."

Shadow Lake may not offer any waves big enough for surfing, but hiking was another outdoor activity Justin enjoyed, and there was plenty of opportunity for that around Larch Haven. Justin worked a lot of hours, but he tried to find time for enjoying the outdoors at least once a week. If he moved here, I figured he'd have more time for such pursuits. The pace of life in Larch Haven was far slower than in Los Angeles. Of course, he'd probably end up working in Burlington, but the commute from Larch Haven wasn't terrible, and hopefully his work hours wouldn't be as crazy as they were now.

Justin carried our drinks over and sat down next to me.

Dizzy took a quick sip of her drink and then wrapped her hands around the cup, fixing her eyes on Justin. "Do you believe in aliens?"

Justin stopped with his coffee cup halfway to his mouth. He set it back down on the table. "Do I . . . ?"

Dizzy nodded. "Aliens."

I fought against the smile trying to stretch across my face.

Justin glanced my way, nonplussed.

"She likes to open with that question," I said.

"It allows me to get the measure of a person." Dizzy stared at Justin, waiting for an answer.

He cleared his throat, taking a moment to gather his

thoughts. "I guess I . . . I suppose it's possible there's life out there somewhere?"

"Is that a question or statement?" Dizzy asked.

"Leave him alone, Diz," I said, taking pity on Justin. "You're going to scare him off."

"Hey," he protested. "I don't scare that easily."

"Glad to hear it." Dizzy took a long sip of her drink and winced. "Brain freeze!" She clapped a hand to her forehead.

Justin glanced over at the display case of baked goods. "I think I'm going to grab a muffin. Can I get something for either of you?"

Dizzy and I weren't hungry, so Justin went in search of a muffin. I wondered if he was truly hungry, or if he wanted a minute to recover from Dizzy's interrogation.

"You didn't warn him," she said.

"About you?" I grinned. "What would be the fun in that?"

She mirrored my grin.

My phone buzzed in my pocket. I pulled it out and read the text message Angela had just sent me.

"Shoot."

"What's wrong?" Dizzy asked.

"Angie forgot her keys to the shop. It wouldn't take her long to go back home to get them, but it'll be faster for me to run over there and open the door for her." I glanced Justin's way. There was still one person in line ahead of him.

"Go ahead," Dizzy said. "I'll let Justin know where you've gone."

"Thanks." I jumped up and dashed out the door.

I jogged to True Confections and slid my key to the shop off my keychain so Angie could keep it for the day. She promised to return it soon, and I left her to open the store. I considered jogging back to the coffee shop, but the sun was already beating down from the sky, despite the early hour, so I settled for a brisk walk.

When I opened the door to Gathering Grounds, my heart did a funny flip-flop in my chest. I hesitated in the doorway for a second, and then hurried forward and dropped into the seat across from Dizzy again.

"Why is Justin talking to Sawyer?" I asked, my voice pitched slightly higher than normal.

Sawyer was in uniform, as always seemed to be the case lately. He and Justin stood over by the counter, talking. Mercedes, the coffee shop's owner, added a few words to their conversation before moving along to the cash register, where another customer waited. I couldn't hear what any of them were saying.

Dizzy shrugged. "No idea."

I wished I had super hearing. "Maybe I should go over there."

"Why?"

"I should introduce them to each other. You know, properly." I tried to read Justin's lips but couldn't figure out a single word. Sawyer had his back to me, so I couldn't even try to guess what he was saying.

"Mercedes already introduced them," Dizzy said.

"But she doesn't know who Justin is."

"I don't think it was hard for her to figure that out."

Okay, that was probably true. Mercedes knew my boyfriend was visiting this week. I'd told her as much a few days earlier when Dizzy and I were in the coffee shop picking up frozen lemonades.

"Relax, Becca." Dizzy took a sip of her drink.

"I'm relaxed." I tore my gaze away from the two men and drank some tea.

A second later, my gaze strayed back their way.

Justin shook Sawyer's hand before heading over to us, carrying a small plate with a blueberry muffin on it. Mercedes handed Sawyer a takeout cup and he turned for the door. He caught my eye and raised a hand in greeting, but he didn't stop. He was out the door a second later.

"What was that about?" I asked Justin as he sat down next to me.

"Nothing. We were just talking. That cop said he grew up with you."

"I wonder if he's competing in the gondola races," Dizzy said.

I wasn't entirely sure why it felt so weird to see Justin and Sawyer together. Whatever the reason, I decided it didn't matter. "He's probably too busy, what with the murder investigation."

I'd filled Justin in on the murder on the drive to Larch Haven. Fortunately, it hadn't put him off in the least. As he'd said, there were far more murders in Los Angeles each year than in the whole state of Vermont.

"Why aren't you racing?" Justin asked me.

"Um. I guess I never really got into the whole gondola thing." I busied myself with drinking down the remains of my tea, but I didn't fail to notice the expression on Dizzy's face. She knew the real reason why I refused to stand up on a gondola and propel it across the water. Thankfully, she had my back and didn't spill the beans to my boyfriend.

Justin devoured the last piece of his muffin. "What about you, Dizzy?"

"This is my only day off this week," she said. "Things have been crazy busy at the library with all the summer programs. Besides, I can give a steady gondola ride, but I've never been particularly fast."

I nudged Justin in the ribs with my elbow. "Maybe by next year you'll be out there racing."

He laughed before taking a drink of his coffee.

When we'd all finished our drinks, we left Gathering Grounds and returned to Venice Avenue. It seemed everyone else had the same idea. Crowds of people had gathered along both sides of the closest canal. The races would start at the main dock in front of the Larch Haven Hotel. The gondoliers would travel along this canal and then out into the open water of the lake, where they had to navigate around a buoy before coming back into the canal and crossing the finish line by the nearest bridge.

One of the preliminary rounds had already started, and people cheered and clapped, encouraging the racers. We had to cross the bridge to find a spot where we could watch. Many people had brought lawn chairs or camp chairs to sit on. Others sat on the grass or stood to watch. We didn't have much choice but to stand. Too many people had arrived ahead of us, and standing was the only way we could see over everyone else.

We found a shady spot beneath a sugar maple that gave us a view of the end of the canal as well as a partial view of the route out on the lake. As we claimed our spot, the current race drew to a close. Minutes later, another one began. This one was for women aged eighteen to forty-nine.

"That's Jolene Doyle-Brodsky in the lead," Dizzy said when the racers came into view, heading for the lake. "She's the defending champion for this age group."

Jolene looked like she meant business. She had her auburn hair tied back in a tight ponytail, and she stayed intensely focused on the path ahead as she rowed past.

"I bet she's going to win again this year," a woman said.

I glanced her way. I recognized the woman, and thought her name was Deirdre, but I didn't really know her. She was talking to a woman with gray hair whose name I didn't know.

"It doesn't look like Archie's death is putting her off her game," the gray-haired woman said.

"Why would it?" Deirdre asked. "It's not as if that man was a father to her. Plus, she and Alex shouldn't have any more problems with the housing development now."

"True," her companion said. "I can't believe Archie did that. It's one thing to be a deadbeat father, but trying to derail his daughter's business? That's a whole different level."

Chapter Eight

THE TWO WOMEN CUT OFF THEIR CONVERSATION SO they could cheer on the stragglers who'd fallen behind the other racers. I remembered when we were talking to Maria after the vigil that Dizzy mentioned Archie had tried to derail Jolene's business. I wanted to ask Dizzy what that was all about, but she was so focused on the gondola race that I didn't think she'd overheard the other women's conversation. I decided not to distract her.

After we'd watched a handful of races, we decided to call it quits for the day. The semifinals and finals would be the most interesting races, and our patch of shade had disappeared with the movement of the sun, leaving us uncomfortably hot.

While most of the tourists were still absorbed with the races, the three of us wandered around town, showing Justin our favorite shops and eateries. After we had lunch at a cozy café, Dizzy left us to run some errands and Justin and I headed back to my cottage.

"I need to make some phone calls," he said as I unlocked the front door.

"Work calls?" I guessed.

"Yes, but they won't take long. I promise."

"No worries," I said, hoping he wasn't wrong about how much time the calls would take. "Actually, I need to go see my brother for a few minutes. How about I meet you back here?"

"Sounds good."

I gave Binx and Truffles each a quick cuddle and then headed for my Jon boat. I always experienced a flash of anxiety whenever I climbed into or out of the boat, but once seated I felt relatively safe. I'd purchased this particular type of boat because of its stability in the calm waters of the canals. I'd been told that it was so stable that it was safe to stand up and walk around the small craft while it was on the water, but I wasn't about to test that theory.

Once safely seated, I turned on the whisper-quiet electric engine and headed away from the crowds of spectators. Although there were living quarters above the Gondolier, Gareth and Blake had decided to rent out that apartment and live away from the restaurant. That way they had some outdoor space as well as some separation from their work life. They still spent most of their time at the restaurant, but it was probably true that it would occupy even more of their life if they lived right upstairs.

Since the Gondolier wouldn't open until the evening today, I figured I might find my brother at home. He and Blake lived in a log house at the edge of town, where generous lots backed up to the forest.

I tied up my whisper boat at the closest dock to their house and finished the journey on foot. I found Blake out front of the house, watering the petunias growing in half barrels on either side of the steps leading to the porch.

"Look at you, actually taking a morning off," I said as I approached.

Blake finished watering one barrel and moved the hose over to the next one. "Hey, I strictly enforce our downtime."

"That's good to hear. Is Gareth around?"

Blake hooked a thumb over his shoulder. "He's working out."

I knew that meant he was out in the shed that he and Blake had converted into a home gym. Also built from logs, the shed matched the house and had an automatic garage door that was currently open. I found Gareth doing TRX exercises with straps suspended from the ceiling. He spotted me when I walked into the gym, but he continued with his workout.

"How did your race go this morning?" I asked, coming to a stop in the middle of the shed.

By the time I'd left the coffee shop with Dizzy and Justin, Gareth's race had already finished.

"I won my heat," he replied. "Semifinals tomorrow."

"Nice. Can you text me the time? I don't want to miss it."

"Sure." His gaze strayed out the open door. "What have you done with Justin?"

"He's at my place, making some phone calls."

"I thought he had the week off work."

"He just needs to check in with a few things."

Gareth adjusted his grip on the TRX straps. "Has he said he's willing to move here?"

I bristled at the question, but tried to hide it. "That's why he's here. To figure that out. He only got here yesterday."

"Okay." It was a simple word, but it was loaded with things left unsaid.

"What does that mean?" I asked.

"It doesn't mean anything."

I didn't believe that for a second. "You don't like him? Why not? What's not to like?"

Gareth finally gave up on his exercises, releasing the straps and resting his hands on his hips. "It's not that I don't like him. He seems like a good guy."

"But?" I knew he had more to say.

"I'm just not sure that he's the right guy for you."

"You've known him all of five seconds."

He held up a placating hand. "Fine. Maybe I'm wrong." He grabbed a towel and wiped the sweat off his face. "What brought you by?"

I had to force myself to shove my irritation aside so I could get my mind back on track. "Have you heard about Pops?"

"You mean about the fact that he's a murder suspect?"

"He should get a lawyer, but I don't think he'll listen to me. Can you talk to him?"

"He doesn't need a lawyer."

"He's a murder suspect!"

Gareth flipped the towel over his shoulder and sat down on a weight-training bench. "He didn't kill anyone."

"I know that," I said, my exasperation building steadily. "But the police clearly don't."

"It'll be fine."

"How can you know that?"

"Because he's Pops."

I let out a growl of frustration.

Gareth rolled his eyes. "Seriously, Becca. Quit worrying. Everything will be fine."

I spun on my heel and marched out of the shed.

Why was he more concerned about my relationship with Justin than he was with Pops being a murder suspect? He had his priorities all mixed-up.

Blake was no longer out front of the house, so I stormed all the way back to the dock, thoroughly frustrated with my brother. I plunked myself down into my whisper boat, causing it to bob up and down. My irritation vanished, replaced with a flash of fear as I gripped the sides of the boat. I shot an apprehensive glance at the murky water of the canal and held my breath.

The boat settled in the water. I breathed in and then out, trying to find a sense of calm.

Gareth didn't think that Pops needed help, and Pops apparently agreed with that position.

If Garcth wouldn't help and Pops wouldn't help himself, then it was up to me to get him out of his predicament.

Somehow, I had to prove that my grandfather hadn't killed Archie Smith.

Chapter Nine

I WAS SO WRAPPED UP IN MY THOUGHTS ABOUT HOW I could help Pops that I didn't notice Sawyer on the bank of the canal until he called my name. I cut my boat's engine and the craft slowed to a gentle glide. Sawyer easily kept pace along the bank.

"On your lunch break?" I guessed.

He was in his uniform, but he had a paper bag in one hand with the Cisco's Sandwich Shop logo on it.

"I was grabbing a sandwich when I got a call about a prowler over at Mrs. Hallwood's place," he said.

"Everything okay?"

"It was just a cat that got into her garden shed."

Mrs. Hallwood was a sweet old lady, but she often dreamed up trouble where there wasn't any.

"I'm glad I spotted you," Sawyer said. "I'm going to have to reschedule our gondola lesson. I'm working on Monday after all."

"That's all right," I said, making sure to hide my relief.

My nonchalance didn't fool him.

"Don't think you're off the hook," he warned. "I'm still getting you on a gondola."

"We'll see." I turned my gaze to a small private dock to my left, a few feet along an offshoot of the canal. "Hold on a second. There's something I want to talk to you about."

I turned the whisper boat's engine on for a few seconds, giving me enough momentum to reach the dock. Sawyer anticipated my next move and stepped down onto the floating platform.

I tossed him the mooring line and he caught it in one hand. He held out his other hand to help me out of the boat.

"Thanks," I said as I stepped onto the dock.

"It's about your grandfather, isn't it?"

My next words came out in a rush. "He didn't kill Archie. He'd never hurt anyone. I know they didn't get along, but Archie had disputes with a lot of people. You've known Pops your whole life. Surely you can't think he's a killer."

"It's got nothing to do with what I think," Sawyer said. "And he's not exactly doing himself a favor."

"What do you mean?"

"His vagueness about his alibi. It makes it seem like he's got something to hide."

"What do you mean, vagueness about his alibi?" I wished Pops had told me more at the restaurant.

"You should ask him that. I shouldn't be talking about the case."

"But he's not the only person who's been questioned, right?"

"Not by a long shot."

That was one bit of good news. "Did you talk to Mike Kwan? Archie was trying to damage his boats, remember?"

"We talked to Mike. He's got an alibi—a solid one. Besides, Archie never actually got around to doing any damage at the Boat Barn."

Sawyer glanced at his watch. "Look, I've got to get going. If your grandfather can fill in the holes in his alibi, that would go a long way to helping him out."

He handed me the mooring line and stepped from the dock onto the grassy bank. "Did you lose your boyfriend?"

"He's making some phone calls."

"An entertainment lawyer, huh? Where's he going to find celebrities to work with around these parts? Aside from you, that is."

"I'm definitely not a celebrity." I didn't bother to answer his question.

Instead, I climbed back into my boat and started the engine. As I steered away from the dock, I glanced back over my shoulder. Sawyer was walking off in the opposite direction.

It irked me whenever anyone brought up the possibility that Justin might not be able to find fulfilling work in Vermont. Probably because I had that same concern myself. While there were entertainment law firms in Vermont—I'd checked online to make sure—I knew the opportunities wouldn't be the same here as in Los Angeles. Justin worked with movie stars and superstar athletes. He wouldn't find work on that same level out here. Of course, that didn't mean he couldn't be happy. But did he really want to leave all that behind?

"That's exactly what he's here to find out," I reminded myself out loud.

A funny feeling that might have been dread tried to settle in my stomach. I quickly kicked it to the curb, determined to remain optimistic.

When I got back to the cottage, Justin was finishing up his last call. We drove up to Snowflake Canyon and spent the rest of the afternoon wandering around the ski resort town. I tried not to let thoughts of Pops and his troubles distract me, but that wasn't easy and I wasn't entirely successful. Fortunately, Justin didn't seem to notice.

After eating dinner at a restaurant in Snowflake Canyon,

we drove back down the mountain to Larch Haven. We left my car in the lot at the edge of town and then walked to my grandparents' cottage in the southeastern corner of town. Instead of going to the front door, I led the way around the cottage, knowing that the back door would be open at this time of year.

We found my grandparents in their vegetable garden. Pops was picking beans and Lolly had a basket full of bright-red tomatoes.

"You're just in time," Lolly declared when she saw us. "I took a blueberry crumble out of the oven a few minutes ago." She headed for the cottage. "Come on in. I'll get out the ice cream."

We hadn't arranged beforehand to stop by, but Lolly was always ready for company, and she loved feeding her visitors. She made the best blueberry crumble I'd ever tasted.

"You go ahead," I said to Justin. "I'm going to talk to Pops for a minute."

I waited as Justin followed Lolly through the screen door to the kitchen.

"How's he liking Larch Haven so far?" Pops asked as he dropped a handful of beans into the bucket by his feet.

"He seems to be having a good time." I didn't want to talk about Justin, so I quickly moved the conversation in another direction. "I talked to Sawyer earlier and he said that you've been vague about your alibi for the time when Archie was killed."

"Hmph." Pops went back to picking beans.

"Do you know when he was killed?" I asked.

Pops straightened up and scratched his mostly bald head. "All I know is that it was after nine o'clock on Sunday night. The police wanted to know where I was from that time until the next morning."

"Weren't you here at home?"

"Most of the time." He got back to plucking green beans from the row of plants.

Getting information out of Pops was like pulling teeth.

"Where else were you?" I pressed.

Pops finally seemed to resign himself to the fact that I wasn't going to give up on my questions. He plunked a few more beans into his bucket and then picked it up off the ground. "I went for a walk. Shortly before ten."

"That's kind of late for a walk."

"I wasn't sleepy. I decided I needed some fresh air."

"So where did you go? Didn't anyone see you?"

"I wandered here and there, on past the canals to the north. I doubt anyone saw me over there."

That part of town, out near where Gareth and Blake lived, was the least populated. I knew Pops was right that there was a good chance no one had seen him in that area, especially since it would have been dark or close to it.

"Did you at least tell the police your route so they can ask people if they saw you?"

"I can't remember exactly where I went." He stepped over the row of beans to get out of the garden. "Now, let's go. I've been waiting to get a taste of that blueberry crumble since your grandmother started making it."

I stood in place for a moment, confused and struggling not to get upset. There was something Pops wasn't telling me. He was being purposely evasive, and I knew that would be as clear to the police as it was to me. Sawyer had already suggested as much.

I fought off a wave of despair. I knew that my grandfather hadn't killed Archie, but he was hiding something, and that didn't look good. I was going to have to figure out how to help him. Hopefully a dish of blueberry crumble and ice cream would give my brain a boost, because at the moment I was at a loss as to how to proceed.

Justin and I spent the remainder of the evening at my grandparents' house, chatting over our dessert and cups of tea and coffee. It was a nice, relaxed way to finish off the day, and I was pleased with how well Justin was getting along with Lolly and Pops.

The two of us set out early on our hike the next morning, before the day got too hot. I wanted to show Justin one of my favorite spots in the forest. Although I used to love climbing to the top of Whisper Mountain, where there was an amazing view of all of Larch Haven, I hadn't gone there for years. I would have liked to show Justin that view, but even before the trail got washed out it was a long hike. Now, with detours required through some difficult terrain, it would take most of the day. I'd recovered well from my ruptured appendix, but I wasn't yet fit enough for a hike as ambitious as that. I wasn't sure that Justin was either, despite his love for surfing and his occasional hikes outside Los Angeles.

So today I was taking him to a waterfall where, in years past, there had been an eagle's nest in a big old pine tree. We followed the walkways along the canals to the northern edge of town and the head of the trail. As we entered the forest, I heard someone coming from the opposite direction. Seconds later, a woman came around a bend in the trail. When she drew closer, I realized she was Carmen Vasquez, Maria's younger sister. She wore shorts and a tank top and carried a small backpack. She had dirt smeared on her knees and on her sneakers. I wondered if she'd taken a tumble, but she seemed unharmed.

"You're out early," I said after we'd exchanged cheery greetings.

"I've always been an early bird," Carmen said with a smile. "Enjoy your hike!"

She carried on toward town, and Justin and I forged ahead. The trail took us in the general direction of Archie's property before veering off to the north. For the umpteenth time since the night before, I wondered what my grandfather was hiding and why. Part of me wanted to turn back and spend the day figuring out how to get his name off the police's suspect list, but I still wasn't sure how to go about that. I hoped the fresh air and exercise would give me a jolt of inspiration since the blueberry crumble hadn't done the trick. After an hour of hiking, I led Justin off the trail. Even though I'd lived in California for years, I still knew my way around this part of the forest.

Within minutes, I heard the sound of rushing water.

"Almost there," I told Justin.

We climbed a small wooded hill, the sound of the water growing louder. At the top of the rise, we broke free of the trees and stopped. We stood on a rocky bank of a swift-running creek. A short distance upstream, the water cascaded down a twenty-foot drop. Rainbows danced in the spray around the waterfall, giving it a magical appearance. It was as beautiful as I remembered.

"Isn't it amazing?" I had to raise my voice to be heard over the rushing water.

"Definitely worth the trip," Justin said as he took in the view.

I picked my way along the bank, heading closer to the waterfall, hoping to find the eagle's nest. I stopped when I noticed footprints in the dirt. Someone else had been here recently. I'd always thought of this place as my secret spot, but there were most likely plenty of other locals who knew about it. I'd never run into anyone else here, though.

After a short distance, the footprints veered off into the forest. I continued on straight ahead, but soon met with disappointment. I found the right tree, but the nest was in tatters and clearly hadn't been used anytime recently. Not surprising, perhaps, since I hadn't visited this spot in years, but I'd nevertheless hoped that the nest was still in use.

Justin and I sat by the waterfall for a rest and then set off on our return journey.

"What do you want to do this afternoon?" I asked as we got back on the trail.

"I've made plans for us," Justin said. "I hope you don't mind."

"What kind of plans?"

He grinned. "That's a secret."

Now I was intrigued. I tried to get a clue out of him, but he didn't crack. He didn't know much about Larch Haven, so I didn't know what he could have possibly planned for us.

My thoughts finally shifted when we got closer to town.

"Mind if we take a short detour?" I asked Justin.

I turned down a smaller trail that took us to a dirt road that led through the forest, providing vehicle access to the lakefront properties. The road connected with the highway after winding around the outer edge of town, always staying within the forest.

From the dirt road, I followed the rutted and bumpy driveway onto Archie's property. When his ramshackle cabin came into view, I stopped. Police tape surrounded the yard and cabin, preventing me from getting any closer.

"Is this where that guy was killed?" Justin asked, sounding uneasy.

"Yes, but we can't get any closer."

"Why would you want to?"

I didn't feel like explaining about Pops being a suspect. "Never mind. Let's go."

We returned to the trail and headed back to town.

Since Archie's property was still off-limits, whatever clues I might be able to find about the identity of his killer would have to come from elsewhere.

Chapter Ten

"I HAVE ONE QUESTION," JUSTIN SAID ONCE WE WERE back at my cottage. "Can we take your boat out on the lake, or do we need to rent a bigger one for that?"

"So you're not planning to serenade me while taking me for a gondola ride?" I joked.

"I don't know how to paddle one of those things, and you know I can't carry a tune, so no."

"That's good," I said. "It's a warm day, but I don't want to end up capsizing in the canal."

I wasn't going to mention just how much I didn't want that to happen. It was bad enough that Sawyer knew about my fear of falling in the water. Justin didn't need to know too.

I picked up Truffles and pressed my cheek against her head while she purred. "The answer is yes, by the way. We can take my Jon boat out on the lake, as long as the water is calm. We'll have to steer clear of the race route, but otherwise we can go wherever you want. Oh, but I need to be back by four to cheer on Gareth."

He'd texted me earlier in the day, letting me know the time of his semifinal race.

"That won't be a problem." He grabbed his wallet from the coffee table. "You wait here. I'll be back soon, and then we'll get going."

I followed him toward the front door with Truffles still in my arms. "Where are you off to?"

He grinned. "That's part of the secret." He gave me a quick kiss and then left the cottage.

I waited out on the back patio, listening to the cheers from the crowds watching the gondola races. Although I was disappointed that I couldn't poke around Archie's property for clues, I doubted I would have found anything helpful. The police had already searched the place. I'd wanted to get a feel for the area where he'd been killed, in case that would give me an idea of who might have committed the crime, but that was out of the question—for now, at least—so I needed to focus my attention elsewhere if I wanted to help Pops.

I could rule out Mike Kwan as a suspect, thanks to the information Sawyer had given me. Oliver Nieminen had fought with Archie over the washed-out hiking trail, and the two men seemed to despise each other. I needed to find out if Oliver had an opportunity to kill Archie. How exactly I'd go about that, I wasn't yet sure, but I'd have to figure that out soon.

Maria Vasquez also harbored a lot of bitterness against Archie. I didn't know why, so that was something else I needed to look into. Karl and Susan Derendorf had a dispute with Archie over the shed that Karl built. That didn't seem like a reason to murder someone, but I knew people had killed for less, and maybe that had been one of many disputes between the neighbors. I hated the thought of putting the Derendorfs on my suspect list after all they'd gone through with their missing daughter, but I couldn't discount them yet.

I surfaced from my thoughts when Truffles leapt to the ground from one of the perches in the catio. She pounced and then batted her paw at something. Binx hopped down from his perch to join her. With tails twitching, they both pounced, nearly knocking their heads together.

"What are you goofs up to?" I got up from my seat to go take a look.

A grasshopper hopped through the wire mesh of the catio, out of the cats' reach. They hunkered down, watching the insect with intense concentration.

"That was exciting," I said.

Both cats ignored me. They were too interested in waiting and watching in case the grasshopper came back their way.

I left them to their entertainment, intending to sit down on the patio again. Before I could get back to my chair, I spotted Oliver walking along the path on the other side of the canal. I hurried around to the front of my cottage. Justin was nowhere in sight. That meant I had at least a few minutes before he'd be back.

I jogged along the canal to the bridge that would take me in Oliver's direction. Halfway across the bridge, I came to a stop. Oliver now stood talking with Estelle Granger. I'd hoped to talk to him alone so I could question him about Archie's death.

As I watched, Oliver and Estelle exchanged a few words. Then Oliver nodded, said something more, and set off at a brisk walk in the direction of Venice Avenue. I continued across the bridge, but unless I wanted to run like crazy, I wasn't going to catch up to him before he reached the crowds watching the races. The conversation I had planned was definitely one I wanted to have in private, not while surrounded by dozens of other people.

"Hello, Rebecca!" Estelle called out as she waved at me.

I smiled and stopped on the pathway as she reached me.

"How are things going?" I asked her.

"Pretty well. I was just talking with Oliver about some fundraising ideas for the hiking trail restoration project."

"I thought you were opposed to the restoration."

"In a way I was," she said. "But it sounds like the hiking

club has come up with a plan that addresses my environmental concerns. And I've since found out that the local search and rescue has had to deal with an uptick in incidents ever since the trail was washed out. People are still determined to get up to the top of Whisper Mountain. Without the trail, a lot of them are getting into trouble. All in all, I think restoring the trail is the right way to go."

"Makes sense." I wondered if I could still collect some helpful information before my date with Justin. "Do you happen to know Maria Vasquez?"

"Of course. I buy soap from her store. It's all natural, you know. Made from local plants."

"I've heard that," I said. "But I haven't been in her shop yet."

"Oh, you should. Maybe once the races are over and there aren't quite so many tourists. I've noticed she's got a steady stream of customers going in and out all the time, as I'm sure you have at the chocolate shop. I personally like it when I can go in there and take my time browsing without getting elbowed out of the way."

"I know what you mean, though the tourists are definitely good for business."

"Absolutely. I'm glad Maria's got her sister here for the summer, helping her out."

"Carmen? I saw her this morning. Has she finished college yet?" I vaguely remembered hearing something about her attending Duke University.

"She graduated a few weeks ago. I think she's looking for a job in Burlington. Probably a good thing. Maria needs the help in her shop right now, but those two working together for any length of time . . . maybe not the best idea."

"They don't get along?"

"Most of the time they do, but they're so similar. They've both got fiery tempers. They burn out quickly, but they ignite in a flash, and each is quite skilled at setting off the other."

"That's life with siblings." I often got exasperated with my brother, as he did with me.

"I haven't got any firsthand experience with that myself, being an only child," Estelle said. "How's your mother doing? I haven't talked to her for a while."

"She's enjoying life in Florida. I'm hoping she and my dad will come here for Christmas."

My parents had moved to Florida for work opportunities more than a decade ago. They planned to move back to Larch Haven eventually, but probably not until they'd retired.

I caught sight of Justin heading our way, a wicker basket in one hand.

Estelle turned to see what I was looking at. "Ah, your young man. I won't keep you from him." She patted my arm. "It's good to have you back in town, Rebecca."

"Thank you."

She continued on past me and over the bridge.

I smiled as Justin drew closer. "Is that a picnic basket?"

He grinned. "I guess the secret's out now. I thought we'd have a picnic on Mad Hatter Island. How does that sound?"

"I love picnics on the island." I hooked my arm through his as we made our way across the bridge. "What's in the basket?"

"You'll see when we get there."

"Then let's go." I released his arm and hurried up to my cottage. I checked on the cats and found them lounging on their perches again, the grasshopper long gone.

Satisfied that Binx and Truffles were fine, I traded my shoes for flip-flops, locked up the cottage, and led the way to the boathouse. As I steered my whisper boat along the canal toward the lake, I firmly put my thoughts of Archie's murder aside for the time being. With any luck, the police would find the real killer and my grandfather's name would be cleared before I had a chance to do any real investigating.

It didn't take us long to reach the island. I took us around to the north side, where there was a small sandy beach. In the shallows, I hopped out and pulled the whisper boat toward the shore. Justin kicked off his shoes and then climbed out to help. With the boat safely out of the water, Justin put his shoes back on and we climbed up the rocks at the top of the beach and entered the small wooded area. Aside from the occasional distant cheer from the race spectators, all I could hear were our footsteps and birds chirping in the trees.

I breathed in the familiar smell of dried pine needles and summer on the lake.

"It feels like I spent half my childhood on this island," I told Justin as we walked through the woods. "We had picnics; pretended we were pirates; and played games like tag, hide-and-seek, and capture the flag."

"Sounds like an idyllic childhood."

"Probably as close as you can get." I smiled at the memories.

When we reached the rock formation that had given the island its name, I showed Justin the easiest way to get to the top. I'd rarely ever gone up that way. Growing up, all the local kids, myself included, had always taken the more challenging—and therefore more fun—route. The easy way involved climbing a rough, steep path that wound its way around three sides of the formation. No actual climbing was required until the last five feet or so.

I climbed up to the rock's flat top and reached down so Justin could pass up the picnic basket. That way he had both hands free to climb up himself.

When we were both safely at the top, we took a moment to enjoy the panoramic view before sitting down on the sun-warmed rock.

"I hope you've got some drinks in there," I said. "I'm parched."

Justin finally opened the picnic basket. He handed me a glass bottle of lemonade. I recognized the brand. The only place in town that sold it was Cisco's Sandwich Shop. That got my hopes up where the food was concerned.

Justin didn't disappoint me. He handed me a sandwich wrapped in the red-and-white-checkered paper used by Cisco's.

"A Veggie Delight sandwich on sourdough. Is that all right?"

"Better than all right," I said, my mouth already watering as I accepted the sandwich. "It's my favorite."

Justin looked relieved.

"This is great," I said, thinking he needed reassurance. "Thank you for doing this."

"I'm glad you're enjoying it."

We dug into our sandwiches with gusto. Between hiking and climbing up to our picnic spot I'd worked up a good appetite, and I was certain Justin had too.

As we ate, I silently chided myself for freaking out about Justin forgetting how I liked my tea. I didn't have any reason to worry. Clearly, he knew me well.

This was my idea of the perfect Larch Haven date.

After we finished our sandwiches, Justin produced slices of chocolate cake from the picnic basket, along with two more bottles of lemonade, kept nice and cold with the help of ice packs.

By the time I finished eating, I wasn't sure I could move, let alone make it down to the boat. Fortunately, we still had plenty of time before Gareth's race. We tidied up and then lay on our backs on the warm rock. Soon, a pleasant sleepiness threatened to overtake me.

After a few minutes of companionable silence, Justin sat up.

"There's something I need to talk to you about."

My eyes had drifted shut, but now I opened them. In a split second, my serenity disappeared, replaced by a hint of apprehensive tension.

"Okay," I said, wondering what he was about to say.

"It turns out that I can't stay an entire week."

I sat up, surprise and disappointment snapping me fully awake. "But you booked the time off."

"I know, but I'm dealing with several important cases and I need to get back."

"When?"

"I'm catching a plane this evening."

"What?" My disappointment intensified. "How long have you known this?"

"I suspected before I even left LA, and I confirmed it this morning. That was one of my phone calls." He took my hand. "I'm really sorry, Becca. You know I want this time with you."

Do you? I wanted to say, but I stopped myself.

I wanted to be understanding, and I definitely didn't want to fight.

"How can you figure out if you want to live here when you've only been here two days?" I asked.

"That's another thing I wanted to talk to you about."

My apprehension made a comeback, stronger than ever this time. I readied myself for another blow.

"I've been thinking about it a lot since I booked this trip," he continued. "My job is really important to me. You know that."

I didn't need him to finish what he was saying. "You don't want to leave LA."

The expression on his face told me I'd hit the nail on the head.

I slipped my hand out of his and gestured around us. "Why do this? Why bring me out here on this picnic just to break up with me?"

A look of horror flashed across his face. "I'm not breaking up with you, Becca."

"You've got me fooled."

"That wasn't what I was getting at." He took my hand again. "Becca, I want you to come back to LA. I want you to live with me there."

I stared at him for a long moment, trying to process everything. "You know I needed to move back here. I was really homesick in LA."

"I was hoping a long visit here would cure that. Aren't

you itching to get back to your career? You love acting. Don't you miss it?"

I slipped my hand out of his again. I didn't know what to say, so I clasped my hands together on my lap and stared at them.

Justin let out a sigh. "I'm sorry. I know I dropped this on you like a bombshell. Take some time to think about it, okay?"

All I could do was nod. It was as if he'd pulled a rug out from beneath my feet, leaving me stunned and unsteady. Our conversation had killed our picnicking mood, so we made the short trek down to the boat and returned to my cottage. Justin disappeared upstairs to pack his bag while I stood in the kitchen, feeling lost.

He returned a minute or two later. He'd barely unpacked anything since his arrival; now I knew why. He'd arranged to take a shuttle from Larch Haven to the airport so I wouldn't have to drive him. Considering my muddled emotions and my gloomy mood, I was glad of that.

I walked with him to the shuttle station at the edge of town, silence stretching between us. When we reached the station, which was really just a covered bench, Justin set his bags down and took my hands.

"I know this isn't how you hoped things would go," he said, "and I'm really sorry about that. But there's nothing I want more than for you to join me in LA. Promise me you'll give it some serious thought?"

"I promise." I got the words out, though they were barely above a whisper.

The shuttle bus pulled up to the station and the door opened with a sigh. Three people disembarked, but I barely noticed them. Justin gave me a kiss and grabbed his bags before climbing on board the small bus. A man in a business suit came running, towing a small suitcase behind him. He darted on board and the door closed.

I stood there with an ache in my heart as the bus drove off.

Chapter Eleven

"I THOUGHT HE WAS STAYING A FULL WEEK."

Sawyer's voice jolted me out of my daze. He was in uniform, walking toward me. I realized I was still standing in the same spot, even though the bus was almost out of sight.

My stomach churned and my heart rate ticked up. I couldn't catch my breath.

Panic squeezed at my chest and the world around me grew hazy.

Then Sawyer's hands were on my shoulders.

"Sit down, Becca."

I sank down on the station bench.

Sawyer sat next to me. "Breathe."

I sucked in a wheezing breath. I let it out slowly, and some of the tension in my chest eased.

The next breath was easier to draw in. As I focused on breathing in and out, my heart settled down and the encroaching fuzziness in my mind slowly cleared.

"Are you okay?" Sawyer was watching me carefully, his dark eyes full of concern.

I nodded.

"You were having a panic attack."

I shook my head. I really needed to find my voice. "Almost," I said.

He'd pulled me back from the edge. Maybe I'd already had a toe or two over, but he'd saved me from falling all the way.

"What happened?" he asked. "Did something go wrong with Justin?"

I managed to stop myself from laughing, knowing that it would have come out sounding hysterical.

"He had to go back to LA for work." I was impressed by how steady my voice sounded.

"Will he be coming back?"

That was a question I didn't want to answer.

For the first time, I truly took in the sight of Sawyer sitting next to me. Police uniform. Kevlar vest. On duty. He didn't need to be wasting his time on me.

I stood up quickly, realizing belatedly that maybe that wasn't the best thing to do. Sawyer seemed to have the same idea because he got up and put a hand to my elbow. I remained steady on my feet, in no danger of passing out. Thank goodness. I didn't need to embarrass myself any further.

I pulled my phone from my pocket and checked the time. "Oh no. Gareth's race is in five minutes. I've got to go." After taking two steps I stopped and turned back. "Thank you. I'm sorry about . . . what happened."

"Don't be. Are you sure you're okay?"

"Yes, I'm fine," I said, not sure how true that was. "I don't want to be late for the race."

"I hope Gareth does well. I'll see you around."

I nodded and broke into a jog, hurrying toward Venice Avenue. Halfway there, I had to slow my pace. Whatever energy I'd had left when I saw Justin off had drained away.

I walked as quickly as I could, but I could practically

hear the minutes ticking away in my head. I'd told Gareth I'd be at his race, and I didn't want to go back on my word.

I figured I had about one minute to spare when I spotted Blake. He had a prime viewing spot halfway along the canal.

When I called his name, he turned around and waved me over. I squeezed my way through the small crowd behind him, hoping no one would get too annoyed by the fact that I was moving to the front. When I reached Blake's side, he tucked an arm around me and scooted me into place in front of him. Nobody protested. Since Blake stood over six feet tall, his frame was already blocking people's views. Me standing in front of him wouldn't make that any worse.

"Did I miss Gareth's race?" I asked.

A group of competitors headed back along the canal, toward the finish line, but my brother wasn't among them.

"They're running a few minutes behind. His race is up next."

I breathed a sigh of relief. At least something had gone right for me.

The crowd cheered as the racers powered toward the finish line. The front two racers were neck and neck. A few feet away from the finish, one of the men pulled ahead and crossed the line mere inches before the second-place finisher.

The crowd continued to cheer, encouraging the stragglers, until every last one had crossed the line. Then the noise died down around us as everyone waited for the next race to begin.

"Where's Justin?" Blake asked.

Another question I didn't want to answer, but I couldn't keep avoiding them.

"He's on his way back to LA."

"What? Already?" Blake put his hands on my shoulders and turned me toward him so he could see my face. "What happened?"

"Work stuff." I tried to sound nonchalant, but I didn't succeed. The fact that I had to blink away tears was a dead giveaway too.

"Becca, I'm sorry."

"It's fine." I tried again to brush it off. "His job is important to him. I totally get that."

"Is he coming back?"

I knew I couldn't dodge that question like I had with Sawyer. "Not anytime soon."

"Does this mean . . ."

I knew what he'd left unsaid.

Does this mean things are over?

"He wants me to move back to LA," I said. "I promised him I'd think about it."

Blake put an arm around me and pulled me to his side. I slid an arm around his back and leaned against him.

"I'm sorry, kiddo," he said. "I know that's not how you wanted things to play out."

"Gareth was right. He didn't think Justin would want to move here."

"He won't take any pleasure from being right. Trust me. He wants you to be happy."

"I know." And I did. As much as we could annoy each other at times, Gareth wanted what was best for me, and I wanted the same for him.

"Are you going to be okay?" Blake asked as Gareth and his competitors maneuvered their gondolas to the start line.

"Yes," I said, knowing that was the truth. I didn't feel great now, but in time I'd figure things out and get back to feeling more like myself.

Blake gave me an affectionate squeeze before releasing me.

I was happy to let the race distract me. When the starting horn sounded, the racers charged forward. Blake and I cheered Gareth on as he took an early lead. He passed us with three other racers on his tail. As the pack left the canal for the lake, I could no longer tell if my brother was still ahead of the others.

Blake had come prepared with a small pair of binoculars. After taking a look through them himself, he passed them to me as he said, "He's still in the lead."

I could hear the pride in his voice.

I watched through the binoculars as Gareth rowed out toward the buoy and navigated his way around it. I handed the binoculars back to Blake. Gareth still had a lead of several feet on the second-place racer. When he reentered the canal, Blake and I cheered him on again.

There was a tense moment when the third- and fourth-place racers nearly crashed into each other on their way back into the canal. The crowd let out a collective sigh of relief when the two men managed to avoid a collision by the skin of their teeth.

The racer behind Gareth was giving him a run for his money now, his muscles straining as he tried to overtake my brother.

Blake and I yelled and cheered as Gareth passed us. Maybe it was my imagination, but I thought hearing us gave him an extra boost of energy. He surged ahead, crossing the finish line half a boat length ahead of the next guy.

Blake and I cheered like crazy. It felt good, after the day I'd had.

With the race over, we left our prime viewing spot and set off toward the dock to congratulate Gareth. On our way there, I noticed a man staring at me. At least, I thought he was staring. He wore sunglasses and a baseball cap, and he was too far away for me to see his eyes anyway, but I had an eerie sense that he was watching me.

He took a few steps in my direction, but then Gareth climbed up from the dock to meet Blake and me. I gave my brother a congratulatory hug, and when I glanced the other man's way again, he was gone. I shook off the incident and listened to Gareth talk about the race. Before his elation wore off, I slipped away through the crowd.

As soon as he realized Justin wasn't with me, Gareth would ask me all the same questions Blake had already asked. I really didn't want to answer them twice. Blake would fill him in.

The farther I walked from the cheering crowds, the more my spirits drooped. Watching my brother win the semifinals had improved my mood, but only temporarily.

My mind kept going in circles. I was still trying to process the fact that Justin had left after only two days in Larch Haven. One moment I was nearly overcome with disappointment, thinking that I wasn't important enough for him to move here. Then I reminded myself that I'd chosen to move away from him and Los Angeles. Did that mean that neither of us was important enough to the other to keep our relationship going?

I didn't want to dwell on that question, even though I knew it was one I would need to find an answer to soon.

Justin had asked me if I missed acting.

I did.

But when I was in Los Angeles, I missed living in Larch Haven.

Why did life have to be so complicated?

Although I didn't make a conscious plan to go to my grandparents' house, that's where I ended up. As usual, I went around to the back, where I found Lolly in her flower garden, picking some gladioli.

"Those are gorgeous," I said, admiring the spikes of flowers in purple, yellow, and white.

Lolly set the flowers in a bucket of water. I knew what she was going to say before she opened her mouth.

"Where's Justin?"

To my relief, I didn't cry. But I did pour out the whole story to her.

Lolly gathered me in her arms and hugged me tight. "I'm sorry, sweetheart."

"What should I do, Lolly?"

She patted my cheek. "You'll figure that out."

"But I'm so muddled."

"It'll take some time, but you'll find clarity."

I wished I felt as confident about that as she sounded.

"I'm having Lois and Carol over for dinner tonight," Lolly said. "Why don't you join us?"

"Thank you, but I'm going to head home. I think I want a quiet evening."

Lolly gave my hand a squeeze. "At least take some tomatoes with you. We have far more than we can use."

"I'm happy to." Store-bought tomatoes never tasted anywhere as good as homegrown ones. "Oh, you don't have to worry about working at the shop tomorrow. I don't need the time off anymore."

"Maybe you should take the time off anyway," my grandmother suggested.

"I'd rather work," I said. "I miss being there when I'm away for more than a day."

Lolly smiled at that. "It's in your blood." She used her clippers to snip off another gladiolus spike. "The piña colada bonbons and those new peanut butter truffles have been flying off the shelves. And we need more of those cute gondolas. The tourists can't get enough of them."

"I'll get on it first thing in the morning," I assured her. "Thanks for stepping in for me today."

"I enjoyed it. Retirement is nice, but I like to feel useful now and then."

I gave her a quick hug. "You're always useful, Lolly. And always needed."

She kissed my cheek and picked up her bucket of flowers. "We've got some pails and baskets in the shed. Why don't you grab one and I'll fill it with tomatoes and beans."

While Lolly took her flowers into the house, I crossed the lawn to the shed at the back of the garden. Talking with my grandmother had helped to make me feel a little better, although my mind was no less jumbled. I really hoped she was right about me finding clarity. At the moment, that seemed a long way off.

My thoughts were still spinning in circles, but when I opened the shed door, they screeched to a halt.

Parked right in the middle of the shed was Pops's vintage scooter.

The one he claimed Archie Smith had stolen.

Chapter Twelve

"OH, POPS, WHAT HAVE YOU DONE?"

I stood staring at the scooter, my own troubles suddenly overshadowed by my grandfather's predicament.

Pops wouldn't have lied about the scooter going missing, and he wouldn't have accused Archie of stealing it if he didn't truly believe that was what had happened. If Pops was right, then either Archie had returned the scooter before his death, or Pops had taken it back, probably from Archie's property. Knowing what I did about Archie's personality, I figured the latter scenario was more likely, and I had a sinking feeling that I now knew why Pops wouldn't go into detail about the walk he took on the night of Archie's death.

Before, I thought it would be a good thing if someone had seen my grandfather out walking, so they could confirm his alibi. Now I worried that any such witness could drop Pops in hotter water than he was already in. If someone told the police that they'd seen Pops heading to or from Archie's place, that wouldn't look good.

My stomach swirled with worry. I really needed to find a way to clear my grandfather's name, and quickly. I had a few suspects in mind, but beyond that I really hadn't made any progress. My problems would have to take a back seat until I knew Pops wasn't in danger of getting arrested for a crime he didn't commit.

I grabbed a basket from a shelf and shut the shed door. Hopefully no one else would happen upon the scooter before I had a chance to talk to Pops. He needed to tell the police what he'd done—if he really had done what I thought—before they found out some other way.

"Lolly," I said as I opened the screen door to get into the kitchen, "is Pops around?"

My grandmother stood at the counter, sprinkling some chopped chives over the top of a potato salad. I almost regretted declining her dinner invitation. Lolly made the best potato salad. I still wanted to head home, though.

"He's gone bowling, dear. I'm not expecting him home for a couple of hours."

I was about to bring up the subject of the scooter when I heard female voices outside. Lolly's friends Lois and Carol appeared on the other side of the screen door. I let them into the kitchen and exchanged pleasantries before making my escape. In time, the conversation might have turned to Justin's absence. Even though I hadn't talked to Lolly's friends any time recently, they probably knew my boyfriend had arrived in town for a visit. That's the way it was in a small town like Larch Haven.

The gondola races had finished for the day by the time I crossed Venice Avenue and headed home. Most of the shops would be closing soon, but tourists still streamed in and out of their doors while others flocked to the local restaurants for dinner. The closer I got to home, the thinner the crowds of tourists grew, but I still passed three or four couples and two families out for a stroll.

When I reached my cottage, I sank down on the front step and texted Dizzy, letting her know about the whole Justin situation. Her response came almost immediately.

OMG!!! Coming right over!

I smiled despite my low spirits. I loved being back in the same town as my best friend.

My smile faded and my stomach gave an unpleasant twist. That was another thing I'd miss if I moved back to Los Angeles.

I tried not to think about anything as I let myself into my cottage.

Binx came careening around the corner from the kitchen, almost skidding sideways before giving a funny hop and running to greet me. I couldn't help but laugh. He was such a goofball. I scooped him up into my arms and pressed my face into his fur. He purred and snuggled closer to me. Truffles came into the hall in a far more sedate manner, padding along at an unhurried pace until she reached me. Then she wound her way around my ankles.

I set Binx down and picked up Truffles for a cuddle. When I set her down next to her brother, they led the way to the kitchen, Binx letting out a series of loud meows, letting me know it was time for their dinner. I fed the cats and poured myself a tall glass of ice water. After drinking down half of it, I got out the ingredients I'd need to make smoked tofu tacos. I nearly had everything ready when Dizzy appeared at the back door and let herself in.

I barely got my hands wiped on a towel before Dizzy launched herself at me, hugging me fiercely.

"Oh my gosh, Becca! I'm so sorry!"

"Thanks," I said as she released me. "And thanks for coming. Do you want tacos?"

"Definitely, but not yet." She took all the food I'd prepared and tucked it away in the fridge. "First we're going to talk."

I poured us each a glass of lemonade and we took our drinks out to the patio. Binx and Truffles had finished eating and now lounged in their catio, lazily watching the world around them. I wished my life were as uncomplicated as theirs.

I told Dizzy about the entire day, even though I'd already given her the basics via text message.

"He wants me to move back to LA," I said to finish. "I promised him I'd think about it."

"You don't sound thrilled about the prospect of moving again," Dizzy observed.

"I'm confused," I said.

"Before Justin told you he won't be moving to Larch Haven, did you have any desire to move back to LA?"

"No." Sometimes I missed my acting career, but I didn't want to move back there.

"So, basically, if you did go back, it would be one hundred percent for Justin."

"I guess you could put it that way," I said. "I could go back to acting, though." But I'd have to leave True Confections, my family and friends, and this town that I loved so much. I didn't say that out loud, but from the way Dizzy was watching me, I figured she knew exactly what I was thinking.

"Do you love Justin?"

I took a second to think about the question. "I really care for him. A lot."

Dizzy took a sip of lemonade, her gaze never leaving my face.

Her silence left me searching for more words. "I think I was on the verge of falling in love with him when I moved home."

"Becca, I'm not going to tell you what you should do, but you came back to Larch Haven because this was where you wanted to be. Do you want to give up everything you've got here for a man you're not truly in love with?"

"When you put it like that, it sounds like a no-brainer."

"And yet you're hesitating. Because you don't want to hurt Justin?"

"I don't know," I hedged. "Dizzy, he was so good to me when I was in the hospital. He visited me nearly every day, even though he was crazy busy with work."

"Becca, you can't stay with a guy just because he was good to you when you were sick."

I dropped my head into my hands. I knew she was right.

"Maybe we should eat now," Dizzy said. "You need to let your thoughts simmer."

She was right again.

I WOKE UP THE NEXT MORNING WITH DREAD SITTING heavily in the middle of my chest. Then I remembered I was going back to work at True Confections. That gave me the motivation I needed to roll out of bed and get ready for the day. Not that Binx and Truffles would have let me laze about in bed for long. They liked getting their breakfast right on schedule, or early. Late, even by a few minutes, wasn't acceptable.

Outside, another gorgeous morning greeted me. This was my favorite time of day in Larch Haven during the summer. Soon, the walking paths and shops would be crowded with tourists, but at this early hour, I had the town almost to myself. The placid water of the canals reflected the morning light, blooming flowers scented the air, and birds twittered in the trees. In my mind, it was pretty much paradise.

The only people I saw were off in the distance, until I reached the bridge that would take me across the last canal to Venice Avenue. Jolene Doyle-Brodsky stood in the middle of the bridge, going through a series of stretches. She wore running shorts and a tank top and had wireless earbuds in her ears.

"Good morning!" I called out when I reached the bridge, making sure to speak loudly enough to be heard over any music she might be listening to. "It's Jolene, right?"

She slipped her phone out of her armband and tapped the screen. "That's right."

I joined her in the middle of the bridge. "I'm Becca Ransom. I'm sorry for your loss."

"My loss?" she said with confusion. "No, I won my race yesterday. I'm competing in the finals today."

"Oh," I said, momentarily taken aback by her misunderstanding. "I meant the loss of your father."

Realization of her mistake dawned on her face, followed by a quick succession of emotions. They appeared and disappeared so quickly that I couldn't pin any of them down for certain. I thought maybe anger and wariness were among them, but by the time that thought occurred to me, she had a neutral expression again.

"Thank you," she said, her voice neutral too.

"Although," I continued, "I heard the two of you weren't close and I know he wasn't easy to get along with. I didn't mean to upset you by raising the subject."

The set of her mouth hardened, just slightly. "I'm not upset. We weren't close. It's no secret he wasn't a father to me in any sense other than biological, but I made my peace with him before he died."

That took me by surprise. I didn't think Archie was the type to make peace with anyone.

"That's good to hear," I said instead of sharing my thoughts. "Anyway, good luck with your race today."

"Thanks." Almost before she even had the word out, she jogged off, heading in the direction I'd come from.

If Jolene had made peace with Archie, that made her an unlikely suspect in his murder. I wasn't sure if I should simply take her at her word, though. Maybe someone else could confirm what she'd told me.

I didn't think I was getting any closer to identifying the real killer. I needed to find out more about my suspects, including Maria Vasquez. She harbored a good deal of anger where Archie was concerned. I needed to find out why.

First, however, I needed to make some chocolates so we'd have enough stock for all the tourists. Then I'd get on with clearing my grandfather's name.

Chapter Thirteen

ON MY WAY DOWN VENICE AVENUE, I WAVED TO A couple of neighboring shop owners. As I slipped my key into the lock of True Confections's front door, a familiar voice called my name.

Sawyer walked along the avenue toward me, two takeout cups in his hands. I tugged my key out of the lock.

"I was hoping I'd catch you before you got to work," Sawyer said. "Do you have a few minutes?"

"Sure."

He held out one of the cups. "Orange pekoe with one cream and one sugar. Is that okay?"

His thoughtfulness brought a smile to my face and sent warmth spreading through my chest. "That's perfect. Thank you."

Sawyer sat on the bench between True Confections and the neighboring store. I joined him, thinking I could guess what he wanted to talk about.

"I wanted to make sure you're okay," he said.

I'd guessed correctly.

I stared at the cup in my hands. "I'm fine. Really. A bit embarrassed, maybe. I got really overwhelmed in that moment."

"You don't need to be embarrassed, Becca. I'm just glad you're all right."

I turned my cup around in my hands. "Thanks for calming me down. I'd say you went above and beyond your duties as a police officer."

He touched my hand briefly. "I might have been in uniform, but I did that as a friend."

I met his eyes and smiled, grateful. "I know."

We sat in silence for a moment, sipping at our drinks.

"How did Gareth's race go yesterday?" Sawyer asked eventually.

I smiled again. "He won. I'll have to text him and ask what time he's racing in the finals." I took in the sight of Sawyer's jeans and T-shirt. "You're not working today?"

"I am, but my shift doesn't start for an hour."

"Will you ever get a day off while the murder is unsolved?"

A slow grin appeared on his face. "Are you eager to get on with your gondolier lesson?"

Laughter almost bubbled out of me but I kept it contained. "No comment."

Sawyer leaned back and rested an arm along the back of the bench. "Things might calm down a bit after the races. We'll still have plenty of tourists, but not quite so many."

"And the murder investigation?" I asked. "Is it likely to be solved anytime soon?"

"That would be nice, but there's still a long way to go." He shifted his weight on the bench. "Becca, I should warn you—or maybe I shouldn't, really—there's a good chance your grandfather will be questioned again."

I closed my eyes briefly. I had worried about that. There was no way I could tell Sawyer about the scooter. It would be far better if Pops told the cops himself. It still wouldn't look good that he'd held back that information, but if the police learned about it from anyone other than him, that would be even worse.

"He's not helping himself," Sawyer said.

"I know. I'll talk to him. He can be so stubborn sometimes."

One corner of Sawyer's mouth quirked upward. "I guess it runs in the family."

I narrowed my eyes at him. "Are you saying I'm stubborn?"

"I've known you to be now and again over the years."

"Name one example," I challenged.

"What about that time when you borrowed my skateboard and then refused to give it back for weeks?"

"It was days, not weeks," I said. "And that was because I was mad at you for dipping the end of my ponytail in paint."

He was enjoying the conversation far too much. "Hey, I was just trying to help you out."

"How was that helping?"

"You were always saying that you wanted purple hair. So, when I had that purple paint out in art class, I thought I'd do you a favor."

"Paint does not equal hair dye."

"I know that now." He tugged a lock of my hair. "I could run over to the drugstore . . ."

I gave him a light shove. "No, thank you."

We settled down again, a comfortable silence falling over us.

Sawyer was the first to break it. "So, are we going to lose you to the bright lights of Hollywood again?" There was something subtly hesitant about the way he asked the question.

My mood dimmed. "No."

"Does that mean . . . ?"

"That Justin and I are done?" My shoulders sagged. "Not officially."

Silence stretched between us again, but this time it felt different, not quite as easy.

"I thought you might miss your acting career," Sawyer said eventually.

"Sometimes I do," I admitted. "The actual acting part, anyway. Some of the other things that went with it . . . not so much."

"The fame, you mean?"

"I'm not sure I'd call myself famous, but people were starting to recognize me on the street. The more successful I became, the more extra stuff there was to deal with." I picked at the sleeve on my takeout cup. "I had to stop looking at the comments on my social media posts. Most of them were positive, but there were always trolls. And I kept putting so much pressure on myself. I felt like I needed to look my best every time I stepped out the door in case someone wanted to take my photograph. Then there were the times I was told I wasn't pretty enough or thin enough for a role."

Sawyer's eyes seemed to darken, and anger rumbled beneath his next words. "People seriously said that to you?"

"It happened a couple of times."

"Those people don't know what they're talking about."

I appreciated his indignation on my behalf.

"To be honest, most of the pressure on me was my own doing," I said. "My anxiety kept getting worse. When I was actually acting, I'd lose myself in the character and the story. But the rest of the time . . . I guess I'm just not cut out for that life."

"Sounds like it's healthier for you to stay right here," Sawyer said.

I held his gaze and smiled, realizing I couldn't have put it better myself. "Definitely."

I broke eye contact and took a long drink of my tea, suddenly worried the conversation might turn back to Justin.

"I need to get Pops out of trouble," I said. "He's not being vague about his alibi because he's guilty. He's . . ." I trailed off, fearing I'd already said too much.

Sawyer didn't miss my hesitancy. "Becca, if you know something relevant to the murder investigation, you need to share it."

"I need to talk to Pops first."

He watched me, his eyes serious and a little too astute for my comfort.

I fought not to squirm beneath his gaze. "I'll talk to him today. I promise." I tried to nudge the conversation along. "Does anyone else look guiltier than Pops?"

"I can't tell you that."

I figured as much, but his answer still disappointed me.

Sawyer stood up. "I should get going."

"Wait a second." I jumped up and unlocked the shop's door. "There's something I want to give you."

I ducked into the kitchen and filled a small paper bag with misfit chocolates. I took the bag out into the shop and found Sawyer checking out a display of chocolate gondolas filled with bonbons and truffles. There were only four left. I really needed to get on with making more.

"Those are cool," he said as he turned to face me.

"Thanks." I held up the small bag. "Some misfits. Peanut butter pretzel truffles, to be exact."

He put a hand to the pocket of his jeans. "How much?"

"On the house."

"You don't need to do that."

"I want to." I pressed the bag into his hand, curling his fingers around it.

My hand lingered over his. He intertwined his fingers with mine and gave them a gentle squeeze. Avoiding his gaze, I dropped my hand and grabbed one of the chocolate gondolas off the shelf, its plastic wrapping crackling with my touch.

"Take this too."

"Becca . . ."

"Really. I want you to have it."

He accepted the gift. "Thank you. From past experience, I'm guessing these won't last me more than a day or two."

"Then you'll have to come back soon."

He looked me straight in the eye when he said, "You can count on it."

When I shut and locked the shop door behind him, I didn't let myself think about the reason why my pulse was fluttering.

Chapter Fourteen

I WORKED UNTIL MIDMORNING BEFORE TAKING A break. By then I had new batches of piña colada bonbons and peanut butter pretzel truffles made, and several chocolate gondolas that would soon come out of their molds. I'd had the molds custom made, and I was glad they'd proved so popular. I was also glad I'd decided to return to work. Keeping busy had helped to clear my mind. Temporarily, at least. I knew what I had to do in terms of my relationship with Justin. I just wasn't eager to actually do it.

After washing my hands and stretching my arms over my head, I peeked into the front. Customers had been coming and going since opening, but at the moment there seemed to be a lull. The only people there were Angela and Milo.

"Looks like a rare quiet moment," I said as I joined them in the shop area.

Milo glanced up from the boxes of chocolates he was straightening on a shelf. "I know steady sales are good, but we needed this breather."

"I'll say." Angie hurried out from behind the counter and pulled me into a hug. "I'm sorry we didn't get a chance to talk earlier, Becca. And I'm sorry about Justin leaving."

I groaned. "Does the whole town know about that?"

She stepped back and held me at arm's length. "I don't know about the whole town. I heard it from Lolly last night."

Hopefully that meant the news was still within the family. It wouldn't stay that way for long, though. Not in this town.

"Are you moving away again?" Milo asked.

The hint of disappointment in his voice surprised me. "You don't want me to?"

He shrugged, trying to be casual. "It's cool having a cousin on TV and in movies, but I like having you here better."

I gave him a hug. "Thank you. You don't know how nice that is to hear." I smiled at him with affection. "You're so adorable."

He made a face. "I'm not adorable. Or cute."

Behind me, Angie giggled. Milo glared at her.

I fought to keep myself from laughing. "How about a very cool and wonderful young man?"

"That I can live with."

The bell above the door jingled as a customer entered the store. Milo greeted the woman as Angie drew me aside.

"I can't believe Pops got questioned by the police," she whispered once we reached the hall that led to the kitchen. "He wouldn't hurt anyone!"

"You and I know that, but it seems the cops need some convincing."

"He's not in any real trouble, is he?"

When I saw the worry in my cousin's eyes, I wanted to reassure her.

"I'm hoping it won't come to that," I said. "I plan to convince the police of his innocence."

The bell jingled again as four more customers came into the shop. It looked like the lull had come to an end.

Angie gave my arm a squeeze. "I'm glad you've got things under control."

She turned her attention to the new customers while I lingered in the hall. I didn't think I had things under control, but I wasn't going to admit that to Angela. I didn't want her to worry. I was already doing enough of that for the both of us.

I checked the time on my phone. I needed to make another two batches of chocolates before calling it a day, but I could spare a few minutes more away from the kitchen. After removing my apron, I made my way through the now-crowded shop and out the front door.

Maria's store, Pure Bliss, sat near the eastern end of Venice Avenue. I'd never been inside, even though I passed the store on a daily basis.

As soon as I opened the door, mingled scents wafted toward me. Two older women were checking out a display of hand lotions and three young women passed me on their way out of the store, but I was the only other customer. Carmen stood behind the counter. She smiled and called out a greeting when I entered the shop. I didn't see Maria anywhere.

The two other remaining customers approached the counter with their selections, so I killed time by pretending to browse the products on the shelves. I barely noticed what I was looking at. I kept hoping that Maria would appear from the back so I would have a chance to talk to her.

By the time the other women left the shop, Maria still hadn't made an appearance.

Carmen came over my way. "You're Becca Ransom, right?"

"That's right. I saw you yesterday on your way out of the woods."

"I really like hiking, and it's so peaceful in the forest. I wasn't quick enough to tell you this the other day, but I loved your show *Twilight Hills*. I was really sad when it got canceled."

"Thank you," I said, pleased to know she'd enjoyed the TV drama. "I was sad too. It was a fun show to work on."

"My sister is a major fan of *Passion City*. She said you were on that show too."

"For a few episodes." I was glad she'd brought up the subject of her sister. "Is Maria around today?"

"She's in the back. I'd go get her, but she's in the middle of making a new batch of soap."

"There's no need to disturb her," I said, although I was disappointed that I wouldn't get a chance to question her. Maybe I could still get some information from Carmen. "I talked to Maria at the vigil the other night."

Carmen nodded, her face solemn. "Lexi was Maria's best friend back in high school. It's crazy how she disappeared without a trace."

"And then there's Archie Smith's mysterious death almost on the anniversary of Lexi's disappearance," I said.

"Yes, but it's not like Archie will be missed as much as Lexi. I know I'm not supposed to speak ill of the dead, but he wasn't a very nice guy."

"I've heard that from a lot of people, and I understand Maria didn't like him much."

"That's putting it mildly."

"Did something specific happen to make her dislike him?" I asked, keeping the question casual.

"That incident with the town house development. Maria is very passionate about plants."

I had no idea what she was talking about. "What do plants have to do with the new town houses?"

"Archie was dead-set on stopping the development. He tried protesting and vandalizing the construction equipment. When that didn't work, he claimed he found an endangered plant growing on the land that was going to be developed."

"Was he telling the truth?"

"Maria went to find out. There was an endangered plant, but it hadn't been growing there. It was transplanted, and it died as a result. Maria was furious."

"I'm guessing it was Archie who transplanted it."

"Nobody ever doubted it, and it turned out he was caught on security camera. The developers put cameras in after the equipment was vandalized."

"Your sister must have wanted to throttle Archie," I said.

"She sure did."

"I hope her history with him didn't get her in hot water with the police when he died."

"They talked to her, but they talked to a lot of people." For the first time, she sounded defensive. "My sister didn't kill the guy."

"I wasn't suggesting that she did," I said quickly, even though the possibility was what had brought me to the shop.

"If you ask me, the person the police should be looking at is Tammy Doyle."

"Jolene's mother? Why?" I asked.

"Tammy doesn't live in Larch Haven anymore, but she's here now visiting Jolene and she had a bitter history with Archie."

"I heard about how Archie refused to acknowledge that Jolene was his daughter."

"And he hardly ever paid any child support," Carmen said. "Poor Tammy raised Jolene all by herself, and she didn't have any family close by to help her out."

"How did Archie get away with paying so little support over the years?"

Carmen shrugged. "I heard he eventually managed to convince the courts that he was broke and unable to work because of some old injury." She rolled her eyes. "A pack of lies, probably."

The door opened and three women came into the shop.

Carmen glanced their way before saying to me, "Is there anything I can help you find?"

"No, thank you," I said. "I'm just browsing."

Carmen turned her attention to the other customers.

I decided to keep up the pretense of being interested in the displays, but it didn't take long before I was no longer pretending. I ended up buying two bars of soap, one honey-oatmeal and the other spearmint. They smelled amazing.

My visit to Maria's shop hadn't allowed me to cross her name off my suspect list. In fact, now I wondered if I needed to add another name—Tammy Doyle.

I had a new appreciation for Sawyer's job. Solving crimes definitely wasn't as easy as it often appeared to be on television. I'd never even played the part of a fictional detective. The closest I'd ever come to a mystery was reading about them in books, so this was all completely new to me. For a second, I wondered if I was in way over my head. Then I realized that didn't matter.

As long as Pops was in trouble, I had to keep digging.

Chapter Fifteen

WHEN I RETURNED TO TRUE CONFECTIONS, A FAMILY of four was pointing out bonbons to Milo to pack in a box. My mom's friend Estelle stood next to one of the cash registers, chatting with Angela over the counter.

I stopped to say hello to them. I was about to continue on to the back when I heard Estelle say, "I thought about organizing a memorial service for Archie, but even his own daughter doesn't want to attend."

"Really?" I said with surprise. "I thought Jolene had made peace with Archie before he died."

Estelle appeared puzzled. "Not as far as I know. I'm not one for eavesdropping, of course, but I accidentally heard her talking to her husband the day Archie's body was found in the canal. I didn't hear every word, but she mentioned his name and said 'good riddance' with a fair amount of vitriol."

"I guess we can't blame her," Angie said. "He wasn't much of a father."

"Not much of a man either," Estelle said. "Such a shame."

"I heard that Jolene's mother is in town for a visit," I said. "Was she here when Archie died?"

"I don't think so," Estelle replied. "I heard she arrived a couple of days after. She likely came to watch Jolene in the gondola races."

She set a box of salted caramels on the counter, and Angela rang up the sale.

On my way to the kitchen, I checked my phone. I'd texted Gareth earlier in the day, asking him about his race. I found a reply from him, letting me know that his race would be at three o'clock. That gave me plenty of time to finish work and head over to the canal.

As I molded chocolates and piped fillings, I thought about what Estelle had said. According to her, Jolene still had a grudge against Archie when he died. Was she mistaken, or had Jolene lied to me? I suspected it might be the latter. Something about Jolene's demeanor when I spoke to her on the bridge made me think she was trying to hide something. Why bother lying about her relationship with Archie if she had nothing to do with his death?

Then there was Jolene's mother. I'd thought of adding her to my suspect list, but according to Estelle, she probably wasn't in town when Archie was killed. If I'd had a physical list of suspects, I would have added Tammy's name just for the satisfaction of crossing it off. Despite my efforts at collecting information, I felt like I was getting nowhere, fast. Maria Vasquez had a motive, but I still needed to find out if she had the opportunity to kill Archie. The same was true of Oliver Nieminen. How the heck I would get that information, I wasn't yet sure, but I needed to figure that out, and quickly.

Time was ticking away. Pops could get questioned by the police again at any time, and as soon as they knew about the scooter sitting in his shed, things could get dicey. If I was going to stop that from happening, I needed to act fast, but I didn't think it would go over well if I asked my suspects straight out for an alibi. I'd have to be more subtle.

While I worked, I imagined a few different conversations, like scenes from a movie playing in my head. Of course, I couldn't expect my suspects to stay on script when there wasn't one, but the exercise left me with a few possibilities of how to broach the subject with Maria and Oliver.

By half past two in the afternoon, I had my chocolates finished and the kitchen clean. Out by the canal, I searched for Blake in the crowd of race spectators without success, until I crossed the bridge. Then I found him on the far side of a weeping willow. He didn't have a viewing spot right next to the canal this time, but his location on a slight rise still gave him a good vantage point.

I joined him there and took in the sight of the other spectators around us. Once again, there was a good turnout, and everyone seemed to be enjoying themselves. Many people sipped cold drinks or munched on pretzels or shaved ice sold by bicycle vendors. My stomach grumbled, protesting the fact that all I'd eaten for lunch was an apple. Food would have to wait, however. Gareth's race would be starting soon, and I didn't want to risk missing it while standing in line for a snack.

"How are you doing today?" Blake asked.

"Better," I replied.

His blue eyes searched my face, as if checking to be sure that I was telling the truth. "Are things settled now?"

"Not quite." That answer made me feel like a coward. I'd made my decision, but I hadn't shared it with Justin yet. I didn't often procrastinate, but I definitely was now.

"Let me know if you need to talk things out some more," Blake said.

"I will. Thank you."

As I turned my attention to the canal, I spotted a man in sunglasses and a baseball cap standing on the far bank. The same man I'd seen the day before. I thought he might have been watching me again, but before I could decide for sure if that was the case, I was distracted by a woman seated on a lawn chair in front of us as she put a hand to her floppy straw hat and jumped to her feet. She scurried around her chair, squeezing past the people standing next to me. She had curly blond hair and round, rosy cheeks, and looked to be in her mid-fifties.

"Tammy!" The woman waved wildly. "Yoo-hoo! Tammy!"

A brown-haired woman of about the same age turned around. When she spotted the woman in the hat, she smiled and came over to meet her. I figured the brown-haired woman was Jolene's mother, and not just because of her name. When she drew closer, I noticed a family resemblance.

The two women embraced as I watched.

"Hi, Celia," Tammy said.

"It's so good to see you!" Celia exclaimed. "Can you believe what happened to Archie? And you must be so proud of Jolene! I bet she's going to be the champion again this year."

When her friend finally stopped for a breath, Tammy smiled. "I hope so. Jolene loves racing."

I noticed she didn't respond to the question about Archie.

"You know," Celia said, "I waved to you on Saturday night, and even called your name, but you didn't notice. So I'm sure glad I saw you here today."

Tammy's face paled. "Saturday? You must be mistaken. I didn't arrive in town until Tuesday."

"Oh." Celia seemed momentarily taken aback, but she recovered quickly. "You must have a doppelgänger running around Larch Haven, then." She laughed and leaned closer to Tammy to say something more.

I wanted to hear the rest of the conversation, but a young couple with three small children squeezed in between us, and their chatter quickly drowned out all other voices. I looked across the canal, searching the crowded bank for the mystery man in the hat and sunglasses. He was nowhere to be seen.

I returned my attention to the race drawing to a close. It was the final for the two-women category. Each gondola had a woman perched in the bow and another in the stern. The speeds they could reach were really impressive. The gondolas practically zoomed by as the crowd cheered.

That race came to a close and nervousness fluttered in my chest. Even though the event was mostly just for fun—with trophies, modest cash prizes, and bragging rights for the winners—I really wanted my brother to be the champion of his category.

He and his competitors lined up at the start, and my stomach did an anxious flip when the horn sounded. Gareth didn't have the best start of the bunch. Another racer pulled out ahead of him, cutting smoothly through the water. Blake and I cheered Gareth on as he passed by us, currently in second place. He held on to that spot as the first three gondolas left the canal for the lake.

As the fifth-place gondola passed us, something funny happened with the racer's oar, causing his whole body to jerk forward. The abrupt movement knocked him off balance, and he tumbled into the canal with a great splash.

The crowd let out a collective gasp.

The racer surfaced and grabbed on to the side of his gondola. Luckily, the other stragglers managed to get past him without crashing into him. A small speedboat immediately left the main dock to come help out the unfortunate man in the water.

I filed the incident away in my mind for future use against Sawyer's claim that gondoliers didn't fall in the water unless they were drunk. I watched anxiously as the man was helped into the speedboat and the gondola was towed back toward the docks. It seemed he hadn't come to any harm.

The canal was cleared just in time. The racers reentered it from the lake, their skin shimmering with sweat as they powered forward through the hot afternoon sun. The guy ahead of Gareth was losing steam. My brother quickly took advantage, digging deep and putting on a final burst of speed. He easily passed the guy in the lead and cruised across the finish line in first place.

The crowd cheered like crazy, but no one was cheering louder or more excitedly than Blake and me. My brother-in-law and I hurried down to the main dock to offer our congratulations. After Gareth took a long drink of water and patted his face dry with a towel, he fixed his hazel eyes on me.

"You didn't tell me about Justin yesterday."

"I knew Blake would fill you in," I said.

He made a brief grumbling sound in response to that. "I hope you cut him loose."

His words put me on edge, but he seemed to regret them right away.

"Hey." He gave my shoulder a squeeze. "I just think you deserve better. You should be the most important thing in your boyfriend's life."

Maybe so, but I hadn't made Justin my top priority either. That spoke volumes to me now, though I'd ignored its significance over the past few months.

"I know you want what's best for me," I said. "And I know what I need to do."

Gareth accepted that with a nod and another squeeze of my shoulder. Then he headed home to take a quick shower before going back to the restaurant. I walked partway to the Gondolier with Blake, and then returned to my cottage, where I texted Dizzy about the man I'd seen watching me twice now.

He's probably a fan, she wrote back. Maybe he's just too shy to talk to you.

I don't know about that.

After wrapping up our text conversation, I ate a snack and played with Binx and Truffles, but I couldn't settle. I needed to help Pops, and I couldn't do that by staying at home. Oliver Nieminen's café served breakfast and lunch and closed in the middle of the afternoon. Since it was nearing four o'clock, I decided to try to catch him at home.

I knew where he used to live, way back when Dizzy and I went door-to-door selling Girl Scout cookies. I had no idea if he'd moved in the many years that had passed since then, but I figured there was a good chance he hadn't. There were a couple of apartments above his café, but I was pretty sure he rented those out, like Lolly and Pops did with the living quarters above True Confections. If it turned out that I had the wrong house, I'd ask around and try to locate him the next day. I hoped I wouldn't encounter a delay, though. I really needed to make some progress with helping Pops, before it got to be too late.

On my way to what I thought was Oliver's house, I cut across Cherry Park. I paused by the oak tree where the vigil for Lexi Derendorf had taken place a few nights earlier. A memorial had been set up beneath the tree. A large photo of Lexi—the same one I'd seen on the posters announcing the vigil—leaned against the trunk. Unlit candles, flowers, and a few stuffed animals surrounded the photo.

A wave of sadness washed over me as I took in the sight. I wished Lexi's parents could get some closure. After all this time, that wasn't likely to happen, but I still wished it could. Hopefully Archie's death wouldn't go unsolved like Lexi's disappearance had. He might not have been well liked in the community—or anywhere—but he hadn't deserved to be murdered, and his killer needed to be locked away. How could the people of Larch Haven feel certain that we were safe until that happened?

A shiver of unease skittered along the back of my neck. I glanced around, expecting to find the mysterious man in sunglasses watching me, but he was nowhere in sight. Aside from me, the only other people in the park were a woman walking two small dogs, three teenagers playing with a Frisbee, and an elderly man seated on a bench.

With a final glance at Lexi's photograph, I continued on my way. It didn't take me long to arrive at the cottage where I thought Oliver lived. I reached the front step and stopped, silently practicing what I was going to say. I told myself that I couldn't stand there all day, so I gathered up my courage and knocked on the door.

Chapter Sixteen

IT TURNED OUT THAT I HAD THE RIGHT HOUSE. OLIVER answered the door within seconds of my knock. He regarded me with a puzzled expression, as if trying to work out who I was.

"Hi, Mr. Nieminen," I said. "I'm Becca Ransom. My family owns True Confections."

"Right." He still seemed confused. He was probably wondering what the heck I was doing on his doorstep.

"Maybe you've heard that my grandfather has been questioned by the police in relation to Archie Smith's death?"

Oliver scratched his jaw and let out a brief grunt that I took as an affirmation.

"My grandfather didn't kill Archie, but he went for a walk that evening, alone, so he doesn't have an alibi for part of thc window of time when Archie was killed."

Oliver scowled. "I'm not going to provide a false alibi for someone I barely know."

"Of course not," I said quickly. "That's not what I was getting at."

"Then why are you here?" He'd never sounded so impatient when Dizzy and I were selling cookies. Of course, most people would find purchasing cookies much more pleasant than talking about a murder.

"My grandfather took a walk around town that night. I was wondering if you were home that evening and if you might have seen him walking along the canal. Or maybe you were elsewhere in town and saw him out and about."

"I was home that evening."

"From what time?"

He scowled again, and I was afraid he'd tell me that wasn't any of my business. To my relief, he gave me an answer.

"I got home around seven. Then I was here all night. I watched some TV and went to sleep. I didn't see your grandfather or anyone else."

"Was anyone here with you?"

"How is that any of your business?"

I hadn't dodged that question after all.

"I thought if you had a neighbor stop by or something, maybe I could ask them if they'd seen my grandfather when they were on their way home," I said.

"I was alone. The whole time." He stepped back and started to close the door. "Is that all?"

I was about to say something more, to ask him if he could think of anyone who might have wanted to harm Archie, but I didn't get the chance. He slammed the door in my face, bringing our conversation to an abrupt halt.

It was my turn to scowl. Okay, so I was poking my nose into his business, but for a legitimate reason. If I was going to clear my grandfather's name, I'd probably have to annoy a few people in the process. That wasn't something I generally liked to do, but I was willing to risk it for the sake of helping Pops.

Perhaps belatedly, I realized that I should be more careful. If I angered the wrong person—like Archie's killer—I could put myself in danger. I suddenly felt very exposed standing there alone on Oliver's doorstep.

The curtain twitched in the window to the left of the front door. The last thing I needed was for Oliver to call the police on me for trespassing or loitering or any other transgression. I got on my way before he had the chance to do that.

I glanced over my shoulder a few times as I walked briskly along the canal, but no one was following me. I told myself to relax. My imagination was making me jumpy when I had no reason to be. Instead of worrying about nonexistent dangers, I focused on my plan to clear Pops's name. Oliver claimed he had been home all evening and night, but no one could verify his alibi. Frustration simmered beneath my skin. I was no further ahead than I was before I'd spoken to him.

Since I didn't yet know which suspect I should question next, I set myself on a path to my grandparents' house. I'd told Sawyer that I would talk to Pops before the end of the day, and I intended to stick to my word. If Pops was out bowling again, I'd get in my car and drive to the bowling alley in Snowflake Canyon to have a few words with him.

Fortunately, that proved unnecessary. I found Pops relaxing in his rocking chair on the back porch, a bottle of beer in hand.

"This is a nice surprise," he said as I walked up the garden path.

I joined him on the porch and kissed his stubbly cheek before settling on the porch swing. "How are you doing, Pops?"

"Can't complain. How about my Hollywood star?"

I smiled at that nickname. Even though I didn't see myself as a star, I liked that he saw me that way. "I'm all right. Did you see Gareth's race?"

Pops nodded as he rocked his chair. "He did the family proud."

My smile faded as I prepared myself to get to the point of my visit. "Pops, when you had that argument with Archie by the Boat Barn, you accused him of stealing your vintage scooter."

It was as if my words caused shutters to slam shut across Pops's face. He went from relaxed to apprehensive in an instant.

He took a long drink of his beer, keeping his gaze averted from mine.

"Your scooter is in the shed again, Pops. How did it get there?"

He tried to take another drink of his beer, but the bottle was empty. He frowned at it before speaking. "Maybe I was mistaken."

"Mistaken that it was stolen? Come on, Pops. We both know that's not what happened."

He sighed and finally met my gaze. "Archie did steal it. I knew he had, but I couldn't prove it. That man had been stealing from the people of Larch Haven for years, but the police could never pin anything on him. I knew I'd never see my scooter again if I didn't do something about it myself."

"Did you confront Archie?" I asked, scared of what the answer might be.

"No. I never saw him again after that scene at the Boat Barn. When I was out for my walk, I went over to his place. He wasn't there, so I poked around. I discovered an old shed in among the trees, and that's where I found my scooter, along with a couple of bicycles and a snowmobile. What do you want to bet that hc stolc thosc things too?"

"I guess the police would be able to find out for sure if that's the case." Maybe they already had, if they'd had the same suspicion about those items when they searched Archie's property.

"No wonder Archie never wanted people going near his place," Pops said.

"He was afraid they'd find his stash of stolen property?"

"I don't doubt it."

That made sense, especially if Archie was transporting items onto and off his land on a regular basis. If he stole things, he probably fenced them too, and he most likely would have done that outside of Larch Haven, to keep his shady practices under wraps.

"Pops," I said, not sure how he'd react to my next words, "you need to tell the police that you took your scooter back from Archie's place."

"That wouldn't look good. It was the same night he was killed."

"It'll look worse if they find out some other way," I pointed out. "Besides, the police know you're holding back about where you were that evening. Sawyer warned me that there's a good chance you're going to get questioned again. You need to tell the police the truth. The whole truth."

"What's this?" Lolly interjected.

I hadn't noticed her on the other side of the screen door. I didn't think Pops had either.

She came out and joined us on the porch, letting the screen door slam shut behind her.

"Did you finally get the whole story out of him?" Lolly asked me.

"You knew about the scooter?" I said with surprise.

"The one Archie stole?"

I could tell by her confusion that she didn't know everything.

"Pops has been cagey about where he went walking on the night of the murder because he went to Archie's place and took his scooter back."

When the significance of that sank in, Lolly fixed her stern gaze on Pops. "Ernest Ransom, you need to do what your granddaughter says and come clean with the police."

Pops avoided her eyes. "I don't want to end up in hot water."

"You're already in it, and it's about to boil," Lolly said. "If the police find out from someone else what you did . . ."

"That's exactly what I was saying," I chimed in. "It'll look even worse."

Lolly nodded her agreement with me. "You're telling the police everything, Ernie. First thing in the morning."

There was no arguing with Lolly when she spoke with that tone. Pops clearly realized that too.

"All right," he relented. "I'll tell the police."

That should have eased my mind, but I still worried about the whole situation. Yes, it would look worse if the police got the information about the scooter from someone else, but the fact that Pops lied to them also didn't look good. Once the cops knew the truth, Pops might seem like an even stronger suspect. They might think he went to get his scooter, ran into Archie, got into a fight, and killed him.

I didn't voice any of those worries out loud. Pops might not have been willing to acknowledge the gravity of his situation, but I thought Lolly had a clear view of things.

My grandmother sent me home with a basket of carrots and sugar snap peas, picked fresh from the garden that day. I snacked on the peas as I walked, thinking once again about who the real killer might be.

I didn't get very far with my thoughts before I heard Dizzy call my name. I stopped and turned to find her hurrying my way.

She peeked into my basket when she reached my side. "What have you got there? Oh, yum! Are those sugar snaps?"

"Delicious ones. Help yourself."

Dizzy grabbed a handful of peas and fell into step with me. "I'm guessing you were visiting Lolly and Pops."

I quickly told her about the scooter situation and how I was hoping to find the real killer so a cloud of suspicion would no longer hang over my grandfather.

"I'll help," Dizzy offered without hesitation. "I'll be the Watson to your Sherlock, the Hastings to your Poirot, the George to your Nancy."

"What about Bess?"

"I'll be George and Bess rolled into one."

That brought a smile to my face. "You're the best, Diz. There's just one problem—I'm not sure how either of us can figure out who killed Archie."

"We'll brainstorm," Dizzy said. "But before we do that, we've got another situation to talk about."

"The Justin situation?" I guessed with a distinct lack of enthusiasm.

"Have you talked to him?"

"Not yet."

"You've come to a decision, though." It was a statement, not a question. Dizzy knew me well.

"I have."

"Don't you think you should get the whole thing over with?"

"He's probably still at the office," I hedged.

"Text him and find out when he can talk."

We stopped in the middle of a bridge and I rested my basket on the railing so I could send Justin a quick text message. Minutes after Dizzy and I reached my cottage, he replied.

"He says he has a few minutes to talk right now," I said as I read his message. A surge of anxiety swirled through me.

Dizzy gave me a hug and then held me by the shoulders. "You can do this." She gave my shoulders a squeeze and released me. "I'll wait out on the patio."

I stood there staring at my phone as Dizzy stepped outside. This wasn't a call I wanted to make, but my best friend was right; I needed to get it done and over with. That would be best for both me and Justin.

With a heavy heart, I placed the call.

Chapter Seventeen

I DIDN'T WANT TO GET OUT OF BED THE NEXT MORNING. As much as I enjoyed working at True Confections, I hadn't had enough sleep to feel ready to face the day. My talk with Justin had left me feeling gloomy, even though we'd ended our relationship as amicably as possible. Dizzy had stayed late, keeping me company and talking about what we could do to clear Pops's name. Our conclusion was that we needed to find out more about Maria Vasquez and Jolene Doyle-Brodsky.

We wanted to know if Maria's passion for plants and her bitterness toward Archie could have boiled over into deadly rage. As for Jolene, the discrepancy between what she'd told me about making peace with Archie and what Estelle had overheard her say bothered me, and Dizzy felt the same.

I rolled over in bed, thinking I'd give myself another five minutes. Binx and Truffles had other ideas. They jumped up onto the bed, Binx landing right next to me. He sat down and let out a loud meow. Truffles padded her way up my back and perched on my shoulder. Once Binx pounced on my feet and attacked them through the blanket, I gave up. My cats were more effective than any alarm clock.

Downstairs, I set out breakfast for the cats and spent the next half hour doing a mixture of yoga and Pilates. That helped to settle my mind and shake off the melancholy that had been clinging to me since making my breakup with Justin official.

After a quick breakfast of yogurt and homemade granola, I left Binx and Truffles watching birds from their catio and hopped into my whisper boat, hoping to make up some time since I was running later than usual. Now that the gondola races had finished, the canals would be quieter. We still had plenty of tourists in town, but the crowds wouldn't be quite so large, and there wouldn't be as many gondolas on the water. At this early hour, I had the canals almost to myself and I made it to the main dock near Venice Avenue in a matter of minutes. From there, I enjoyed the short stroll to True Confections.

As I got to work putting chocolate in the tempering machine and setting out the ingredients I needed for the fillings I was going to make, I realized I felt lighter and could breathe more easily. I hadn't wanted to end things with Justin, but I knew it was the right decision, and now that it was done, it was like a heavy weight had lifted from my shoulders.

After Angela opened the shop, but before it got too busy, Lolly stopped by. During a quiet moment, without any customers, I joined her out front with my cousin.

"I just came from the police station," Lolly announced.

My heart jumped into my throat. "Has Pops been arrested?"

All the color drained from Angie's face. "Arrested? Pops?"

I grabbed her arm, worried she might faint.

Lolly put a comforting arm around her. "Shh. Don't

worry. He hasn't been arrested. He's playing darts with his friends."

Some of the color returned to Angie's face. "But why were you at the police station?"

I added my own question. "Did Pops go with you?"

"Of course," Lolly confirmed. "I wasn't going to let him get away with putting it off."

I quickly filled Angie in on what Pops needed to tell the police. Although she no longer looked like she was going to faint, worry practically radiated from her brown eyes.

"How much trouble is he in?" she asked.

Lolly patted her back. "I'm not sure. The police seized your grandfather's scooter, but Hilda McIntosh's grandson is a lawyer. She gave me his name and number. I'm heading home to give him a call. Better safe than sorry."

"I think that's a good idea," I said with a touch of relief.

At least if the police wanted to question Pops again, he could get some legal advice first. Hopefully he could even have a lawyer present with him.

"I don't like this," Angie said to me after Lolly had left the shop. "I can't believe Pops is a murder suspect. It's crazy!"

"I know. But if I have anything to do with it, he won't be a suspect for long."

Angie eyed me as she stacked boxes of chocolates on a shelf. "What are you up to, Becca?"

"I'm just making some discreet inquiries." At least, I hoped I was being discreet enough not to tip off the killer to the fact that I was trying to identify them.

"Please be careful. I know I said earlier that I was glad you were involved, but maybe that was hasty of me. This isn't a murder mystery movie or TV show. There's a real killer out there."

"I know," I assured her.

A family of five came into the shop then, putting an end to our conversation. I returned to the kitchen for a couple more hours and then took another break since Dizzy and I had arranged to get together during her lunch hour. I met her on the front steps of the library with two bubble teas in hand, lychee for her and taro for me, both with tapioca pearls.

"Thank you," Dizzy said with enthusiasm when she accepted her bubble tea. "How did you know I was dying for one of these?"

"Our BFF psychic connection."

We bumped fists.

"Are you hungry?" I asked.

She shook her head as she took a drink. "I had some pasta salad at my desk. What about you?"

"My boba will tide me over."

"Then let's get sleuthing."

We set off up the hill toward the new town house development that overlooked Shadow Lake. From the front, the town homes were accessible only by foot, bicycle, or golf cart. From the back, however, the units would be accessible by car. Since the development sat at the edge of town, a road would lead from the highway to a parking area behind the town homes. The road wouldn't be visible from the rest of town, maintaining the car-free character that tourists and so many of us locals loved.

The town houses offered a gorgeous view of the town and the lake, and from the pictures I'd seen online, they would look fantastic inside and out. I wasn't tempted by them, though. In my opinion, the best Larch Haven living was done right by the water. I loved that I could step out my front door and hop into my kayak or whisper boat. Anyone who wanted to get to the nearest canal from the town houses would have to walk down the hill and around the shops on Venice Avenue.

"So, what are we hoping to find out?" Dizzy asked as we followed the cobblestone walkway up the hill.

"Whether Jolene has an alibi for the time Archie was

killed," I said. "Or anything else that might point us in the direction of the real killer."

Dizzy chewed on a tapioca pearl before speaking again. "I don't know if they're offering tours of the units yet, but I guess it doesn't matter. As long as we can get Jolene or her husband talking, that's what counts."

We'd decided the night before that we would pretend Dizzy was interested in purchasing one of the new town homes. Hopefully, once we got a conversation going with Jolene or her husband, we'd be able to steer it in the direction of the murder.

Temporary fencing surrounded the town houses, and the front yards remained unfinished, with dirt instead of grass and pieces of construction equipment and materials lying here and there. A portable office with its door standing open sat outside the fence. I could hear the sound of some sort of saw whining in the distance, and three men in hard hats stood conversing outside the farthest unit, but I didn't spot Jolene or her husband anywhere.

"Do you know Jolene's husband's name?" I asked Dizzy.

"Alex, I think."

"Right." I'd known that at one time but had forgotten.

We both fell silent, drinking our bubble tea as we approached the office. We'd nearly reached the open door when I heard terse voices coming from inside.

"What if the cops find out?"

I couldn't be sure, but the woman who asked the question sounded like Jolene.

Dizzy and I both stopped in our tracks.

"They won't find out. Nobody will," a man said.

Dizzy and I exchanged a glance and crept toward the open door, sticking close to the outer wall of the portable office.

"Sometimes I think even the trees in this town have ears," the woman said.

Carefully, I raised myself up on my tiptoes and peeked

in through the window. As I suspected, the woman's voice belonged to Jolene. I recognized the man with her as her husband. I'd never met him, but I'd seen his picture on the development's website when Dizzy and I took a quick look at it the night before.

"Then don't say anything more about it," Alex said.

He turned toward the window, and I dropped down out of sight.

"But if the cops *do* find out . . ." Jolene said.

"Babe. Relax. Nobody's going to find out. The old geezer can't talk now that he's dead, and no one else knows. It's smooth sailing from here on out. Okay?"

I chanced another quick peek through the window. Alex took Jolene into his arms and kissed her. She wrapped her arms around him and kissed him back.

I ducked down and took Dizzy's arm, pulling her with me as I scurried back the way we'd come.

Chapter Eighteen

ONCE WE'D PUT SOME DISTANCE BETWEEN US AND the open door of the portable office, Dizzy and I drew to a stop.

"Oh my gosh!" Dizzy exclaimed. "Alex and Jolene were in on it together! They killed Archie!"

"Maybe." I was still turning over everything in my mind.

"What did you see when you looked in the window?" Dizzy asked. She wasn't tall enough to peek into the office like I had.

"Not much. They were just standing there talking, until they started making out."

Dizzy clutched my arm. "Look, here they come. Should we still talk to them?"

Alex and Jolene descended the three steps from the trailer door. Jolene gave her husband a kiss and then hopped into a nearby golf cart.

"Shoot," Dizzy said. "There goes Jolene."

She zoomed past us in the golf cart, barely casting a glance our way.

"Let's see what we can get out of Alex," I suggested.

He stood outside the portable office, texting on his phone. He glanced up when Dizzy and I approached. Tucking his phone into the back pocket of his jeans, he flashed us a smile.

"Afternoon, ladies. How can I help you?"

"My friend here is interested in the new town houses." I gave Dizzy a subtle nudge, reminding her to play her part.

"That's right!" she said. "Is it possible to get a tour of one of the units?"

"Not yet," Alex replied. "But the show unit will be open for viewings in a couple of weeks. In the meantime, I've got floorplans and an artist's rendering I can show you."

"That would be great," Dizzy said with what sounded like sincere enthusiasm. Maybe she was catching the acting bug.

"Come on and join me in the office." Alex led the way inside.

Dizzy and I followed close on his heels.

"There will be two- and three-bedroom units," Alex said as he grabbed a remote control off the top of a desk. "Do you know what number you're looking for?"

"Oh . . ." Dizzy pretended to think about it. "Two would suit my needs."

Alex punched a button on the remote and a flat-screen mounted on the wall came to life. He navigated through an onscreen menu until a floorplan appeared.

Dizzy and I stepped closer for a better look. As Alex pointed out the various rooms and features, and Dizzy pretended to be interested, I glanced surreptitiously around the office. I didn't see any incriminating evidence that would help me in my investigation. Not that Alex would have left any such thing lying out in plain view.

While Alex and Dizzy chatted about the town houses, I edged closer to the wastepaper basket sitting next to the desk. A quick look inside showed me that it held nothing but a couple of crumpled tissues and a receipt from Pure Bliss, Maria's store.

"Let me get you a couple of printouts to take with you," Alex said to Dizzy as he shut off the screen. He opened a desk drawer and pulled out some papers.

I decided it was time to do some fishing for information.

"I hope the police haven't been giving Jolene too much trouble since Archie Smith died," I said as Alex flipped through the papers.

He glanced at me before pulling two pieces of paper out of the small pile in his hands. "Why would they?"

"I understand she didn't have a good relationship with Archie. The police questioned my grandfather because he'd argued with Archie recently. But I guess as long as Jolene has an alibi, she's in the clear, right?"

Alex's hand tightened around the papers, almost crumpling them. "Jolene wouldn't have bothered to kill that guy. He meant nothing to her. The cops talked to her, but if they're smart, they'll know she had nothing to do with the murder. She has an alibi because she and I were together that whole night."

"I'm glad that's the case." I decided to shift the conversation back to real estate before he got suspicious about the true reason for our visit. "The town houses really look great. When do you think the development will be complete?"

"By the end of September, but we expect to be sold out by then." He addressed Dizzy. "If you leave me your name and number, I can give you a call when the show unit is ready for viewing."

"That would be great," Dizzy said.

She sounded convincing, but the quick look she shot my way told me she'd rather not leave her number.

Fortunately, Alex's phone rang, giving us a chance to escape.

"We'll let you get that," Dizzy said. "I need to get back to work, anyway."

Alex fished his phone out of his pocket. "Tell you what, you can drop me a line through the contact form on my website. Then I can get back to you."

"Great idea!" Dizzy practically shoved me out the door. "Thanks! Bye!"

We walked briskly down the hill, away from the new town houses.

"What do you think?" Dizzy asked me once we were well out of Alex's earshot.

"He and Jolene are each other's alibi," I said. "As far as I'm concerned, that doesn't get them off the suspect list."

Dizzy nodded in agreement. "He would totally lie for her."

"They could be lying for each other."

"So they really could have been in on it together."

"Maybe." Once again, I found myself unwilling to fully commit to that theory, or any other, for that matter.

"What's wrong?" Dizzy asked.

"I need something more," I said, frustration creeping into my voice. "Suspicions aren't enough to clear Pops's name."

We slowed our pace when we got closer to Venice Avenue.

"Take this information to Sawyer," Dizzy advised. "Maybe he can figure out if Jolene and Alex are lying about their alibi. Oliver too, for that matter."

"He might have figured it out already," I said. "Not that he'd tell me if that's the case."

"It's worth talking to him."

Maybe she was right. Sawyer hadn't been willing to tell me much about the investigation so far, but he had warned me that Pops would likely get questioned again. It was at least worth a try. I could tell him what we'd found out and see what happened from there.

"You know what?" Dizzy said as we approached the library. "It would be really helpful if Archie's spirit would make an appearance. Then he could tell us who killed him."

I chewed on the last of my tapioca pearls. "Somehow I doubt that's going to happen. He wasn't very agreeable in life. He probably isn't any more so in death."

"Good point," Dizzy conceded. "But we shouldn't discount the possibility completely. We could hold a séance if need be. I think the most likely place for his spirit to linger would be around his home. He spent most of his time there."

"I walked past his place the other day and there was still police tape cordoning off the property. It might be gone now, though."

"If it is, we should go and have a look around."

"I don't know what we'd find there," I said. "I really don't think Archie's ghost is going to pop out and announce who killed him."

"Okay, neither do I," Dizzy admitted. "But we could always check for signs of his spirit being close by. You know, cold spots and stuff like that. If we think he might not have moved on, we could give the séance idea a try."

"How about we try some more earthly investigative techniques first." I wasn't a complete skeptic when it came to the paranormal and supernatural, but I also wasn't quite as eager as Dizzy to believe in things. Except for the lake monster. That I definitely believed in, probably even more than my best friend did.

"Fair enough," Dizzy said. "But I still think we should poke around Archie's place. If he stole from more than just Pops, maybe one of those people got in a fight with him and killed him. If we could figure out whose stolen property Archie stashed away, that could give us a lead."

I considered that. "Good point. I'll go around later and see if the police tape is still up."

We drew to a stop at the base of the library's front steps.

"Text me when you know?" Dizzy requested.

"Of course."

She tapped her bubble tea cup against mine. "Here's to us solving the case and clearing Pops's name."

"I'll drink to that," I said before sipping up the last of my bubble tea. "I couldn't have asked for a better partner in crime. Or I guess I should say partner in solving crime."

"I've always got your back." Dizzy headed up the steps, waving at me over her shoulder. "Talk soon!"

I walked away from the library, feeling happier and more hopeful than I had in days.

Chapter Nineteen

AFTER PARTING WAYS WITH DIZZY, I RETURNED HOME in my whisper boat. I checked on the cats and applied some sunscreen before climbing into my kayak and navigating my way out to Shadow Lake. I was craving some time out on the water, so I figured I'd paddle along the shore to Archie's property. I took a small pair of binoculars with me, so I could check for the presence of crime scene tape. I also wanted to keep my mind off of Justin and our breakup. Even though I knew I'd made the right decision, and even though ending our relationship had lifted a weight off my shoulders, I knew I would miss him. We'd stayed in contact on a near-daily basis for months. Adjusting to his complete absence from my life would take time.

I stopped paddling when I reached the shoreline abutting Archie's place. As it turned out, I didn't need the binoculars. Even without them, I caught a glimpse of yellow police tape. I raised the binoculars to my eyes anyway, wanting to make sure that I wasn't seeing remnants of tape that had been cut down.

No, I quickly realized. That wasn't the case. The tape was still intact and outlined a large area around Archie's cabin.

I wondered how much longer it would remain a closed scene. Sawyer might know. That was another reason to pay him a visit.

He likely wouldn't be finished with his shift for a while yet, so I took my time and enjoyed a paddle around the entire lake. By the time I got home, I was hot and thirsty. After texting Dizzy about the crime scene tape, I sat in the shade on my patio with a book and a tall glass of ice water flavored with some fresh lime juice. As much as I was enjoying the mystery novel I was reading, my mind kept wandering away from the story. I couldn't seem to stop thinking about Archie's murder and my grandfather's sticky situation.

Eventually, I gave up on reading and fixed myself a light dinner. After eating, I texted Sawyer to see if he was off work. When he didn't reply in the next ten minutes, my impatience got the better of me. I decided to take a walk over to his place. If he wasn't home, I'd at least get some more fresh air.

Sawyer lived in a timber-frame town house in the northeast corner of town. The back door opened to a set of concrete steps that led down into the canal. Out front, each home had a small grassy yard. I approached from that direction and found Sawyer in the sun, reclined halfway back on a lounge chair, a black baseball cap tipped forward to cover his eyes.

He nudged the hat up when he heard me coming and then tugged it off, dropping it on his lap. I sat on an old tree stump next to his lounge chair and picked up the hat. It had a red, green, and white embroidered eagle on the front and a small Mexican flag on the side.

"From your last trip to visit family?" I guessed as I set the hat down.

"My mom sent it to me."

After Sawyer's dad passed away a few years ago, his mom moved back to Mexico, where she was from, and where many of her relatives still lived. She traveled a fair bit, but Mexico City was now her home base.

"How's she doing?" I asked.

"Pretty well. She's in London at the moment. Then she's heading to Paris."

"Nice."

"What about your parents?"

"Enjoying life in Florida." I paused for a beat before changing the subject. "I guess you know Pops's full story now."

"He would have been better off leaving the scooter at Archie's place for me or another officer to find."

"He didn't know Archie was going to end up dead." I steeled myself for what I was about to ask. "How much trouble is he in? Is he the prime suspect?"

"I wouldn't say that. We're still looking at other people as well, but his name is up there on the list."

Even though I'd expected it, hearing the words from Sawyer sent an unsettling swirl through my stomach.

"Dizzy and I overheard a conversation earlier today that we thought you should know about," I said. "Jolene and Alex Brodsky are hiding something."

"What kind of something?" Sawyer asked.

"I don't know exactly, but they don't want the police knowing about it." I repeated what I'd heard Jolene and Alex say, as accurately as I could.

Sawyer eyed me with suspicion. "And you just happened to overhear this?"

"Yes . . ." Even to my own ears, I didn't sound very convincing.

"Where were you at the time?"

"Up by the new town house development."

His suspicion hadn't faded. If anything, it was getting stronger every time I answered one of his questions.

"Why were you there?" he asked.

"So Dizzy could ask Alex about the town houses."

"Dizzy wants to buy one of them?" He didn't believe that for a second. He knew as well as I did that she was saving up to buy a cottage on the water.

"Well, not exactly."

Sawyer regarded me quietly for a moment. It felt like he was trying to see inside my head.

"Whatever you two are doing, you should stop," he said eventually.

"We should stop trying to help Pops?"

"You should stop talking to murder suspects."

I latched onto those last two words. "So Jolene and her husband are official suspects?"

"I didn't say that."

"Didn't you?" I didn't give him a chance to say anything before I continued. "They're each other's alibis. One could be lying for the other. Or they could have been in on the murder together."

Sawyer sat up. "See, that's what I'm talking about. You two shouldn't be asking potential murder suspects about their alibis or anything else. What happens if you question the killer and they get ticked off about it?"

"I've considered that."

"Consider it more," he said. "What you're doing could be dangerous. Leave the investigating to me and my fellow officers. We're taking care of it."

"I just want to help Pops."

Something in his gaze softened. "I know, but I don't want you or Dizzy getting hurt."

"I don't either, but what about the stolen property Archie had stashed away? Do you know who the owners are?"

Sawyer scrubbed a hand down his face. "We're working on that."

"I noticed the crime scene tape is still up around Archie's place."

The suspicion was back in Sawyer's eyes. "Where were you when you noticed that?"

"Out on the lake, in my kayak. I'm not about to duck under police tape and sneak onto an active crime scene."

"Good to hear," he said with a wry note in his voice.

"So, I was wondering if you could take me there?"

He looked at me like I'd gone insane. "No."

"Why not?"

"Have you not been listening to our conversation?"

"But I might notice something . . . different."

"Do I even want to know what you mean by that?"

"Dizzy thinks we should check for signs that Archie's spirit might be hanging around his cabin."

Sawyer rolled his eyes heavenward. "Next the two of you will be wanting to hold a séance."

"Dizzy did suggest that as a possibility."

Sawyer groaned and leaned back in his lounge chair. He picked up the baseball cap and placed it over his eyes again. "Not happening."

I took the hat off his face. "Okay, so I'm not totally on board with the séance idea either, but when it comes to helping Pops, I'd try just about anything."

Sawyer sat up again. This time he turned on the chair so he could face me, his feet on the ground and his knees nearly touching mine. "Becks, I know this is hard, but I promise you that we're going to investigate thoroughly. You can trust me on that."

"I do trust you," I said. "It's just hard to sit back and do nothing."

He took my hand. "Get your grandfather some legal advice. That way he'll be as prepared as possible if Detective Ishimoto wants to talk to him again."

"Lolly was going to phone a lawyer today. I should find out how that went."

Seconds ticked by as we sat there in silence. I drew comfort from his gentle hold on my hand, but when I raised my gaze to meet his, I slipped my hand free and stood up.

I placed the hat on his head. “I’ll let you get back to your beauty rest.”

“Relaxation,” Sawyer amended as he adjusted the hat. “I can walk you home.”

I put a hand on his shoulder as he moved to get up. “That’s all right. I’m going to stop by my grandparents’ place.” My hand lingered on his shoulder until I realized it was still there. “Thanks for listening.”

I hurried off before he could insist on walking with me. It wasn’t that I didn’t like his company—because I did—but I wanted a few moments alone, and I didn’t want to take up any more of his evening.

When I reached my grandparents’ cottage, I found them on the back porch, enjoying drinks with their neighbors. I didn’t want to intrude, but Lolly insisted on feeding me a slice of the rhubarb coffee cake she’d made earlier in the day. While the two of us were alone in the kitchen, I asked her about the lawyer and she told me that she and Pops would meet with him the next day. That news brought me a tiny sliver of relief.

After I polished off the coffee cake, Lolly convinced me to hang around a while longer. I accepted a cup of chai tea and sat out on the porch, chatting with my grandparents and their neighbors. As the light faded from the sky, I gave my grandparents each a kiss and set off for home.

I hadn’t gone far when the front door to a cottage down the road opened, spilling light out into the darkening night. Maria Vasquez emerged and took pains to close the door quietly before creeping down the two front steps. She glanced back at the cottage and then picked up her pace.

She turned onto the road and set off in the same direction that I was heading, not noticing me behind her. I paused when I reached the cottage she’d emerged from. A light glowed in the front window. Without giving myself a chance to think about what I was doing, I darted quietly up the path to the cottage and peeked in the window. A television was on in the cozy living room and someone was curled up on the couch. Carmen, I realized a second later. She appeared to be sleeping.

That explained why Maria had tried to be quiet when she left the cottage. Didn't it?

I hurried back out to the cobblestone road. Ahead of me, Maria disappeared around a corner. I broke into a jog, not wanting to lose track of her. She probably wasn't doing anything out of the ordinary, but since she was on my suspect list, I wanted to make sure that wasn't the case.

Once I had her back in my sights, I slowed to a brisk walk, matching her pace. I followed her to the parking lot at the edge of town. I hung back in the shadows, not wanting to step into the bright light of the streetlamps that kept the parking lot illuminated all night long.

A red four-door sedan chirped and its lights flashed once as Maria approached it. I expected her to climb in the car and drive away, but instead she opened the trunk. She pulled out a large shopping bag and then slammed the trunk shut. The car chirped again as she locked it with her key fob.

I ducked behind a hedge when I realized she was heading back my way. I stayed in my hiding spot until she passed by and the sound of her footsteps began to fade away. There was some sort of logo on the shopping bag she carried, but I couldn't make it out from my vantage point.

Most likely I was wasting my time by following Maria, but I stayed on her tail. She was heading in the direction I needed to go to get home anyway. By the time we neared Venice Avenue, I had myself convinced that she'd simply gone to her car to pick up some shopping she'd forgotten to take home earlier. When she struck off along Amsterdam Avenue, I decided not to bother following her any farther, even though she clearly wasn't heading home. Her actions no longer seemed suspicious to me, and I wanted to get home to my cats.

I crossed the nearest bridge and set off along the canal. After a few steps, I paused. Across the water, Maria approached the main dock. Somebody else was there, seated in a whisper boat, appearing to me as nothing more than a dark shadow. Maria descended the steps to the dock and handed the shopping bag to the person in the boat. A murmur of voices drifted across the water to me, but I couldn't decipher any words. I thought the other voice belonged to a man, but I couldn't even be sure about that.

Maria turned away and jogged up the steps before heading back along Amsterdam Avenue. The light at the boat's bow lit up and the craft moved quietly away from the dock. The person steering the boat turned their head, and the light from the rising moon illuminated their profile. In the second or two before the boat slid away into the night, I got a good look at its sole occupant.

The man in the boat was Alex Brodsky.

Chapter Twenty

AFTER TWO HOURS SPENT MAKING CHOCOLATES THE next morning, I decided to take a break so I could walk to the coffee shop. Angela was getting ready to open True Confections, so I offered to bring something back for her. She'd be on her own out front until Milo arrived in the afternoon.

As I walked to Gathering Grounds, I wondered for probably the thousandth time what Maria had handed off to Alex Brodsky the night before. Maybe what I'd witnessed was nothing significant, but two of my suspects had been involved in what might have been a clandestine rendezvous, and I couldn't get it off my mind. I didn't think Maria was having an affair with Alex. I certainly hadn't witnessed anything romantic between them. Still, she'd met him after dark, and it had looked like she had been sneaking away from her cottage. I wondered if there was a way I could find out if she'd done that simply because she didn't want to wake her sister, or if there was a more sinister reason behind her stealth.

I recalled Sawyer's warning about grilling the wrong

person and putting myself in danger, but I thought I could pose my questions in a way that wouldn't raise Maria's suspicions. I hoped that was the case, anyway. I wouldn't get a chance to talk to her until the afternoon, at the earliest, so I had some time to come up with a mental script for myself.

A handful of customers sat scattered throughout the coffee shop, but no one stood waiting at the counter when I arrived. I placed an order with Mercedes for an iced chai tea latte for myself and a cold-brew coffee for Angie. After paying for the drinks, I moved down to the other end of the counter to wait.

"I was sorry to hear things didn't work out with Justin," Mercedes said when she set the drinks on the counter in front of me. "He seemed like such a nice guy."

"He is a nice guy," I said, wondering if the whole town knew about my breakup. "I guess our lives just didn't fit together."

She nodded sagely. "Been there. But I thought it was so sweet how he wanted to take you on a perfect Larch Haven date."

Which didn't stay perfect for long. I kept that to myself, saying instead, "You knew about that?"

"Sure, he asked me if I could give him any ideas. I told him Sawyer has known you forever. He was here at the time, remember?"

I nodded.

"Sawyer told him you always loved picnics on Mad Hatter Island, and sandwiches and lemonade from Cisco's." She sighed. "But I guess the perfect date isn't really perfect when you're not right for each other."

I wasn't sure what to say. Fortunately, another customer approached the counter, and Mercedes hurried over to serve her. I grabbed the two drinks off the counter and made my way out of the coffee shop.

A gray-haired woman stopped me right outside the door. I recognized her as a local, but I didn't know her name.

"Hello, dear," she said. "How are you holding up?"

"Holding up?" I echoed with confusion.

She leaned closer and patted my arm. "I understand you not wanting to talk about it. Just remember, we all get blindsided at some point in life." She opened the door to Gathering Grounds and paused. "Maybe not always to such a degree but . . ." She gave me a look full of pity and disappeared into the coffee shop.

My cheeks burned. That was one of the pitfalls of small-town living. Everyone knew your business.

I shook off the encounter and got on my way.

Tourists were emerging from their lodgings and True Confections had three customers when I got back to the shop. Angie had everything under control out front, so I left the cold-brew coffee with her and returned to the kitchen. My thoughts kept circling back to what Mercedes had told me, until I silently scolded myself. I needed to focus on making chocolates and narrowing down my suspect list. The latter would have to wait, so I fixed my attention on my work.

By noon, the shop was bustling. Milo arrived for his shift, and I spent some time out front helping him so Angie could go in the back and eat some lunch. I slipped a box of salted caramels and two chocolate gondolas into a bag and rang up the purchase. As I tucked the receipt in with the chocolates, Dizzy came into the shop, carrying an insulated lunch bag.

She waved to me and then browsed the shelves while I attended to another customer. By the time I finished ringing up the latest purchase, Angela had returned. She took over for me, so Dizzy and I headed into the back.

"I made your favorite lumpia, so I thought I'd share," Dizzy said as she patted the bag. "I prepped them last night and just ran home to fry them, so they're still hot."

My stomach gave a loud rumble. "You're the best, Diz."

We took the spring rolls into the kitchen. While Dizzy set the lumpia out on plates, I collected a bag of misfits for her to take home, and a second one for her to share with her colleagues at the library. I almost filled her in on what Mercedes had told me at Gathering Grounds earlier, but for some reason I stopped myself. Maybe I simply didn't want to talk about Justin anymore.

I fetched us each a glass of ice water, and we sat down on stools at the large island to enjoy our lunch.

Dizzy took a bite of one of the vegetarian lumpia and chewed thoughtfully. "Even though I use my mom's recipes, I can never get things to taste quite as good as hers. She says there's no secret she's hiding, but everything she makes has a little something more than anything I make."

"I don't know," I said after savoring a bite. "Your food always tastes amazing to me."

"Thanks. I still think hers is more amazing, but I'll take the compliment."

"How is your mom, anyway?" I asked. "And your dad?"

"They're doing pretty well. They'll probably come visit for several weeks over Christmas."

"That's fantastic."

"You know what will happen, right? My mom will try to feed us until we're ready to burst."

"I doubt you'll find me complaining," I said with a smile.

Dizzy's parents had immigrated to the United States from the Philippines shortly before she was born. Now, with aging family members in Manila, her parents split their time between the two countries.

"So, anything new to report on the investigation?" Dizzy asked as we ate.

"I might have witnessed something odd last night." I told her about what I'd seen when I followed Maria.

"But you don't think she's having an affair with Alex?"

"That's not what it looked like. I'm just not sure what it *did* look like. I'm going to try to find out what it was all about."

"Let me know if you need your sidekick," Dizzy said. "We could always do a good cop/bad cop routine."

I laughed. "Which one of us is supposed to be the bad cop?"

"You. Not because you're like that in real life, but because you can act out any part."

"I don't know," I said. "You can be pretty scary when you're in your ticked-off librarian mode."

Dizzy smiled with pride. "That is true."

I brushed crumbs from my hands. "I'll try going solo, but if that doesn't work, I'll call you in as my reinforcement."

"Deal."

We chatted about other things as we finished up our lunch, and then Dizzy returned to her work at the library.

I wanted to do some experimenting with fall flavors that we could hopefully offer for sale once summer was over, but first I wanted to at least try talking to Maria. My conversation with Dizzy had left me itching to get on with my quest to find out if she had killed Archie.

Out front, Angela and Milo were busy with customers, but although the place was hopping, they had things under control and didn't mind me stepping out for a while. When I reached Pure Bliss, I peered through the large front window. At first I saw only Carmen in the store, standing behind the sales counter as a middle-aged woman set out the goods she wanted to purchase. I almost turned away, but then I noticed Maria across the shop, speaking with a customer by one of the displays.

I hesitated, wanting the right opening to speak with Maria. At the same time, I didn't want to look suspicious, loitering outside the shop while peering through the window.

The customer at the cash register turned and came out of the shop with a Pure Bliss bag in hand. Before the door latched behind her, I caught it and entered the store. The customer who was chatting with Maria picked a bottle of lotion up off the shelf and headed for the sales counter, leaving Maria alone. I saw my opportunity and jumped at it.

"Hi, Maria," I said. "This is a great shop you've got here."

She smiled at the compliment. "Thanks. Is this your first time coming in?"

"My second, actually. I bought some soap the other day, and I liked it so much I thought I'd pick some up for my grandmother."

"Did you have a particular scent in mind?"

"I think she'd really like the rhubarb."

"That's on sale today." She led me over to a display of sale items.

"Perfect." I selected two bars off the shelf. "I saw you last night when I was on my way home from the parking lot, but you were too far away to talk to. It looked like you'd been on a successful shopping trip."

The smile disappeared from Maria's face, quickly replaced with wariness. She darted a glance toward her sister. "What do you mean?" she asked me.

The other customer in the shop thanked Carmen and headed for the door.

"You were carrying a shopping bag," I said. "I just assumed—"

Maria cut me off. "You're mistaken. That wasn't me."

"Oh . . ."

"Have you found everything you needed?" she asked, her words clipped.

I glanced down at the soap in my hands. "Yes, thanks."

Almost before I had the words out, Maria was talking again. "Carmen will be glad to help you. I'm sorry. I need to go in the back for a few minutes. It was nice to see you again."

She vanished before I had a chance to say anything further.

Carmen looked at me expectantly from behind the sales

counter, so I quickly took the bars of soap over and purchased them.

Maria didn't reappear before I left the shop.

Instead of going straight back to work, I plunked myself down on the bench outside True Confections and texted Dizzy about my latest encounter with Maria.

It was so strange, I wrote after detailing Maria's words and demeanor. I know it was her I saw last night. She's definitely hiding something.

I knew my best friend would be busy with work, so I didn't bother waiting for a reply.

Back in the True Confections kitchen, I got out the notebook I used for developing recipes and started experimenting. I tried out a couple of potential new flavors and then made some notes about what I should tweak for a better result. I liked what I'd come up with so far, but the flavor of one variety wasn't quite where I wanted it to be yet. Good wasn't good enough for me. I wanted everything in our shop to taste delicious.

I left some of the samples for Milo and Angela to taste and also put some aside for Lolly and Pops. They were my official taste-testers. Once I had feedback from everyone, I'd take another stab at the recipes.

I enjoyed the familiar process of developing new bonbons, even when they didn't turn out exactly right the first time or two. With a few adjustments, I usually achieved what I was aiming for.

If only I could have such success with finding Archie's killer.

Chapter Twenty-One

ANGIE DECLARED THE NEW CHOCOLATES TO BE PERfect just as they were, but Milo agreed with my opinion that the flavor of the pumpkin cheesecake truffles could be more intense. That didn't stop him—or me—from sampling a couple more, though. As we finished up the taste test, Susan Derendorf came into the shop, followed by two small groups of tourists.

"I'll help Mrs. Derendorf," I said to Angie before slipping out from behind the counter.

"Good morning," I greeted. "Is there anything I can help you with today?"

She glanced around the shop. "I had a hankering for your ice wine truffles."

I smiled at that. "One of our most popular products."

I led her to the shelf that held a stack of the boxed truffles. I'd made the chocolates with ice wine purchased from a winery in Quebec, Canada. Even though I didn't drink much in the way of wine, or any other alcohol, I loved the ice wine ganache that filled the popular truffles.

"Is there anything else I can help you find?" I asked.

"I think I'll have a box made up of an assortment of chocolates to share with my husband. I'd like to include at least four salted caramels. Those are his favorite."

"Of course," I said. "I can help you with that."

Milo was showing one group of tourists around the store while Angie was gift wrapping a box of chocolates. I grabbed a box and a set of tongs from behind the counter so I could remove chocolates from the display case. Susan pointed out which ones she wanted, and once a dozen bonbons sat in the box, I closed it up.

"How are you and your husband doing?" I asked as I punched the sale into the cash register.

"We're all right, thank you," Susan replied. "A little unsettled, maybe, but that's probably the case with everyone here in town."

"Because of the murder?" I guessed, before telling her the cost of her purchase.

"Yes. It's a terrible thing."

"I imagine it's particularly frightening that Archie was killed right next door to you," I said.

"Dreadfully," Susan agreed. "I hope the police find the killer quickly so we can all rest easier." She dug her wallet out of her purse. "Do you know if there's going to be any sort of service for Archie?"

"I haven't heard of one," I said. "It feels terrible to say this now that he's dead, but he wasn't well-liked. I guess you know that firsthand. I understand he caused a lot of trouble for you and your husband over a shed."

Susan nodded as she slid her credit card out of her wallet. "Archie kept insisting that the shed Karl built encroached on his property, but that really wasn't the case. Karl made sure to keep it well within our property line."

"I heard he even tried tearing the shed down," I said.

She nodded and tapped her credit card to pay for the

chocolates. "I had to call the police, but after that incident, things calmed down."

"Because the police got involved?" Somehow, I couldn't picture that being enough to cool Archie's temper.

"I don't think that was the reason," Susan said. "I'm really not sure what happened. He was still spitting mad when the police walked him off our property, but then two days later he told my husband not to worry about the shed. Karl said that Archie's demeanor was completely different, like he felt sorry for causing us trouble."

"Really?" I tucked the chocolates into a paper bag and added the receipt.

"I know," she said in response to my surprise. "It was so un-Archie. I can't explain it, but I'm glad that he and Karl were on better terms before he died." She picked up the bag of chocolates. "Anyway, thank you so much. My husband and I both love your chocolates."

"I'm so glad," I said with a smile. "Enjoy."

I stood there, lost in thought as I watched Susan leave the shop. I didn't move until Milo came around the counter and gave me a nudge. The tourists were ready to pay for the impressive stack of boxes they'd collected off the shelves.

I smiled at the customers but didn't linger any longer. In the shop's office, I woke up the desktop computer and got online. In under two minutes, I'd found a social media profile for Jolene. Her privacy settings didn't stop me from looking through her photos. She'd posted a picture of herself with her mother, but it was dated one day ago, and there were no other recent photos of Tammy. A little more snooping led me to Tammy's profile. Fortunately, she didn't have high privacy settings either. I scrolled through her photos, not entirely sure what I was looking for, but hoping I'd know when I found it.

I did.

A few weeks ago, Tammy had taken a selfie while standing by the hood of a blue car. I noticed a sticker on the windshield. When I zoomed in on the photo, I smiled with satisfaction. It was a parking sticker for a hospital in Maine. I knew from the information on Tammy's profile that she worked there, which meant there was a good chance that the blue car belonged to her.

A plan formed in my head. If I could locate her vehicle in the town's parking lot and get a better idea of what it looked like—the photo didn't allow me to see much other than the color of the car and part of the windshield—then I might be able to find out when Tammy arrived in Larch Haven. That would require getting access to the security footage of the parking lot. I'd need help to do that, but I knew who to ask.

The sun beat down on me as I left True Confections and walked toward the edge of town. I considered stopping to get a frozen lemonade to cool me down, but I didn't want to delay my mission. According to the weather app on my phone, we had some rain—and possible thunderstorms—headed our way, but the blue sky, sunshine, and warm temperatures were supposed to stick around for another day or so. I didn't mind getting some rain here and there throughout the summer, but I was glad that the gondola races had taken place during a stretch of beautiful weather.

When I reached the parking lot, I had to hold back a groan. The place was packed with cars. I should have expected that, considering that it was the height of tourist season. Even though the gondola races had ended on the weekend, Larch Haven typically enjoyed a steady stream of tourists all summer and on through to the end of leaf-peeping season.

Normally I wouldn't have complained. High numbers of tourists meant good business at True Confections and other local businesses. Today, however, the row upon row of parked cars meant my task could take a while. I didn't want to give up before I got started, though, so I got on with the search, walking up and down the rows of cars, stopping every time I found a blue one in a similar shade to the one in Tammy's photo.

It took me around ten minutes—which felt more like thirty—to locate a blue car with a circular sticker on the lower corner of the windshield. After glancing around to make sure no one was watching me, I moved closer so I could get a good look at the sticker.

I smiled with triumph. After noting the car's make and license plate number on my phone, I left the parking lot. I considered heading straight to the town hall but decided to stop back at True Confections first. When I reached the shop, I drank down a tall glass of ice water and snagged a bag of misfits off the shelf.

"See you at the barbecue?" I asked Angie and Milo, both of whom had just finished ringing up sales.

Lolly had planned a family barbecue to celebrate Gareth's gondola race win. I thought she herself deserved a trophy for convincing my brother to take enough time away from the restaurant to attend the gathering.

"You bet," Angie said.

"I wouldn't miss Lolly's food," Milo added.

I laughed at that as I left the shop.

Once outside, I set off to the east, my destination the town hall. Angie's husband, Marco, was a computer whiz. I didn't know his exact job title, but he worked as a tech guy for the town of Larch Haven. I was hoping that meant he had access to its video surveillance system. Larch Haven didn't have a lot of security cameras, but I knew that there were at least two aimed at the parking lot.

Like True Confections, the town hall had the air-conditioning running. I paused inside the door, enjoying the cool touch of the air, before crossing the lobby and heading down the hallway that would take me to Marco's office. The door stood open, so I knocked lightly on the doorframe. Marco looked up from where he sat behind his desk, a computer in front of him.

"Becca," he said with surprise. "Hey. What's up?"

I stepped into the office, glad to find that he was alone. "I have a favor to ask." I held up the bag of misfit chocolates I'd brought with me. "And I come bearing gifts."

"Are you trying to bribe a town employee?" He tried for a serious expression when he asked the question, but humor shone in his dark eyes.

I plunked the bag of chocolates down on his desk. "Would that be a problem?"

He peeked inside the bag. "Not in this instance." He picked out a bonbon and took a bite.

"Hazelnut," I said, able to recognize the flavor from the design on its chocolate shell. "Isn't that your favorite?"

He didn't respond right away, too busy enjoying the rest of the chocolate. Then he eyed the bag before sending a suspicious glance my way. "Maybe I should have asked what the favor is."

I made a move to take the bag back, but he snatched it out of my reach. "Never mind. Surely it can't be anything too bad."

"Of course it's not," I said, hoping that was really the case.

I pushed the office door shut. Marco raised an eyebrow but ate another chocolate instead of saying anything.

I dropped down into the chair across the desk from him. "Do you have access to the security footage of the town's parking lot?"

"I do," he said, his expression quickly changing to one of concern. "Did something happen to your car? We had a couple of smashed windows and thefts two weeks ago, but I haven't heard about any incidents from the last couple of days."

"Nothing happened to my car. I'm hoping to find out when a certain vehicle arrived in town."

As succinctly as possible, I outlined my reasons for

wanting to determine when Tammy Doyle showed up in Larch Haven.

"This sounds like something the cops should be doing," Marco said when I finished.

"I take it they haven't looked at the video footage recently?"

"Not since those thefts that I mentioned. At least, not as far as I know. And I probably would know."

"You'd think Tammy would be a suspect, or at least someone the police would want to talk to, seeing as she had a history with Archie." I was mostly talking to myself as I thought things through. "But maybe they did talk to her and she managed to convince them that she wasn't in town when the murder happened."

"But you think she was."

"I think it's a definite possibility. One worth looking into."

"Do you know how many hours of footage you'd have to go through?" Marco asked. "Looking for one specific vehicle during tourist season would be like looking for a needle in a haystack, especially when you don't have much of an idea of when she really did arrive, if it's not when she said she did."

"I don't think she could have arrived all that many days before she claims. Someone would have been bound to figure out she was in town, unless she stayed in hiding. If she did come earlier than she wants people to believe, at least one person *did* see her. I think there's a good chance that we wouldn't need to look back any further than a day or two before the murder."

"That's still a lot of hours of video," Marco said. "And a lot of cars coming and going."

"If you set me up with the footage, I'll do all the looking."

"I don't know, Becca."

"Tracking down the real killer would help Pops. And

before you say anything," I added quickly, "if it turns out Tammy arrived in town before she claims, I'll give that information to the police."

Marco got up from his chair. "All right. If it's possible to help Pops, we should do that. It's totally crazy that the police suspect him, but I guess from their perspective, they have reason to."

"Unfortunately."

Marco grabbed a laptop off a nearby shelf and set it on the desk. "I'll bring up the footage and let you go through it. I've got other things I need to get on with."

"I know. I'm sorry for interrupting your day."

He waved off my apology. "A few minutes don't matter. Besides, like I said, I definitely want to help Pops."

Once the laptop booted up, Marco navigated to the surveillance footage. He set it to two days before the murder and then nudged the laptop over my way. Fortunately, the video was in color, so I could watch for blue cars as I fast-forwarded through the footage. Unfortunately, as Marco had warned, and as I had expected, a lot of cars came and went from the parking lot on any given day during tourist season.

I had to stop the footage many times to take a closer look at a blue car entering the lot. I couldn't always be sure that the car wasn't Tammy's because I couldn't get a clear look at all of the vehicles that were possible matches or at the person or people who exited the cars. Whenever I wasn't certain, I noted down the time on a scrap piece of paper that Marco gave me. If I had no luck definitively identifying Tammy's car, I could go back and take another look at the ones I wasn't sure about.

One hour of my life and many hours of footage later, I was almost regretting my decision to look into Tammy's time of arrival. A dull headache was beginning to form behind my eyes, which were watering from staring at the screen for so long.

I'd made it through another hour of footage when Marco got up from his desk.

"I need to go down the hall for a while," he said. "If you leave before I get back, just close my office door. It will lock automatically."

My eyes nearly sighed with relief when I looked away from the screen. "Thanks, Marco. I really appreciate this. Will I see you at the barbecue?"

"You bet. And remember what you said about taking anything you find to the police."

"I promise."

Marco left and I got back to watching the fast-forwarding footage. I didn't know how much longer I could keep going. Maybe I'd have to finish the task the next day. My headache was getting worse, and I was growing thirstier by the minute.

When I checked the timecode, I realized I was getting close to the end of the first day of footage. Dusk was falling on the video when I brought it to a halt a few minutes later. I rewound and played the footage at normal speed. A blue four-door sedan drove into the parking lot and pulled into a pool of bright light beneath one of the lamps. I couldn't tell if there was a sticker on the windshield, but that didn't matter in the end.

When the driver climbed out of the car, I got a good look at her face.

Tammy Doyle.

I checked the timecode and smiled.

"Gotcha."

Chapter Twenty-Two

I MADE A NOTE OF THE DATE AND TIME WHEN TAMMY had arrived in Larch Haven, storing the information on my phone. Then I shut down the laptop and left Marco's office, pulling the door closed behind me as he'd requested. I checked to make sure that it locked, and then I was on my way.

After that long and tedious task, I figured I deserved a frozen lemonade, so I stopped and got one on my way home. I was so thirsty that I drank far too fast, giving myself several painful brain freezes as I walked. On the upside, my headache had disappeared by the time I reached my cottage.

I considered texting Dizzy about what I'd discovered, but I decided to tell her in person. I'd see her at the barbecue later. She counted as family, so I knew Lolly had expected me to invite her.

I thought about inviting Sawyer to the barbecue too, but wasn't sure if I should. Despite Pops's current predicament, I knew he wouldn't mind Sawyer joining us, but would it look bad for Sawyer to attend a social event hosted by one of the suspects in an ongoing investigation?

Maybe.

In the end, I decided not to invite him. Instead, I texted him to say I had some information to share and asked if we could meet up sometime soon. He replied as I was getting ready to head over to my grandparents' place. He'd be working for a while yet, but he was free later in the evening. I told him I'd be having dinner at my grandparents' house and would swing by his place after.

When Dizzy and I arrived at Lolly and Pops's house, we helped carry food out to the folding table that would serve as the buffet. We set out salads, veggies, chips, dip, and all of the condiments and fixings for the burgers that would soon be grilled on the barbecue.

By the time we had everything set up, almost everyone had arrived. Angie's kids, Bella and Luca, ran around the yard with Milo's younger sister, Sage, playing tag and having a great time. Angela's parents—my aunt Elizabeth and my uncle Jonah—showed up, as did my uncle Jack and his wife and Milo's parents.

When Gareth arrived with Blake, everybody cheered.

"Where's the trophy?" Marco asked.

"He refused to bring it," Blake said with an affectionate eyeroll aimed at my brother. "He's too modest to show off."

Laughter burst out of me. "Since when?"

That earned me a glare from Gareth. "Careful, or I'll throw you in the canal," he warned.

That put an end to my laughter. Knowing my brother, he might actually carry out that threat.

Lolly, who looked tiny next to Gareth and Blake, put an arm around each of them and ushered them into the heart of the gathering. "Never mind that. I'm glad you two took some time away from work. Let's get some food into you."

My uncle Jack helped Pops at the grill and soon everyone had a burger to eat.

I was seated at the wooden picnic table with Dizzy and Sage, finishing up my veggie burger, when Marco sat down across from me, bringing a bottle of beer with him. Soon after, Dizzy and Sage left to go get more food, leaving me alone with Angie's husband.

"How did your search go?" he asked. "When I saw you'd left the office, I didn't know if you'd found something or if you'd given up."

"It took a while, but I found what I was looking for."

He seemed surprised by that. "Tammy Doyle seriously lied about when she got to town?"

"She lied to her friend, at least, and I'm betting there's a good chance she did the same to the police."

"Have you told them yet?" Marco asked.

"I'm meeting Sawyer later tonight. I'll tell him then. I haven't forgotten my promise."

"Good."

Dizzy, Angela, and Bella joined us at the table then, so we dropped the subject.

After I'd finished eating, I managed to get Dizzy alone, out of earshot of anyone else. I filled her in on what I'd found with Marco's help.

"She's totally the killer!" Dizzy said after hearing the story.

"I thought you were convinced Jolene and Alex killed Archie."

"Maybe it was all three of them."

"That might be a bit too far-fetched."

"Okay, so it probably wasn't all three of them who actually committed the murder," Dizzy conceded, "but they could all be in cahoots. Maybe Tammy murdered Archie, and Jolene and Alex are covering up for her. It's possible."

"I'm with you there," I said.

Gareth wandered over our way, and I gave Dizzy a nudge to alert her. I definitely didn't want my brother knowing what I'd been up to. I'd only end up getting a lecture from him, something I wanted to avoid if at all possible.

"Do I even want to know what you two are whispering about over here?" Gareth asked before taking a drink of his beer.

"No," Dizzy replied with a devious smile.

"I figured as much," my brother said.

Blake came over and joined us. "Did you ask them yet?" He directed the question at my brother.

"I was just about to," Gareth said. He addressed me and Dizzy next. "I've got a couple of new recipes we're thinking of adding to the menu. Do you two want to come by the restaurant and give us your opinions?"

"Free food?" Dizzy said. "Count me in!"

I laughed. "Me too. When do you want us to show up?"

After a short discussion, we decided that we'd stop by the Gondolier during Dizzy's lunch hour the next day.

Lolly came out of the cottage, carrying a homemade strawberry shortcake, and Angie followed behind her with ice cream. All the kids came running when they saw the desserts. Blake and Dizzy headed that way too, but Gareth hung back with me.

"Hey," he said once we were alone. "I'm sorry about what I said the other day about cutting Justin loose."

"That's all right." I'd forgotten all about it until he mentioned it.

"Are you okay?" he asked. "Breaking it off couldn't have been easy."

I thought about the question before answering. "I'd be lying if I said it didn't hurt, but I know things turned out for the best. And I'm managing not to dwell on it too much."

"I'm glad to hear it."

We wandered over to join the others.

After everyone had enjoyed some dessert, Dizzy and I played a round of croquet with Milo and the kids.

"I wish Gareth had brought his trophy," seven-year-old Bella said as we waited for our turns. "I wanted to see it."

"I bet he'll show it to you some other time if you ask him," I said.

"One day I want to win a trophy." She smiled. "Becca, can you teach me how to race a gondola?"

Milo overheard and coughed in an attempt to cover up a laugh. He knew I had no experience with rowing gondolas, and the reason why. He liked teasing me about my fear now and then.

"You're probably better off asking Gareth to do that," I told Bella. "After all, he's the champion."

"Good idea!" She ran off to find my brother.

"Smooth," Milo said, his eyes bright with laughter.

"Just take your turn," I told him.

Milo won the game—as he usually did—but everyone had a good time.

Dizzy and I were the first to leave the barbecue. I liked to start work at True Confections early in the day, and I wanted a good night's sleep. I also didn't want to leave my meeting with Sawyer too late. I didn't know how long it had been since he last had a day off, but I didn't want to be responsible for keeping him from going to sleep at a decent hour, if that was what he was hoping for.

When I texted Sawyer to see if he was home yet, he sent a message in response saying that he was just leaving the Oar and Anchor, the local pub, after having some dinner. He said he'd walk in our direction and meet up with us. Dizzy and I set off, and within minutes we spotted Sawyer up ahead.

"We have a new theory about the murder," Dizzy announced as soon as we met up with him.

He didn't roll his eyes, but I suspected he was tempted to.

"Let me guess," he said. "Aliens? Sasquatch?"

"Don't be ridiculous," Dizzy admonished. "Aliens wouldn't have killed him with a branch to the head. They probably would have used some sort of technology that we wouldn't even recognize. And why would Sasquatch ever bother with Archie Smith?"

"What if the aliens wanted it to look like a human had killed Archie?" I asked.

Dizzy considered that for a second. She was about to say something, but Sawyer cut her off.

"I'm not arguing with you two about aliens or Sasquatch," he said.

"You're the one who brought them up," Dizzy pointed out.

"It's Tammy Doyle we want to talk about," I said quickly, worried Sawyer might walk off on us. "Has she been questioned? Did anyone ask her if she was in town when Archie was killed?"

Sawyer regarded me with suspicion. "Why are you asking me that?"

"Because if she told you she didn't arrive in Larch Haven until Tuesday, that was a lie, and I can prove it."

"Becca, what have you been up to?"

I didn't miss the exasperation behind the question.

"Nothing dangerous," I said in my defense. "All I did was look at the security footage of the parking lot. Tammy Doyle drove into Larch Haven on Saturday. Before the murder. But when a friend or acquaintance of hers mentioned that she'd seen Tammy on Saturday evening, Tammy denied that she was here."

To my disappointment, Sawyer gave no indication of what he thought of that information. Instead, all he said was, "What was your role in all of this, Dizzy?"

"She wasn't involved," I said, wanting to spare her from receiving any blame Sawyer might want to dish out.

"But I fully supported Becca's investigative efforts," she said.

Sawyer leveled his gaze at me. "Remember what I said about leaving the investigation to the professionals?"

"There was no danger involved," I said. "And I'm passing the information on to you."

He let out a breath. "Okay, message received. I appreciate you telling me. But no more investigating, okay?"

"It's good information, though, right?" Dizzy asked.

I was grateful that she'd spoken up, preventing me from having to respond to Sawyer.

"I'm not discussing that," he said.

"It's all right, Dizzy," I said before she could protest. "He's got the information. That's the important thing."

She frowned. "I guess that's true."

I understood her disappointment, because I shared it. I wanted to know what Sawyer thought about what I'd told him, but I knew we wouldn't get anything more out of him. Not at the moment, anyway.

At least he didn't seem too annoyed with Dizzy and me. He walked with us, talking about how this year's gondola races had brought in a record number of tourists. Dizzy left us when we reached her apartment over the local bookstore, Hooked on Books, and Sawyer and I continued on.

"Do you want to head home?" I asked him when we reached a fork in the road. "I don't want to disrupt your evening too much."

"I'll walk with you, if that's all right," he said. "It's a good evening to be out."

He was right about that. With the sun setting behind the mountains to the west, the heat of the day was disappearing, and the gentle evening breeze was scented with the smells of summer.

As we drew close to Venice Avenue, a lady with gray-streaked brown hair stopped us as we were about to pass by her. I knew her name was Glenys, but I'd never actually spoken to her.

"Rebecca, I heard what happened," she said.

I stifled a groan. I didn't want to talk about my breakup with Justin, especially with someone I didn't really know.

She peered at me. "Do you ever wear glasses?"

"Um." The question took me aback. "Sometimes. Mostly I wear contacts." I glanced at Sawyer, but he was as mystified by the conversation as I was.

Glenys shook her head, and I almost expected her to tsk at me. "You should wear them more often. They'll make you look more intelligent."

"Sorry?" I was too stunned to be sure I was hearing her correctly.

"And maybe you should try going blond," she added.

"She looks great just the way she is," Sawyer spoke up, sounding annoyed.

Glenys acted as though she hadn't heard him.

"I had blond hair for a movie I was in once," I said, still confused about why we were having this strange conversation. "Trust me, dark hair suits me better."

"Hmm." She pursed her lips, not looking convinced. "But dark hair didn't help you keep the man now, did it?"

She walked off without further comment.

"Is she for real?" Sawyer said, watching her go. "Who does she think she is?"

I put a hand on his arm. "Don't worry about it."

He was still glaring after Glenys. "She shouldn't be saying things like that to you."

I tugged on his arm so he'd start walking with me again. "Seriously, forget about it. It doesn't matter. I just don't get why people are so concerned with my breakup with Justin. She isn't the first person to say something. People seem to think that he dumped me. It was a mutual decision to go our separate ways. Not that it's any of their business."

"Exactly. It's not any of their business. And to tell you to change your appearance—"

"Never mind," I said, cutting him off. "Let's talk about something more pleasant."

"Good idea, because that excludes the murder."

I smiled. "It definitely does." My expression became more serious. "But you know I can't help but worry about Pops."

"And I can't help but worry when you get mixed up in a murder investigation."

"Fair enough," I conceded.

Fortunately, he didn't ask me to promise to keep my nose out of the investigation.

That was a promise I couldn't make.

Chapter Twenty-Three

AFTER SEVERAL HOURS OF MAKING CHOCOLATE gondolas, chocolate bars, and delectably filled bonbons, I wrapped up my next day of work. With Angie and our aunt Kathleen looking after the shop, I took a leisurely stroll along the canals to the Gondolier.

Since the restaurant would be open only for dinner service that day, the patio was empty. Dizzy had texted me moments before to let me know she was leaving the library, so I knew I had a few minutes to wait. Instead of heading straight inside, I wandered to the end of the patio, where I leaned my forearms against the wrought iron railing and gazed out over the canal.

A gondola glided past, steered by Caden Barnes, a professional gondolier. A family of four sat in the gondola, snapping photos and pointing out the sights. Caden raised a hand in greeting as he passed me, and I returned the wave.

Not for the first time, I felt a twinge of something like longing. It really was crazy that I'd grown up in Larch Haven and had never rowed a gondola. Sawyer was right about that. I'd ridden in gondolas a few times—while safely seated—but standing up and rowing was something I couldn't work up the courage to do. Sometimes, like at the moment, I wished I could hop on board one of the boats and take it along the canals without a worry. Briefly, I entertained the idea of taking Sawyer up on his offer to teach me. Not that it was an offer, exactly. More like a command.

A small splash off to my left caught my attention. By the time I turned my head, there was nothing but a slight ripple on the water. I almost shuddered, despite the heat of the summer afternoon. The splash had brought my line of thought to a screeching halt. No way did I want to risk falling in the water.

I missed the days before I knew about the large creature lurking in the lake, back when I would swim to and from Mad Hatter Island with the other local kids. Even though I'd done that countless times without incident, I couldn't forget that one occasion when something large, solid, and scaly had brushed against my leg. The memory of that touch was as fresh as the day it happened.

By the time Dizzy arrived, my thoughts had drifted in another direction.

"You look so pensive," Dizzy said she joined me at the railing.

My gaze wandered into the distance, where Mad Hatter Island sat out in the middle of the lake. "Mad Hatter Island is one of my favorite places. Now it reminds me of the end of my relationship with Justin. I don't want it to have negative associations."

"Then you need to reclaim it," Dizzy said. "Let's go tomorrow. Once you create more positive memories there, you'll feel better about it."

"That's a good idea."

I texted Blake from the patio, and he showed up seconds later to unlock the front door of the restaurant for us. Inside, Dizzy and I perched on stools at the bar and Blake brought us glasses of iced tea. Gareth came out of the kitchen a few minutes later, carrying two plates, which he set before us.

"Vegetarian mushroom stroganoff," he said. "I used three types of mushrooms and some sour cream to add a nice tang. Served with an egg dumpling."

"Smells delicious," Dizzy said as she picked up her fork.

My stomach rumbled. "It looks good too."

Dizzy's eyes widened when she took her first bite. "Oh my gosh. Gareth, this is amazing."

All I could do was nod in agreement because I was too busy enjoying a second forkful right after the first. Once I'd swallowed, I added my own compliments as well.

When we finished off the first sample, Gareth brought us another one. This time it was a dessert.

"Apple and cinnamon crème caramel cakes," Gareth said as he set the individual cakes on the bar before us.

Dizzy inhaled the delicious aromas. "I think I'm in love, and I haven't even tasted it yet."

"Seriously," I said after taking a bite and savoring it. "I don't know how you guys haven't won every award in the restaurant business."

I could see relief in Gareth's eyes.

Blake put an arm around him and gave him a squeeze. "See? Delicious." He addressed Dizzy and me. "He never takes my word for it, even though he knows I'd tell him the truth if I didn't like something."

"I just like to get a broader base of opinions," Gareth said. "You like pretty much everything. Dizzy has good taste and Becca is picky, so if I can win them over, I know we're good."

"I'm not picky," I objected.

"You won't eat meat," Gareth said to start.

"Hello, vegetarian here."

He continued as if I hadn't spoken. "You don't like any shellfish other than shrimp. You won't touch beets, water chestnuts, green olives, or goat cheese."

I made a face. "Goat cheese is gross."

"I don't know," Dizzy said. "You are a little bit picky, Becca."

"Traitor," I grumbled.

"Dizzy knows the truth," Gareth said with a grin. "Thanks for helping out, you two. I need to go get some prep work done for this evening."

Dizzy and I finished off our cakes while Gareth returned to the kitchen and Blake disappeared into one of the back rooms.

"Okay," Dizzy said after she'd licked her fork clean. "So Tammy's on our list of suspects."

"Definitely." I eyed my empty plate with longing, but I knew I shouldn't ask for another serving of dessert. My stomach was already full.

"I still want to know what Maria was up to with Alex," Dizzy said.

"Me too."

"Did I hear you mention Maria?" Blake asked as he returned from the back with some liquor bottles in hand. "Maria Vasquez?"

"The one and the same," I replied. "I saw her sneaking around a couple of nights ago. It was strange."

"Maybe it had something to do with the surprise party." Blake placed the bottles on the shelves behind the bar.

Dizzy and I exchanged a confused glance.

"What surprise party?" she asked before I had the chance.

Blake placed the final bottle on the shelf. "Maria came by a week or so ago, asking if we could cater a surprise birthday party for her sister. I had to tell her we don't do catering and our banquet room was already booked for the night she wanted. I suggested she ask the Oar and Anchor if they could help her out."

"And here I thought she might be up to something criminal," I said.

"Don't cross her name off our suspect list yet," Dizzy

cautioned. "Even if her meeting with Alex had something to do with the party—which we don't know for sure—that doesn't mean she didn't kill Archie."

"Whoa." Blake had been checking something under the bar but now he straightened up so he could look at us. "You think Maria might have killed Archie?"

"She's one of our many suspects," I said.

"You make it sound like you two are amateur detectives or something."

Dizzy and I shared another glance.

"Wait a second," Blake said, watching us. "Don't tell me you've actually been investigating."

"Okay. We won't." I looked anywhere but at my brother-in-law.

"Becca . . ."

"We've made some discreet inquiries," I said. "That's all."

Dizzy nodded in support of my statement.

Blake eyed us with apprehension. "I don't like the sound of that. This is a cold-blooded killer we're talking about."

"You don't need to worry," I assured him. "We really haven't done much. We overheard a couple of conversations, and I looked at some security footage."

That wasn't quite all that we'd done, but I didn't need to go into every detail.

Judging by the suspicion in Blake's blue eyes, he knew I wasn't telling him everything.

"You two need to be careful," he said.

"We will be," I promised.

"Extremely," Dizzy chipped in.

I slid off my barstool, and Dizzy did the same.

"We'd better get going," I said. "Thanks for the food."

Blake stacked our empty plates. "Thanks for lending us your taste buds."

Dizzy and I hurried out of the restaurant before he had a chance to turn the conversation back in the direction of our recent activities. As we walked away from the Gondolier, Dizzy and I made a plan to meet up the next day and take my boat out to Mad Hatter Island. I really didn't want my last experience on the island to change how I felt about the place. Spending some carefree time out there with my best friend would help make sure that didn't happen.

After parting ways with Dizzy, I stopped by True Confections, even though I didn't plan to make any more chocolates that day. Angie and Aunt Kathleen had their hands full with a big crowd of customers so I helped them out with some gift wrapping and boxing of chocolates. When the rush of business slowed slightly, I took the opportunity to go into the back and bring out more chocolates to refill the display case and restock the shelves.

I was adjusting the placement of the bonbon-filled chocolate gondolas on the shelf when Maria entered the shop. At the sight of her, my mind raced through all the questions I wished I could ask her. I kept them to myself, however, and simply smiled and asked her how she was doing. Giving her the third degree and scaring her out of the shop wouldn't be good for business. It could also put me in danger if she was Archie's killer. If I wanted information from her, I would have to find a way to be subtle about it.

"I was hoping to get some chocolates for a party," Maria said to me. "I was thinking of giving the guests treats when they leave. Maybe small boxes with four or six chocolates each? Do you have anything like that?"

"Absolutely." I led her toward the appropriate display. "We've got these small sampler boxes with six different bonbons in each."

Maria took the box I handed her. "This is perfect. Exactly what I was looking for."

"Is this party the one you're holding for your sister?" I asked.

Her eyes widened with surprise and alarm. "How did you hear about that?"

"Oh . . ." I wasn't sure what to say. I didn't want to throw

Blake under the bus by bringing up his name. "I'm not sure. Someone mentioned it in passing, I guess."

Maria frowned with annoyance. "It's impossible to keep a secret in this town. It's supposed to be a surprise party. I really don't want Carmen finding out about it before it happens."

"She won't hear about it from me," I promised. "Is the party the reason you didn't want to talk about your shopping trip the other day?"

Maria's shoulders relaxed and some of her annoyance faded away. "Yes. I'm sorry I was so evasive about that, but I didn't want Carmen overhearing."

"I understand. Do you have help organizing the party? It seems like a lot to take on." I wasn't sure if that was really the case, but I was hoping to keep her talking.

"Jolene's helping out. She and Alex are storing the decorations and presents for me. Carmen is staying at my place for the summer, and I don't want her accidentally finding everything."

"Sounds like a good plan." I patted the stack of small boxes on the display table. "How many of these would you like?"

"Two dozen, if you've got that many."

I counted the boxes. We had two to spare on the table, and a few more in the back, so it wasn't a problem. I helped her carry the boxes over to the cash register, where Angela rang up the sale.

It didn't look as though my cousin and aunt needed my help any longer, so I wandered out of the shop and toward home.

I thought there was a good chance that Maria had told me the truth about why she'd denied that she'd been shopping. Her explanation made sense. She was probably handing off decorations or presents to Alex the other night.

That didn't mean Maria absolutely wasn't the killer, but it did explain her suspicious behavior. I figured that meant I could bump her down to the bottom of the suspect list. I wasn't ready to forget about her entirely, but in my mind, it was time to focus on some of my other suspects.

Chapter Twenty-Four

DIZZY HAD THE NEXT DAY OFF FROM WORKING AT the library, so she purchased sandwiches and drinks for us and showed up at True Confections around noon. As soon as I'd finished cleaning up the kitchen after another good session of chocolate making, we walked over to my cottage. We checked in on the cats, and then climbed into my whisper boat and took it over to Mad Hatter Island.

Once we'd pulled the boat up onto the beach, we raced to the top of the rock formation, just as we'd done dozens of times in the past. Dizzy got there a few seconds ahead of me, which I blamed on the fact that I was carrying our lunch. We collapsed onto the rock, out of breath and laughing.

I stared up at the dark clouds drifting across the sky. It looked as though the predicted rain was heading our way, but for the moment it was holding off.

"This was the best idea, Dizzy," I said as I relaxed. "Thank you."

We spent close to an hour up on the rocks, chatting and eating our lunch. Once we'd finished our meal and the clouds were growing darker, we climbed down and returned to my whisper boat. On our way back to my cottage, I slowed the boat.

"Check it out," I said as I looked toward Archie's property. "I don't think the police tape is up anymore."

Dizzy followed my line of sight. "Perfect! Let's go take a look around."

"I doubt there's anything to find there," I said.

"But we can't say that for sure."

"That's true."

"So let's go and find out if there's anything to see," Dizzy urged.

I glanced around, not liking how easy it would be for our movements to be observed.

"How about we go there on foot?" I suggested. "That way we won't draw any unnecessary attention."

"Good idea. We may as well avoid any trouble if we can."

After tying up the whisper boat in my boathouse, we left the remnants of our lunch in my cottage and set off in the direction of the north end of the lake. On our way across a bridge, I spotted Oliver and Estelle up ahead, chatting together. They both wore muddy hiking boots, shorts, and T-shirts.

Dizzy and I called out greetings as we approached.

"You two look so serious," Dizzy said. "Is everything all right?"

She shot a conspiratorial glance my way. I knew she was hoping we could get some sort of clue out of Oliver since he was one of our suspects. I was hoping for that too, although I had no idea what to say to make that happen.

"Everything's fine," Estelle said. "We're discussing the latest fundraising ideas for the trail restoration project."

"Is the project definitely going forward now?" I asked.

"The club gave it the green light this morning," Oliver said with a satisfied smile. "We're going to apply for some grants, but we're also going to raise money on our own."

"We're hoping to hold a silent auction and a bake sale." Estelle turned her full attention on me. "Would True Confections be interested in donating some chocolates for the auction?"

"I don't think that would be a problem," I said.

Estelle made a note on her phone. "I'll be in touch later so we can discuss it more."

"Sounds good." I didn't know what else to say so I simply added, "Have a nice day."

Dizzy and I left them to their fundraising discussion.

"We didn't get anything interesting out of Oliver," Dizzy said with disappointment once we were out of their earshot.

"I didn't know what to say," I admitted.

"Neither did I. We can't exactly come right out and ask him if he lied about his alibi. If he did lie, he'd just do so again."

"And he'd get mad at us." I sighed as we crossed another bridge. "Solving a murder sure isn't easy."

"You can say that again."

We entered the woods a short time later and followed the narrow dirt road that provided access to the lakefront properties. We hadn't gone far when Carmen came around a bend, heading our way.

"Hi there! We meet again," she said cheerily. "Enjoy your walk!"

Dizzy and I thanked her, and she didn't hang around for any further chitchat.

Over lunch, I'd filled Dizzy in on my latest conversation with Maria, and she agreed that Maria's name should be dropped to the bottom of our suspect list.

After Carmen disappeared from sight, we couldn't see or hear any other people. It seemed we were alone with the trees and the birds, which was exactly what we wanted. Another minute or two of walking got us to Archie's property. As we'd observed from out on the water, the police tape had been removed, leaving no obstacle to us entering the property. Nevertheless, I hesitated before leaving the road.

"You don't think we'll get charged with trespassing if anyone finds us here, do you?" I asked.

"The only person who would want us charged is Archie, and I doubt his ghost will have much clout with the cops."

She had a point. Besides, as long as we stayed away from the edge of the lake, we'd be well hidden from any prying eyes. Evergreen trees grew thickly around the property, with several close to the cabin and outbuildings as well.

I pushed aside my hesitations. "All right. Let's do it."

We started our search at the nearest outbuilding, a ramshackle shed that looked like it would collapse if a strong gust of wind came along. The door was unlocked and opened with a creak when Dizzy tried it.

Inside we found a couple of rakes that had seen better days, two shovels, and hedge clippers. Aside from the tools, the place was home to an impressive number of cobwebs, some currently occupied, but nothing else.

Dizzy made a face and let the door swing shut. "Creepy crawlies, but no clues."

"Let's try that building." I nodded at a larger shed tucked among the trees, closer to Archie's cabin.

A padlock was lying on the ground by the shed door. It looked as though it had been cut off, probably by the police. The door groaned with protest but moved fairly easily when I opened it. Between the thick clouds overhead and all the tall evergreens on the property, the natural light was limited, but I still managed to notice a tire track on the dirt floor.

I pointed it out to Dizzy. "This is probably where Archie had Pops's scooter stashed. The bikes and snowmobile Pops said he saw are gone."

"Maybe the police knew they were stolen and took them," Dizzy said.

"Probably."

I ventured into the shed, hoping for a better look at its contents. The far end of the old building was thick with shadows, leaving me to wonder what kind of creatures might be lurking there. I wasn't terrified of spiders and other insects, but I didn't like them crawling on me.

"See anything?" Dizzy asked from the doorway.

"Not yet."

I dug my phone out of the pocket of my shorts and switched on the flashlight app. I aimed the light into the corners, but there wasn't much to see. Archie had piled some old lumber by the back wall, and everything else appeared to be junk.

"Nothing here," I declared once I'd had a look at everything.

Dizzy wrapped her arms around herself as I joined her outside the door. "I've got the chills."

"From paranormal activity or the changing weather?" I asked.

"I think it's just because this place gives me the creeps."

"Me too." I shut the shed door.

A fat raindrop hit me on the shoulder. Another one pinged on the metal roof of the shed. More followed, drumming against the roof. Dizzy and I moved beneath the shelter of a towering pine tree.

"So far I haven't seen anything that looks like it might have been stolen," Dizzy said. "If there were any such thing, I guess the police took it along with the bikes and snowmobile."

"Most likely." A thought struck me. "We've considered the possibility that someone Archie stole from could have killed him out of anger, but what if Archie stole something that no one other than the owner was ever supposed to see?"

"As in something that might reveal a terrible secret?"

"Exactly. And once Archie saw . . . whatever it was—documents or who knows what—then he had to be silenced, in the killer's opinion."

"But then we're still not likely to find anything. If something was so important to the killer, they would have taken it once they'd silenced Archie for good."

"That's true. Unless they couldn't find it."

Dizzy warmed to the idea. "Because Archie hid it too well."

She hurried over to the cabin, and I followed on her heels, raindrops pelting us whenever we weren't beneath the trees. When we reached the window next to the front door, we peered inside, cupping our hands around our eyes so we could see better.

"I was thinking maybe the killer trashed the place while searching for whatever they were after," Dizzy said as we peered into the murky interior of the cabin. "But it doesn't look like it."

There was a lot of what looked like junk in the cabin, but it was all stored in a fairly tidy way, on shelves or piled against the walls.

"Do you think the cops would have tidied up while they were searching?" Dizzy asked.

"I don't know." I stepped away from the window, my enthusiasm for the investigation waning. "All our theories are nothing but speculation. We've got no evidence of anything. We don't even have a solid lead to take us in any particular direction."

If there had been a bench or seat nearby, I would have dropped down onto it in defeat. Instead, I leaned my back against the outer wall of the cabin and crossed my arms.

As if wanting to reflect my mood, the clouds overhead opened up, and the steady rain turned into a downpour.

Dizzy joined me beneath the overhang of the cabin's roof. "We are speculating about everything, but we're here now. We may as well finish what we started. We'll give the place a good once-over. If we don't find anything, we'll have a brainstorming session so we can figure out what to do next."

"You're right," I said, shaking off my glum mood. "We might as well finish looking around now that we're here."

Dizzy tried the cabin door. It didn't budge. "Locked."

I reached up and ran my fingers along the top of the doorframe. "No spare key."

"Maybe he hid one somewhere else," Dizzy said. "Let's check."

I picked up a rock not far from the front door, but all I found were some creepy crawlies. "Ugh." I dropped it back down.

Dizzy found a scarred section of a tree trunk that looked as if it had been used for chopping wood. She tipped it to one side and peeked underneath. "Nothing. Let's keep looking. You go around that way," she said, pointing to the right of the cabin, "and I'll go this way." She disappeared around the corner to the left.

I set off in the opposite direction. Along the side of the cabin, I paused to check under a couple of rocks. One hid nothing but dirt. A worm squirmed beneath the other so I quickly replaced it. An old tree stump sat a few feet away from the exterior wall of the cabin. I left the shelter of the roof's overhang so I could inspect it. Fat raindrops pelted me, so I searched quickly among the moss and fragments of tree bark. Again, my search came up empty.

I dashed back beneath the roof's overhang and pushed strands of wet hair away from my face. A branch snapped nearby.

My gaze darted in the direction of the sound. I couldn't see anything, but the snap had come from the woods at the edge of the property. I stood frozen, watching for any sign of movement. An eerie sensation creeped over my arms and up my neck, leaving goose bumps in its wake.

Even though I couldn't see anything, and even though I couldn't hear any other noises over the sound of the rain drumming against the rooves of the sheds and cabin, I could have sworn someone was watching me.

"Hello?" I called out.

Nobody responded.

I raised my voice. "Dizzy?"

She peeked around the corner from the back of the cabin, appearing so suddenly that I jumped.

"Find anything?" she asked.

"Nothing." I glanced toward the woods again. "Did you hear something out there?"

"No." She followed my line of sight. "If there's an animal out there, I bet it's more scared of us than we are of it." She disappeared from sight.

I joined her behind the cabin. I wasn't worried about an animal in the woods. It was the thought of a human sneaking around out there that unnerved me. I relaxed once I was with Dizzy again, though.

We spent another minute or two searching the area behind the cabin, but we came up empty.

"No key." Dizzy rested her hands on her hips and looked up at the sky as raindrops hit her face. "I say we get out of the rain and come up with a better plan."

"Good idea."

I glanced toward the woods, but I still couldn't see anything there. I was letting myself get spooked too easily.

Shaking off my worries about being watched, I led the way around the side of the cabin.

When I turned the corner, I collided with something solid.

Chapter Twenty-Five

I LET OUT A YELP AS I TEETERED OFF BALANCE.

Strong hands gripped my upper arms.

"*Sawyer?*" I pressed a hand over my pounding heart.

He released his hold on me now that I was steady on my feet.

Dizzy appeared at my side. "You nearly gave her a heart attack," she said to Sawyer.

"Seriously." I dropped my hand from my chest. "I thought you were the killer. Or maybe the mystery guy in the sunglasses. What the heck are you doing here?"

"I'm the one who should be asking that question." Sawyer's unimpressed gaze swept over both of us and then zeroed in on me. "Hold on. What mystery man?"

"Forget about that for the moment." I took in the sight of his uniform. "I thought the police were done with this place. The tape's gone."

"It's no longer an active crime scene, but I wanted to take another look around. What are *you* doing here?"

"Looking for clues," I said.

"And signs of paranormal activity," Dizzy added. "In case Archie's spirit is still hanging around."

"You two are going to give me high blood pressure." Sawyer leveled his gaze at me. "Becca, we already talked about this amateur detective thing."

I took his arm and tugged him beneath the overhang. "I know, so we don't need to repeat the conversation."

"Really? Because it looks to me like you didn't listen to a word I said."

"I listened." I stood up on my tiptoes and ruffled his wet hair.

He swatted my hand away.

"You look way more intimidating when your hair isn't all plastered to your head," I said.

Dizzy nodded her agreement. "She's right."

Sawyer raked a hand through his hair, looking thoroughly annoyed now.

"Much more effective," Dizzy said, stepping behind me so I had to take the brunt of his glare.

"Were you going inside?" I asked.

Sawyer turned for the door, muttering under his breath. I thought I heard him say something about two Miss Marples, but I wasn't certain.

He produced a key from his pocket and unlocked the door to the cabin. "You two stay out here."

"It's pouring!" Dizzy protested.

He pushed open the door. "That didn't stop you from coming here and nosing around."

"It wasn't raining when we got here," I said.

He entered the cabin without saying anything more, but I was pretty sure I saw him roll his eyes as he stepped over the threshold.

Dizzy looked my way. I shrugged. Together, we followed Sawyer into the cabin.

I considered leaving the door open, but then a gust of wind blew up from the lake, sending the rain in at us. I quickly closed the door and combed my wet hair out of my face with my fingers. Dizzy did the same with her hair. I pried my purple T-shirt away from my skin. Luckily it was only wet in splotches, aside from the shoulders.

Dizzy and I lingered near the door, watching Sawyer as he opened cupboards in the kitchen, running his now-gloved hands along the inside of each unit before shutting it and moving on to the next. I let my attention wander as he continued his search. The cabin was quite basic. The kitchen and small living area were all one room, and two closed doors along the back wall led to what I assumed were a bedroom and a bathroom. I looked around from my vantage point near the door, but didn't see anything of interest.

Sawyer had his back to us, and at first, I wasn't sure if he even realized that we'd followed him into the cabin. I should have known better.

After checking a few cupboards, he stepped back and rested his hands on his hips as he stared at the kitchen. "So, who's this mystery guy and why would he be here?" he asked without looking our way.

"I don't know who he is," I said.

"Hence the mystery part," Dizzy added.

"And I don't think he would be here unless he followed me."

"Which he might do," Dizzy said.

Sawyer turned to face us, his forehead furrowed with concern. "Why would he be following you?"

"He wouldn't," I replied at the same time Dizzy declared, "He's obsessed with Becca."

"No, he's not," I said quickly.

"Has he been bothering you?" Sawyer asked.

"No. Not exactly."

He had his full attention on me now. "What does that mean?"

"I've seen him watching me a couple of times. Once he

started heading my way, but then when he saw me with Gareth and Blake, he took off."

"Can you describe him?" Sawyer got back to his search, checking the lower cupboards this time.

"Not in any detail." I thought carefully. "He's white. Maybe a little shorter than you, so just under six feet? Late thirties or early forties, probably. I think he has dark hair, although it's hard to tell because he's always wearing a baseball cap."

"I bet he wants your autograph," Dizzy said.

"I doubt it." Even though I'd been asked for my autograph many times, I still had trouble understanding why anyone would want it. Despite my relative success with my acting career in the past few years, I was a far cry from the celebrity A-list.

"Dizzy's probably right," Sawyer said. "But if you see him again, give me a call. If you can point him out to me, I'll have a chat with him."

"I think that would be going overboard. He really hasn't done anything much more than look in my direction."

"Then if he does anything to make you feel uncomfortable, give me a call," Sawyer amended.

"I will." I watched as he surveyed the room. "What are you looking for?"

"I don't know." He tugged off one of his gloves and ran a hand through his hair again, leaving it disheveled.

I liked the look on him.

"I feel like we're missing a piece of the puzzle," he said. "Probably several pieces. If nothing else, I was hoping that coming here would jog some new ideas."

"It did that for us," Dizzy said. "Well, for Becca, anyway." She told Sawyer about our theory that Archie might have stolen something that would reveal a dark secret, one worth killing Archie to keep it under wraps.

Sawyer raised an eyebrow. "I'm guessing you're basing that on nothing but conjecture."

"You guessed right," I admitted.

"But it's an idea, at least," Dizzy said.

Sawyer nodded, but he seemed distracted. He opened one of the doors along the back wall and disappeared into the next room.

Dizzy and I wandered farther into the living area. I stopped in the middle of the room. From there, I could see Sawyer in Archie's bedroom. I opened the other door and peeked through it. As I'd thought, it led to a bathroom. I made a face and backed out, closing the door again. Archie hadn't exactly kept up on his housekeeping.

Dizzy stood by the stone fireplace, inspecting a collection of odds and ends lying scattered across the mantel. I stepped into the bedroom, where Sawyer was now searching through a closet to the left of the door. As with the kitchen cabinets, he was running a hand along the inside of the closet. He moved all the way into the small space, which held only a few garments, and looked up toward the ceiling. He pushed at a panel above his head and it lifted up.

"Access to the attic?" I guessed. "Did that get missed during the previous search?"

"No," Sawyer said. "It was checked." He let the panel fall back into place and stepped out of the closet, closing the bifold doors behind him. I stared at the wall next to the closet. I retreated to the hall and looked at the wall out there.

Dizzy appeared by my shoulder. "What's up? Did you find something?"

"I'm not sure." I returned to the bedroom. "It's probably nothing."

"But?" Sawyer prodded.

I squeezed between him and the foot of the double bed so I could get to the far side of the closet. I was about to touch a hand to the wall when Sawyer caught my arm in a gentle grip.

He handed me a glove. "Just in case."

I tugged on the glove and rested my hand against the wall. "The closet only extends halfway along this wall. There's no other closet out in the hallway, so doesn't that leave a big space between the bedroom wall and the one in the hall?"

I started knocking on the wall, moving from the end of the closet toward the corner of the room. The first knock sounded slightly different than the ones that followed. Less hollow.

Sawyer and Dizzy noticed the difference too. They came over to join me as I started pressing at the white-painted wood paneling on the walls. One of the panels seemed to give more than the others. I leaned my weight into it and something clicked. A portion of the wall opened toward me.

"A secret room!" Dizzy bumped my fist. "Way to go, Jessica Fletcher."

"Don't encourage her, Dizzy," Sawyer admonished, but I could tell he was interested in my discovery.

I pulled the paneled door open wider. "More like a secret hidey-hole than an actual room."

I stepped back so the others could see into the space between the bedroom and hall walls. It was the same height as the closet and roughly half as wide.

"Jackpot," Dizzy whispered as she got a look inside.

Rough shelving filled the space. The shelves held all manner of small items, from cell phones and jewelry to video game consoles and a couple of laptop computers. A series of pegs had been driven into the wall above the shelf that stood level with my eyes. Several necklaces, bracelets, and watches hung from the pegs.

Dizzy reached toward some of the jewelry.

Sawyer stopped her with a hand to her wrist. "Don't touch anything. Not even with gloves."

Dizzy snatched her hand back. "Right. You'll want to

photograph the evidence as we found it." Her eyes lit up. "Archie must have stolen all this stuff. Maybe something in here is the reason why he was killed."

A phone rang. For a second, I thought it was one of the phones on the shelf, but then Sawyer pulled his out of his pocket.

He checked the display. "I have to take this." He pinned Dizzy and me with his gaze. "Remember, don't touch anything."

I tucked my hands behind my back.

He stepped out into the hall and answered the call.

I whipped out my own phone and snapped a few photos of the contents of the hidey-hole.

"Good thinking," Dizzy said with approval.

"I don't know that it'll help us at all."

"You never know. And we need all the help we can get right now."

I couldn't deny that. Despite the find, I didn't think I was any closer to proving Pops's innocence. Clearly, I was far better at making chocolates than I was at detecting.

I slipped my phone back into my pocket a split second before Sawyer returned to the room.

"I need to call this in," he said. "I'll walk you two out to the road."

"Don't you trust us to leave on our own?" Dizzy asked, all innocence.

"Nope."

He motioned us out of the bedroom and toward the front door. I stepped outside first, with Dizzy right behind me, and Sawyer following after her.

A twig snapped off to my left. I whirled around.

"Sawyer!" I exclaimed with surprise.

He swore under his breath and took off after a dark figure that was running away from Archie's cabin like greased lightning.

Chapter Twenty-Six

AFTER A SECOND OF HESITATION BROUGHT ON BY surprise, Dizzy and I raced after Sawyer. By that point, the mystery person had already disappeared from my line of sight. Sawyer's brief head start and the fact that he was a faster runner than me meant I didn't catch up to him until I reached the dirt road. Sawyer stood there, hands on his hips, not looking happy.

"Where did they go?" I asked, scanning the forest around us.

Dizzy ran up behind me. "They got away?"

"They were gone by the time I got to the road," Sawyer grumbled. "I have no idea which way they went."

I couldn't hear any sounds of someone crashing through the underbrush, but that didn't mean much. Aside from the road, there were nearby trails leading off in different directions. Even though it was raining, the dirt on the road was so hardpacked that there weren't any discernible footprints. The three of us walked up and down the road, checking each trailhead, hoping we'd have more luck with footprints, but we didn't come up with anything.

Finally, when we were all well and truly soaked from the rain, we gave up and huddled beneath the broad branches of a pine tree, where it was still relatively dry.

"Did you get a look at the person before they took off?" Sawyer asked me. "Did you see their face?"

I shook my head, disappointed. "I don't even know if it was a man or a woman." The hood of the roomy coat had been pulled up, hiding the person's face and hair. "What about you?"

He looked as disappointed as I felt, plus a bit frustrated. "Whoever it was, I'm pretty sure they're shorter than I am, but that's it. Dark pants and a black raincoat. It could have been almost anyone."

"I did notice one thing," I said, remembering a small detail. "The back of the raincoat was torn at the bottom."

Sawyer nodded. "I saw that too."

I rubbed my goose bump–covered arms. "I don't think that will help much, though."

"It might," Dizzy said.

Sawyer sounded less hopeful. "We'll see. I need to call Detective Ishimoto about what we found in the cabin. Do you want me to walk you home?"

"That's all right," I said after exchanging a glance with Dizzy. "We'll be fine."

Despite that assurance, Sawyer walked us around the bend in the road and then stood and watched us until we left the woods. Either he wanted to make sure that we really did leave, or he wanted to be certain that the mystery person wouldn't leap out at us before we made it into the open. Maybe both.

"You know," Dizzy said as we crossed a bridge, "what just happened fits with our latest theory."

"Because the person who ran away could have been the

killer, coming to search for whatever Archie stole from them?" I guessed.

"Exactly."

"Or the murder could have had nothing to do with any of Archie's thefts, and the killer was returning for some other reason. Maybe to get rid of some other type of incriminating evidence that they think the police haven't found yet."

Dizzy stopped in her tracks. "We should search the whole property again."

I tugged her back into motion. "The police will do that, considering what just happened."

"True." She shivered and tucked her wet hair behind her ear.

"We should probably get warm and dry. How about hot drinks at my place?" I suggested.

Dizzy readily agreed to that idea.

Back at my cottage, I changed into dry clothes and loaned some to Dizzy. Everything of mine looked ridiculously large on her, but since we didn't plan to do anything but lounge around inside, she didn't care. She put her wet clothes in the dryer so she could change back into them later before heading home.

I filled the kettle and turned it on while Dizzy got mugs down from the cupboard. Once the tea was made, we settled at the kitchen table with our drinks. Binx and Truffles brushed up against our legs but then returned to the couch, where we'd found them upon our arrival. The rain continued to pour down outside, and the cats showed no interest in heading out to their catio.

I felt bad for Sawyer. He was probably still out in the rain, unless he'd taken shelter in Archie's cabin while waiting for Detective Ishimoto to arrive. Either way, if the police did decide to search Archie's entire property again, Sawyer probably had a very wet couple of hours ahead of him. I considered taking some hot coffee over to him later, but I didn't think he'd be too impressed by me showing up at Archie's place twice in one day. Plus, if his colleagues were with him at the time, they might wonder how I'd known where to find him. I didn't know for sure, but he might not want to explain that Dizzy and I had been with him earlier. It was probably best to leave things be in that respect.

"So," Dizzy said, once we'd both taken time to get some tea into us, "regardless of what the mystery person was after, we know Archie stole more than Pops's scooter."

"It's pretty hard to think otherwise after what we found," I agreed. "Have there been a lot of thefts in town in recent years? I remember occasional break-ins, especially with the summer homes when they were unoccupied, but crime was never a major issue here before I moved to LA."

Dizzy took a sip of chai tea. "It's been a problem on and off. Every so often there'll be a rash of thefts or break-ins, then things go quiet for months at a time. Same thing up at Snowflake Canyon. Sometimes the police catch the culprits, but not always."

"I think it's safe to assume that Archie was responsible for at least some of the unsolved thefts."

Dizzy set down her mug of tea with a thud. "We still have no way of knowing what the mystery person was after."

"Or who they were." I stared into my empty mug, wishing we had more to work with.

Dizzy sat back in her chair after finishing her tea. Her cheeks had turned pink. "That was good tea, but now I'm hot."

"Me too."

Although the temperature had dropped when the rain started, it was still fairly warm out. The inside of my cottage felt muggy and oppressive now. I opened the windows, and Binx and Truffles immediately got up from the couch and hopped onto the sill of the largest window. They looked out through the screen at the rain while Dizzy and I collected our mugs and put them in the dishwasher.

The cats remained on the windowsill, and Dizzy and I got comfy on the couch. We spent the next half hour or so brainstorming how we could narrow down our list of suspects. Our ideas were limited, unfortunately. We decided we needed to keep a lookout for anyone with a torn black raincoat. Although we didn't know if the person who'd run away from us at Archie's cabin was definitely the murderer, their shifty behavior made that a good possibility.

The rest of our meager plan involved taking a closer look at Tammy Doyle and Oliver Nieminen. We thought maybe we could chat with members of the hiking club in an effort to find out more about Oliver's problems with Archie, and whether any of the hikers had reason to suspect Oliver of being the murderer. We wanted to do that in a subtle way. Hopefully that was possible.

Eventually, the rain stopped, and Dizzy decided to head home in case the break in the weather was only temporary. After she'd changed back into her own clothes and had set off for home, I curled up in an armchair with a notebook and pen. I wrote down the names of all our suspects, hoping that seeing them in print would somehow spark new ideas. It didn't, so I gave up on sleuthing for the day, and lost myself in a good book.

WHILE MAKING CHOCOLATES THE NEXT MORNING, I tried to figure out what kind of questions I could ask the hiking club members to subtly gather more information about Oliver. As I thought things over, I realized that the questions I would ask weren't the only things I needed to figure out. First, I had to locate members of the hiking club. I thought back to the snippet of the meeting I'd witnessed in the library the day that Archie had intruded. I couldn't remember recognizing anyone aside from Oliver and Estelle. That didn't really matter. I could start with Estelle and go from there. There was probably a way to get her to reveal the names of other club members without me saying exactly why I wanted to track them down.

After I'd finished working for the day, I decided to go for a jog before turning my mind back to Archie's murder. The rain had stopped the day before, but the weather was cloudy and cooler than it had been lately. I planned to do a loop around the town, and maybe stop in at Lolly and Pops's place on my way home. I ran along the canal paths, following a route that took me around the north side of the Larch Haven Hotel and then on to Cherry Park. When I reached the oak tree where we'd stopped during the vigil for Lexi, I slowed my pace. Her photo, the flowers, and the toys were all still there, the flowers now well past their prime.

I was about to continue on when I stopped short. I moved in for a closer look at Lexi's photo. Tugging my phone out of my armband, I pulled up the photos I'd taken at Archie's cabin the day before. When I found the one I was looking for, I zoomed in.

I didn't think there was much room for doubt.

One of the pendants mixed in with the other jewelry Archie had stashed in his hidey-hole was a perfect match for the one Lexi was wearing in the photo.

The one she'd been wearing the day she disappeared.

Chapter Twenty-Seven

I TEXTED SAWYER RIGHT AWAY, TELLING HIM I NEEDED to talk to him about the murder case as soon as possible. He wouldn't be impressed when he saw the text, considering that he wanted me to stay out of the investigation, but once he heard what I had to say, he'd probably forgive me. Maybe the police had already made the connection between the pendant in Archie's stash and the one Lexi Derendorf wore, but there was a good chance they hadn't, and they needed to know about it. It could possibly change the course of the investigation. It was certainly making me look at things from a new angle.

Sawyer didn't respond to my message right away, which didn't surprise me. He was likely on duty and might not see my text for a while. I considered heading straight for the police station to share my discovery, but in the end, I decided to give Sawyer a bit more time to respond. That way I could finish my run, which would give me a chance to think.

Before leaving Cherry Park, I snapped a photo of Lexi's

picture, making sure the necklace was in focus. As I jogged along the tree-lined avenue leading out of the park, I tried to calm my spinning thoughts so I could make sense of them. If Archie was in possession of the necklace Lexi was wearing when she disappeared, that suggested that he'd had something to do with her disappearance.

A cold, sickly sensation trickled through me, despite the fact that I was sweating from jogging on a warm summer day. After an entire decade with no sign of Lexi, she was most likely dead. It was also highly likely that she died very soon after storming out of her family home on the night she was last seen. Last seen by everyone except Archie or whoever had harmed her, anyway. If Archie had stolen Lexi's necklace when he killed her, perhaps as a sick memento, that would explain why he had it hidden away in his cabin.

My steps faltered. What if all that jewelry hadn't been stolen in break-ins? What if at least some of it consisted of mementos taken from other murder victims?

My stomach churned, but then I had second thoughts about that theory.

I started jogging again, thinking things through. If Archie had been some kind of serial killer, surely we would have been aware of more people getting murdered or disappearing. I didn't know how many unsolved missing persons cases there were in Larch Haven and the surrounding area. Lexi's disappearance was the highest profile one in my lifetime. I couldn't think of any unsolved murder cases other than the present one. Of course, I'd been away for years, and Archie could have traveled farther afield, although I didn't know if that would fit with the typical behavior of a serial killer. Didn't they usually stick close to where they lived? I'd have to ask Sawyer about that.

I shoved aside all thoughts of other potential murder victims for the time being and focused on Lexi. The Derendorfs lived right next door to Archie. Their houses weren't visible from each other because of all the trees, but both properties stretched down to the open shoreline of the lake. It was likely that Archie had seen Lexi around, at least now and then. Had he become fixated on her and waited for an opportunity to murder her, or had it been a spur-of-the-moment crime when the opportunity presented itself? I didn't know, and for the moment it didn't really matter.

What I wanted to figure out was whether Archie's murder really was related to Lexi. If Karl or Susan Derendorf had somehow found out that Archie had killed Lexi, maybe they'd decided to take matters into their own hands instead of going to the police, especially if they only had suspicions, and not any solid proof.

My heart sank. Lexi's parents had been through so much. I hated the thought of being responsible for bringing information to light that could make them suspects in a murder investigation. My feelings didn't matter when it came down to it, though. I had to share what I knew with the police.

I hadn't seriously considered Karl and Susan as suspects in Archie's murder, especially since the dispute over the shed had fizzled out before Archie's death, but now I had to put their names on the list, and bump them right up to the top. Susan Derendorf wasn't a tall woman, but if angry enough, I thought she could have wielded a tree branch with enough force to deliver the fatal blow to Archie's head. I didn't know if Karl was any taller than Archie, but he was a good deal younger, with a stronger build. It wouldn't have been a problem for him to hit Archie in the head with a branch and dump his body in the lake.

I didn't want either of Lexi's parents to be guilty of murder, but they had a strong motive, if they knew what I knew. I wasn't sure how they would have come to realize that Archie had killed their daughter—if he really was responsible for her disappearance—but maybe one or both of them had been in Archie's cabin for some reason and had found his secret stash. That was possible, especially if they'd suspected him of stealing something of theirs. I wondered if Sawyer knew if any of the items had been traced back to the Derendorfs. The police hadn't had much time for that yet, but I'd ask Sawyer anyway. Whether he'd share such information with me would remain to be seen.

When I reached my cottage, I still hadn't heard back from Sawyer. I took a quick shower and dressed in my favorite denim shorts and a lightweight V-neck T-shirt. I decided to head over to the police station. If Sawyer wasn't available, I could share my discovery with another officer. I'd rather talk to Sawyer, but I didn't think I should be too choosy under the circumstances.

I hopped into my whisper boat and navigated the canals to a dock not far from the police station. The station had its own private dock behind the building, where it had a couple of official police boats moored, but the public wasn't allowed to use that one. I tied up my boat at the small public dock and walked along the cobblestones to the front of the station, which was housed in a two-story brick building with white trim. It didn't exactly blend in with the rest of Larch Haven's architecture, but that wasn't a big deal since it was near the edge of town. Besides, it made the station easy to find since it stood out from all the buildings around it.

Broad concrete steps led to the double doors. When I stepped inside, the air-conditioning sent a chill over my skin. One of the first things I saw was a poster about Lexi's vigil pinned on a large noticeboard. It featured the same photo as the one at the memorial in the park.

I approached the front desk, where a female civilian member of the department was talking on the phone. She signaled to me that she'd be another minute, so I wandered back over to the poster. As I'd done at the park, I took out my phone and compared the Viking rune pendant from the photo of Archie's stash with the one around Lexi's neck. I was still just as certain that they were one and the same.

The woman behind the desk hung up the phone, so I turned away from the poster and asked if Sawyer was available. I waited while she checked, and I was relieved to see he was with her when she returned. I'd feel much more at ease talking to him than the detective in charge of the case.

"Did you see my text message?" I asked once he'd joined me in the lobby.

"Sorry, no." He produced his phone, checking it.

"Do you have a few minutes to talk? There's something you need to know."

He finished reading the text message and leveled a suspicious gaze at me. I thought he was about to lecture me again, but instead he simply tucked his phone away and said, "What is it?"

I took his arm and tugged him over to the noticeboard. I tapped a finger against the poster. "See this pendant Lexi is wearing in the photo?" When he gave a slight nod of acknowledgment, I continued. "My understanding is that she was wearing it the day she went missing."

"Right . . ." He didn't know where I was going with this.

To me that indicated that the police hadn't yet made the connection I had.

I woke up my phone and showed him the screen. "I took this photo at Archie's cabin."

Sawyer looked at the photo and then up at me, unimpressed.

"I know," I said quickly before he could get a word in. "You don't like that I was there and I probably shouldn't have taken the photo. But stick with me."

Sawyer let out an exasperated breath, but gave another nod.

I zoomed in on the photo. "Check it out. That's Lexi's pendant. Right there in Archie's stash."

He took the phone from me. His eyes seemed to darken as they focused on the enlarged photo. His gaze bounced from the phone to the poster, then back to the phone, and up at me. "Let's go."

He took off with long strides, down a hallway that led off from the lobby, still with my phone in hand.

I scurried to keep up with him. "Where are we going?"

He pushed open a door and held it for me. I stepped into a stairwell with concrete steps and a metal railing painted blue. Sawyer led the way down toward the basement. The fluorescent lights flickered overhead, and it crossed my mind that the stairwell would make a good location for a scene from a horror movie. That thought was still with me when we left the stairwell for a corridor with cement floors and cinder block walls painted off-white. Here and there were speckled stains on the concrete floor. I didn't want to know what had caused them.

We rounded a corner and came to an alcove with a desk in the middle and a door behind it. I hung back as Sawyer talked to the man seated behind the desk, requesting evidence that had been logged the day before. I gathered the door behind the desk led to the evidence lockup.

Within a couple of minutes, Sawyer had a plastic evidence bag in hand, with the Viking pendant inside. In Lexi's photo, the pendant had been tied around her neck with a leather cord. The fact that the cord was now missing did nothing to dissuade me from my theory that the pendant in the bag was Lexi's. I moved up closer to Sawyer, until our arms touched, getting a good look at the pendant through the plastic.

Sawyer held the bag next to my phone.

My breath hitched. I pointed to the grainy, blown-up photo I'd taken of the vigil poster. "Look at that little scratch." I tapped the pendant through the plastic. "It's got the same one."

Even though I'd already been sure that the pendant taken from Archie's cabin was Lexi's, seeing the proof right there in front of me still shook me.

I wasn't sure I'd ever seen Sawyer look so serious.

He handed my phone back to me. "I need to show this to Detective Ishimoto."

He thanked the guy behind the desk and then headed back along the hall toward the stairwell. Again, I had to scurry to keep up with him.

"This means Archie could have killed Lexi, right?" I said as we entered the stairwell. "Do you think some of those other items in the hidey-hole could be mementos of other victims?"

Sawyer cast a glance my way before starting up the stairs. "You think he was a serial killer?"

"Isn't it possible? Have there been many unsolved disappearances in the area over the years? Or could he have gone farther afield sometimes? Would a serial killer do that?"

Sawyer paused by the door on the landing. "Most serial killers operate within a defined geographic area, one that's familiar to them. They often kill close to home, but there are exceptions."

"So Archie could have been a serial killer?"

He didn't appear convinced of that. "Most likely not, but it's something we'll consider."

He was about to open the door to the hallway, so I touched a hand to his arm to stop him.

"Do you think Karl or Susan Derendorf could have somehow figured out that Archie killed Lexi?" I asked.

"And killed Archie in revenge? That's one possibility."

"Have you traced any of the stolen property we found back to the owners?" I wondered again if the Derendorfs had been among Archie's theft victims. If so, and they suspected him of stealing their belongings just as Pops had, maybe one of them had gone searching for their missing items and found the pendant. Although, I wasn't sure they would have left the pendant in the hidey-hole and kept quiet. Wouldn't they have gone to the police? Sure, they might have worried about getting in trouble for breaking into Archie's cabin, but I had a feeling that would be far less of a concern to them than getting to the truth about what happened to Lexi.

"We haven't had a chance to do that yet," Sawyer said in response to my question.

"So will someone be questioning the Derendorfs?" I asked. "Are they strong suspects now?"

He held up the evidence bag. "I should get this to Detective Ishimoto."

It didn't surprise me that he'd dodged my questions, but it did disappoint me. I really wanted to fit all the puzzle pieces together and figure everything out. The sooner the case was solved, the sooner Pops would be free of suspicion. Even if Pops weren't involved, I'd still want to know who had killed Archie and why. With the killer behind bars, the whole town would feel safer again. Plus, unsolved mysteries had a tendency to drive me nuts. I wasn't good with unanswered questions.

"Does this make things better for Pops?" I asked as Sawyer held the door open for me.

He followed me out into the corridor. "Things already were a bit better for him."

"Really?" I asked, hopeful.

"That lawyer he's got is a good one."

My shoulders sagged. "That's the only reason things are better for him?"

Sawyer stopped halfway down the hall. He glanced up ahead and then back behind us. We were alone.

He lowered his voice. "Archie was about the same height as your grandfather, but he was twenty years younger, and probably weighed a fair bit more. Maybe your grandfather could have hit him in the head. Physically speaking," he added when I was about to protest. I relaxed, and he continued. "But whoever killed Archie dragged his body down to the lake afterward. It's possible that your grandfather could have done that, but it would have been difficult for him. It would have been easier for some of our other suspects."

Happiness and relief welled up inside of me. I wanted to throw my arms around Sawyer and hug him, but I refrained, not wanting to chance embarrassing him while he was at work.

A uniformed officer came down the hall and nodded at Sawyer as he passed us.

"So Pops is in the clear?" I asked quietly once we were alone again.

"I didn't say that," Sawyer cautioned.

"But surely this new information points in a completely different direction."

"It's definitely going to open new avenues of investigation," Sawyer said. "That's all I can say at the moment."

We started walking along the hall again. After a few steps, I stopped short as a thought struck me.

"Oh . . ." I quickly turned things over in my mind.

"What is it?" Sawyer asked.

I raised my eyes to meet his. "What if Archie didn't kill Lexi, but he stole her pendant from the person who did kill her. And maybe the killer found out and killed Archie because he or she was worried that Archie would figure out the connection, or because Archie had made it clear that he'd already made the connection."

Sawyer touched a hand to my shoulder. "Okay, Becca. No more theorizing."

"But it's another possibility, right?"

"Sure, but I'll take it from here, okay?" His gaze softened when he saw my disappointment. "I'll run everything you said by Detective Ishimoto, and we're going to look into it. I promise. But we're dealing with a killer here, and I want you safe."

It was hard to argue with that, so I nodded. "I'll leave it to you."

"Thank you. And we need to keep quiet about the pendant for now. We might hold back the information for a while, and I don't want the Derendorfs hearing about it through anything but official channels."

"Of course," I said as a wave of sadness washed over me. The news would likely stir up more questions and heartache for Lexi's parents, if it would indeed be news to them.

Sawyer walked me to the lobby and opened the front door for me. "I appreciate you coming to me with this information, Becca."

"I hope it helps to catch the killer," I said.

I descended the front steps. When I reached the bottom, I turned back and waved at Sawyer, who was watching me through the glass door. Then I set off for home.

Chapter Twenty-Eight

DIZZY CAME OVER THAT EVENING, AND WE TALKED for ages about the pendant and its possible meanings. I couldn't keep a secret from Dizzy, and I knew the information wouldn't go any further, so I didn't worry about sharing it with her.

"I don't know for sure if the police are going to keep the discovery of Lexi's pendant a secret from the general public," I said, "but if they do, maybe they think the killer knew Archie had it but couldn't find it when they killed him."

Dizzy caught on quickly. "So the person who ran from Archie's cabin really could have been the killer. And whoever it was might go back and search for the pendant again."

"So if the police are watching Archie's place, they might catch the killer," I added.

Dizzy flopped back on the couch. "In which case, the investigation could be wrapped up before long and Pops will be completely free and clear."

"I sure hope so."

Of course, if the pendant had nothing to do with Archie's death, then our hopes were groundless, but I decided to stay optimistic.

That optimism buoyed my spirits, all the way through the next morning as I made bonbons and truffles and chocolate gondolas. Even though the races had ended several days earlier, the gondolas remained popular, and I had to make more every day just to keep up with the demand.

Angie was looking after the shop on her own that day, so when it got busy around midmorning, I took a break from my work to help her out. Eventually, the rush died down, leaving only a couple of customers left in the shop. Angie was helping them out, chatting with them over by the display shelves, so I considered returning to the kitchen. Before I made a decision, the bell over the door jingled, announcing the arrival of another customer.

"Good morning, Mrs. Lawrence," I said, recognizing the senior citizen as a local. "How are you doing today?"

"Not too bad, thank you," she replied. "I wanted to come by and pick up a dozen of your delicious salted caramels for my friend's birthday, and a box of mint melties for me and my husband."

"Of course. Would you like the caramels gift wrapped?" I asked.

She did, so I quickly took care of that and fetched a box of mint melties. As I rang up the purchase, Mrs. Lawrence moved closer to the counter. She cast a glance across the shop at Angie and the other customers and lowered her voice.

"Dear, I wanted to let you know that your former boyfriend made a big mistake. Well, several mistakes, really. That woman has nothing on you. Sure, she might be a stunner, but you're gorgeous too and you've got a lovely personality to boot."

Her words took me aback, so a second or two ticked by before I responded. "Thank you," I said when I found my voice. "But what woman are we talking about?"

"Oh, what's her name?" She closed her eyes in concentration. "The actress from that daytime drama. Tessa something-house?"

"Tess Oosterhouse?"

She brightened and opened her eyes. "That's it."

"I'm a little confused." That was an understatement. "What does she have to do with Justin?" Tess was one of the stars of *Passion City*, the soap opera I'd appeared on for a few episodes. As far as I knew, Justin had never met her.

Mrs. Lawrence leaned closer and lowered her voice further. "You know, the *baby*."

"What baby?" I asked, even more baffled now.

Mrs. Lawrence didn't seem to hear me. The other customers had come over to the display case with Angie, and her attention flicked their way.

She grabbed her credit card and tapped it to pay for the chocolates. "We'll say no more about it. Thank you so much, dear."

I remembered to slide her receipt into the bag just before she grabbed it off the counter and sailed out of the shop.

I stared after her, dumbfounded. "A baby? What baby?"

"Sorry?" Angie said.

I realized I'd spoken out loud without meaning to.

"Nothing," I said quickly, not wanting to share the strange conversation with the other customers.

Instead, I retreated to the kitchen, where I sent a text to Dizzy.

People have been saying the strangest things to me about my breakup with Justin, I wrote.

I knew Dizzy would be busy with work, so I didn't expect a response right away. I got busy myself, and managed to sooth my confused brain by making more chocolates.

An hour or so later, my phone rang with the ringtone I'd assigned to Dizzy. I quickly washed smears of chocolate from my hands and grabbed the device.

"What kind of strange things have people been saying?" Dizzy asked after we'd exchanged brief greetings.

I filled her in on my baffling conversation with Mrs. Lawrence.

"Okay, that really is strange," Dizzy said.

"And a few days ago, another woman told me I should consider dyeing my hair, and she suggested that Justin and I might still be together if I were blond."

"Oh, right. Sawyer mentioned that one."

"He did?" I said with surprise. "When?"

"This morning. I ran into him at Gathering Grounds and he brought it up. He was pretty ticked off that someone had said that to you, and he wanted to make sure you weren't upset about it. I told him you probably weren't, since you hadn't even mentioned it to me."

"There's been so much going on lately that I forgot all about it until my conversation with Mrs. Lawrence."

"Well, this is one mystery you can leave to me. I'll figure out what's going on."

"Thanks, Dizzy."

We ended the call and I got back to work.

Lolly showed up later, as I was cleaning the kitchen.

"How's your day been?" I asked as I washed down the countertops.

"Busy but good," Lolly replied. "I just finished my volunteer shift at the thrift shop. We had a steady stream of customers."

"That's definitely good."

The local thrift shop was a community venture. It was run by volunteers and the profits were donated to local charities.

"How's everything with the chocolates?" Lolly asked, surveying the tray of bonbons and truffles I had ready for refilling the display case in the morning.

"I'm keeping up with demand, but I'm glad you're here. I have a couple of potential new flavors I'd like you to try."

"Your grandfather will be sorry he didn't come with me," Lolly said with a smile.

"There's no need for him to be disappointed. I'll send some of the new flavors home with you."

Lolly happily sampled the test batches. She loved the apple cider caramels as they were, but agreed that the pumpkin cheesecake truffles could use an extra punch of flavor. Otherwise, she wholeheartedly agreed that adding them to our product line for the fall would be a good idea.

"I'll make another test batch of the pumpkin ones tomorrow," I said. "Hopefully, I can get them right."

"You will, sweetheart." Lolly gave me a hug. "You're a truly talented chocolatier."

I hugged her back. "Thank you, Lolly. That means so much coming from you."

I tucked most of the remaining test chocolates into a small paper bag for Lolly to take to Pops.

"I missed a lot of local news while I was living in LA," I said as I packed the chocolates. "Dizzy mentioned that there's been break-ins and other thefts on and off over the years."

"That's true."

"We know Archie stole Pops's scooter, but I'm wondering how many other thefts he might have been responsible for in recent times."

"It wouldn't surprise me if he was behind a whole lot of them," Lolly said. "A couple of young men were arrested a few years back, but many of the crimes are still unsolved."

"Do you know who any of the victims have been in the unsolved cases?"

Lolly thought for a moment. "Sometimes it's the summer homes that are hit, when they're unoccupied. It's usually things like television sets that get taken, and other electronics that people leave behind. Sometimes year-round homes get hit too, though, usually more on the outskirts of town. It seems like more items are taken in those cases, probably simply because there's more to take. People don't tend to leave jewelry and such behind at their summer homes when they leave at the end of the season."

"And a lot of jewelry has gone missing?" I wanted to tell Lolly about what I'd seen at Archie's place, but aside from Sawyer wanting to keep things quiet, I wasn't sure that she'd be too impressed to know that Dizzy and I had gone poking around in search of clues.

"Jewelry and small electronics have been some of the items stolen the most, I believe."

"All things that are probably easy to fence," I said.

"But you asked about the victims. Sheryl and John Wagner had their house broken into last fall. Same with Delilah Robinson and Ellen McKellar up at Snowflake Canyon. I believe Oliver Nieminen's cottage got hit late last year. That was probably shortly before you came home."

"Really?" I mentally placed an asterisk next to Oliver's name on my suspect list. If he'd gone searching for his stolen property at Archie's cabin, maybe that could have led to a deadly confrontation.

Lolly continued, cutting off my thoughts. "Rachel Stephanopoulos had her home broken into, but I think that was a couple of years ago now. Oh, and a few months ago, during the latest rash of break-ins, one of the houses hit belonged to that nice young woman who owns the soap shop."

"Maria Vasquez?"

"That's her," Lolly said with a nod. "She was a few years behind you in school, wasn't she?"

"Yes," I replied as I added another asterisk to the suspect list in my head, this time next to Maria's name.

"Anyway, hopefully the truth about Archie and his death will come out before long."

"Hopefully," I echoed. "Pops needs to have his name cleared."

Lolly patted my arm. "I have faith that will happen.

Now, I'd better run." She picked up the bag of chocolates. "I'll take these to your grandfather."

"Thank you," I called as she left the kitchen.

Once alone, I stood in the middle of the room, thinking.

Maybe it was time to see if I could poke holes in Oliver's alibi.

As for Maria, I needed to find out if she even had one.

I didn't feel like I was getting any closer to identifying Archie's real killer, but I couldn't give up. Not until I knew my grandfather was completely clear of suspicion.

Chapter Twenty-Nine

LATER IN THE AFTERNOON, WHEN I WAS AT HOME playing with my cats, Dizzy texted to ask me to meet her for dinner. She'd done some sleuthing and had information to share with me. I was ready to burst from curiosity, but since she was still at work, she only had time to arrange to meet me at the local pub. I'd have to wait to find out what she wanted to tell me.

In the early evening, I headed to the pub on foot. The Oar and Anchor was located toward the eastern end of Giethoorn Avenue. The timber-frame building was white with brown timbers that were so dark they were nearly black. The proprietors, Mr. and Mrs. Appleton, lived in the two-story apartment over the pub. Their son, Jonathon, had been a year ahead of Dizzy, Sawyer, and me in school. He'd left Larch Haven for college and now lived in Houston, where he worked for NASA. He was often referred to as Larch Haven's own rocket scientist.

When I arrived at the pub, the sun was only just beginning to sink in the sky, but the lighting was dim inside the establishment, as it always seemed to be. The two front windows let in the waning daylight, but it didn't reach the back of the pub. The dark wood of the floors, the bar, and the beams overhead probably added to the dimness, but they also gave the place plenty of character. The padded seats of the booths that lined the walls were dark red, and dozens of framed photos lined the walls. Most captured moments from local events over the years. A few featured minor celebrities who had visited Larch Haven and the pub.

I wasn't surprised to find that the place was quite busy. Business tended to be brisk at all eateries during the tourist season, and the Oar and Anchor was popular with locals as well as visitors. I scanned the large room for any sign of Dizzy but didn't spot her, so I claimed one of the two remaining free booths and texted her to let her know I'd arrived. She sent an immediate response, letting me know that she was only a minute or two away.

Noise behind me caught my attention. I leaned slightly out of the booth and turned to look. It appeared as though there was a party going on in the back room. Colorful helium balloons hovered by the ceiling. A young couple carrying wrapped presents entered the pub and headed straight for the back room. As I watched, Carmen greeted them with hugs and a huge smile.

"I can't believe my sister managed to keep this a secret from me!" she exclaimed before pulling the new arrivals farther into the room and out of my line of sight.

I faced forward in my seat again, in time to see Dizzy coming into the pub. I waved to get her attention. She spotted me and hurried over, sliding into the seat across from me. We barely had a chance to say hello to each other when Nikki, one of the waitresses, appeared by our booth.

Dizzy and I were both familiar with the menu, so we ordered right away, Dizzy requesting a mushroom burger while I asked for the fish tacos. I also ordered one of the mocktails from the drinks menu, but Dizzy asked for a Bellini.

"No mocktail for me, not after the day I had," Dizzy said as Nikki swept off to get our drinks.

"Uh-oh," I said. "What was today's library drama?"

"No drama. Not really. But the place was hopping. We had a parent-tot reading group in the morning, a teen book club in the afternoon, and a constant stream of patrons." She went on to tell me about a few of those patrons who had taken up a good deal of her time with questions, complaints, and requests for assistance with research.

"Then I shouldn't have bothered you with my strange conversations," I said with a pang of guilt.

"No way! I'm glad you told me. I don't want to be left out of the loop. Besides, it wasn't hard to track down the source of the strangeness."

Nikki returned with our drinks, so we paused our conversation. After the waitress had left and Dizzy had taken a long, appreciative sip of her Bellini, she picked up where we'd left off.

"It turns out you've fallen victim to the Gossip Grannies," she said.

I groaned, knowing what that meant. "Delphi and Luella. That can't be good."

"It never is."

"So they're telling everyone that Justin dumped me because he prefers blondes?" I guessed.

"Um. Not exactly." Dizzy took another drink.

"It's worse than that?"

"Are you sure you don't want any alcohol?" She nudged the drinks menu toward me.

"Just tell me, Diz," I requested. "Let's get it over with."

She didn't have a chance to do that right away. Nikki returned, bringing our meals. My mouth watered, despite my apprehension over what Dizzy had yet to tell me.

"All right," she said once Nikki had left. "So, according to Delphi and Luella, Justin dumped you—"

"He didn't dump me," I protested. "It was a mutual decision to break up."

"You and I know that, but do you really expect the Gossip Grannies to stick with the truth?"

"Sorry. Continue." I picked up one of my fish tacos.

"Their story is that Justin dumped you because he decided he wanted to be a one-woman man."

I almost choked on my taco. I quickly took a drink of my fruity mocktail. "Excuse me? They think Justin was cheating on me and had an attack of conscience so he decided to go with the other woman?"

"According to them, *you* were the other woman."

"That's ridiculous!" I sputtered. "Justin and I might not have been meant for each other in the end, but he's a good guy and never would have cheated on me or anyone else."

"Again, you and I might know that, but Delphi and Luella are telling a different story."

I sighed, but another bite of my delicious taco tamped down my growing annoyance.

"Unfortunately, that's not all," Dizzy said after she'd taken a moment to eat some of her burger.

"Seriously?" I wasn't sure how much more I could handle.

"Apparently, Justin has a child with this other woman. And you'll never guess who the other woman is."

"Considering that she doesn't exist, you're probably right about that." My conversation with Mrs. Lawrence came crashing back to the forefront of my mind. Puzzle pieces clicked together in my head. "Wait. I can guess, after all. Tess Oosterhouse from *Passion City*. That's the baby Mrs. Lawrence was talking about."

"You got it," Dizzy said.

"That's completely nuts. Justin and Tess don't even know each other, let alone have a kid together. How do the Gossip Grannies even come up with this stuff?"

"They've got vivid imaginations. You've got to give them that," Dizzy said. "I don't think they know the difference between fact or fiction, though."

"With a storyline like that, they should write for *Passion City.*"

"Right?" Dizzy said. "Although, I suspect some of their stories would be too far-fetched even for the soap opera."

"And that's saying something." I sighed again. "Is that seriously what people believe about me?"

"I doubt it. I don't even know if Delphi and Luella believe the stories they spin, or if they churn out lies knowingly, just for the fun of it."

"Even if they don't believe the rumors they spread, some people obviously do. Otherwise, I wouldn't have been getting the comments I received lately."

"The Gossip Grannies have a few followers who latch onto everything they say, but for the most part, the people of Larch Haven know full well that Delphi and Luella make things up."

"I hope that's true." After I took another bite of my taco, an unpleasant thought struck me. "Please tell me the Gossip Grannies don't use the Internet. The last thing I need is for the story to get out online. It's one thing to have it contained to the town, but if it spreads over social media, and Tess's and Justin's names get dragged into it, the tabloids would have a field day."

"It doesn't matter what the tabloids say."

"Maybe not, but they can create a firestorm and I'd really rather not have to deal with that." I'd seen such things take a toll on other actors.

"I don't think you need to worry about that," Dizzy said, to my relief. "Delphi and Luella have smartphones, and they might be on social media, but I don't think they have much of a reach outside their own circle. If they did, their other wild rumors would have gained more traction in the past."

“What about their faithful followers?” I asked with trepidation. “Could they have a greater reach?”

Dizzy’s expression turned skeptical. “I’m not so sure. Their followers are mostly elderly women, and I know for a fact that at least a couple of them don’t know how to use a computer, let alone use the Internet. I’ve had to help some of them with the most basic computer tasks at the library. Mrs. Lawrence barely knows how to use a mouse.”

“I guess that’s comforting,” I said with relief. “Thanks for solving that mystery.”

“You bet, but try to forget about the ridiculous rumors. They’ll die down in time and everyone will forget about them.”

“Hopefully you’re right.”

I decided not to worry about the Gossip Grannies anymore that evening. Dizzy and I polished off our food while chatting about more pleasant subjects. After Nikki cleared away our dinner plates, we shared a decadent slice of Mississippi mudslide cake. We were halfway through the dessert when Nikki came out of the kitchen carrying a birthday cake, candles alight. She carried it into the back room, where a rousing cheer went up. Then the partygoers burst into an enthusiastic rendition of “Happy Birthday.”

“Carmen’s surprise party?” Dizzy asked once the singing finished.

I nodded as I enjoyed another forkful of cake. Thinking about Carmen’s party sent my thoughts traveling in Maria’s direction. As I was about to sink my fork into the cake once again, I paused.

“Hey,” I said, speaking barely above a whisper. “We considered that the Derendorfs might have killed Archie because they thought he was responsible for Lexi’s disappearance.”

“Right,” Dizzy agreed.

“But maybe that could be true of Maria. I was talking to Lolly earlier, and she mentioned that Maria had her cottage broken into a while back.”

Dizzy caught on. "And if she suspected Archie was responsible, she could have gone looking for whatever was stolen."

"And stumbled upon the you-know-what," I added.

"And she would have recognized it right away, being Lexi's best friend."

"Exactly," I said.

"Hmm." Dizzy thought for a moment before speaking again. "Could it have been Maria that we saw running from Archie's cabin? You got a better look than I did."

"Yes, but it could have been almost anyone."

"Sawyer thought the person was shorter than him," Dizzy said. "Karl and Susan Derendorf both fit the bill. Maria too."

"The only clue is the torn raincoat."

"And until the weather changes again, we aren't going to be seeing anyone out and about in a raincoat."

She was right about that. The weather was back to being sunny and hot.

We didn't come up with any further conclusions before leaving the pub. By the time I stepped outside, the sun had set and darkness had fallen over Larch Haven. The temperature was still warm, but pleasantly so. Dizzy and I parted ways, both of us heading for our respective homes on foot. Other pedestrians strolled along Giethoorn Avenue, but once I crossed a bridge and set off along one of the narrower pathways, I was alone.

At least, I thought I was at first.

After a minute or two of walking, I heard footsteps behind me. I glanced back and could have sworn that I saw a person amid the shadows.

That didn't mean I had anything to worry about.

Nevertheless, unease thrummed along my skin. I picked up my pace.

Somewhere behind me, the footsteps moved faster too. I glanced back again as I crossed another bridge. Whoever was behind me wore a dark hoodie with the hood pulled up. Not exactly suitable for the current weather.

My heart rate kicked up and fear spread through my limbs.

I walked even faster and tried digging my phone out of my pocket.

The footsteps behind me got faster too.

I yanked my phone free of my pocket and broke into a run.

Chapter Thirty

I SLAMMED THE FRONT DOOR OF MY COTTAGE AND turned the lock. I leaned against the door, gasping for air, my thumb hovering over the glowing screen of my phone.

Binx gave a meow of welcome, and he and Truffles weaved around my ankles.

"Hey, guys," I said in a breathless voice. "Do you think I overreacted?"

My cats offered no opinion, not that they knew what had happened.

I disentangled myself from them and hurried to the front window, leaving the lights turned off. I peered out into the night, searching for any movement, any shadows that seemed out of place. I saw nothing of the sort.

I closed the curtains and performed the same check at every window on both floors. Each time I looked outside, the coast appeared to be clear.

My heart settled back down to its normal rate, but tension still hummed through my muscles and I kept a firm grip on my phone. The device chimed, making me jump. Dizzy had texted to let me know she'd arrived home safely. It was our practice to do that when walking home alone at night.

I'm home too, I wrote in a text message. I thought I was being followed but I got inside safely.

What?! Dizzy wrote back right away. Call the police!

What if it was nothing and I'm overreacting? I typed out.

I think you should trust your instincts, but at least call Sawyer. Please?

Okay.

I felt silly calling Sawyer, now that I was doubting myself. At the same time, I couldn't shake my residual fear. I hadn't imagined the footsteps keeping pace with me, or the hooded figure. Maybe someone was playing a prank on me, trying to scare me for fun, but with a killer still on the loose, it was best to err on the side of caution.

Sawyer picked up after two rings, and I gave him a brief rundown of what had happened on my walk home.

"Stay inside," he said. "Keep the doors and windows locked. I'll be there soon."

I was about to voice my concern that I might have overreacted, but he'd already hung up. Now that I had all the curtains closed, I turned on several lights, not wanting any shadows around me. I sat down on the couch to wait. Binx and Truffles both jumped up to my lap, purring. I stroked their fur for a moment but then had to get back to my feet. I had too much nervous energy bouncing around inside of me to remain still.

I paced up and down the hallway, and then hurried to the front window when I heard a noise outside. I spotted a shadowy figure climbing out of a boat by my dock, a beam of light bobbing with the figure's movement. I flicked on the exterior light. A rush of relief left my legs weak when I saw Sawyer striding across the lawn, a powerful flashlight in hand. I scooped up Binx, who'd followed me to the foyer, and opened the door.

Sawyer paused by the front step but didn't come in. "Shut and lock the door again. I'll take a look around."

I did as he'd told me. Then I resumed pacing, this time with Binx in my arms. Truffles glanced up from her spot on the couch, but then returned her attention to grooming herself.

A loud knock on the front door nearly sent my heart leaping into my throat.

I relaxed when I heard Sawyer's muffled voice.

"Becca, it's me."

I hurried back to the door and let him in. He locked it as soon as I had it closed again.

He rested his hands on my upper arms. "Are you okay?" he asked, searching my face.

I nodded, hugging Binx close to me. "I'm fine. Just a little scared."

"There's no sign of anyone hanging around out there."

A hint of embarrassment mixed in with my relief. "I'm sorry for calling. Someone was probably just playing a prank and I interrupted your evening for nothing."

He dropped his hands from my arms and I immediately missed the comfort of his touch.

"You definitely should have called," he said. "If not me, then 9-1-1."

"Even if I was overreacting?"

"Better to overreact than to come to harm," he said. "Besides, I think you've got good instincts, Becca, and you should trust them."

"That's what Dizzy said. She convinced me to call you."

"Good thing you listened to her."

"But there's no one out there."

"Not now. They probably took off as soon as you got inside."

A shudder ran through me. Binx squirmed in my arms, so I set him down. I wrapped my arms around myself, suddenly chilled, despite the warmth of the night.

"Are you sure you're okay?" Sawyer asked, his dark eyes concerned.

"Yes. It's just . . . do you think it could have been Archie's killer? What if Archie wasn't a targeted victim? What if there's a person out there who wants to kill at random?" The thought sent a wave of nausea crashing through my stomach.

Sawyer stepped closer and pulled me gently into his arms. I leaned into him, wrapping my arms around him and resting my head against his chest.

"I know it's a scary time," Sawyer said. "It wouldn't hurt for everyone to be on high alert until Archie's murderer is caught. If anything happens again to make you the slightest bit worried or uncomfortable, call 9-1-1, okay? I don't want anything bad happening to you. I'll take an overreaction over that any day."

I smiled at that, although my eyes watered with unshed tears, a product of my heightened emotions.

"Is there any chance that it could have been your mystery man following you?" Sawyer asked.

"It could have been. It could have been anyone." Just like the person in the raincoat who'd fled from Archie's property. "I think that guy is harmless, though."

"He's not if he was the one out there tonight."

I suppressed a shiver, or at least I tried to. I must not have been entirely successful, because Sawyer seemed to sense my unease and held me closer. It felt good to be in his arms. Maybe a little too good. That thought sent confusion rushing through me.

I released him and stepped back, doing my best to ignore my confusion and to rein in my emotions.

"Can I get you anything?" I asked. "Maybe a drink or a snack? Or do you need to get going?" I realized I was babbling and snapped my mouth shut.

"I'm good," he said, "but I can stay a while if you want company."

I definitely did want company, but I didn't want to impose on him any longer. I'd already disrupted his evening enough.

"I'll be okay," I said. "I should probably get some sleep."

"Then I'll be on my way." He rested a hand on the doorknob. "Lock up behind me, and remember what I said about calling 9-1-1."

"Thanks, Sawyer. Really. I appreciate you coming over here."

"I'd do it again in a heartbeat, Becca."

I saw through the sidelight that he waited on the front step until I turned the lock. I watched from the front window as he made his way to the dock, the beam of his flashlight cutting through the darkness. He climbed into his boat, and I let the curtain fall back into place.

"What was that?" I asked of my heart, which had glowed with warmth with Sawyer's last words, and while he held me.

I shook off the memory, and ignored my own question, not sure that I was ready to answer it.

After checking every window and door to make sure they were locked up tight, I texted Dizzy to let her know that Sawyer had come by and made sure I was safe. Then I got ready for bed, even though I wasn't sure if I'd be able to sleep.

Truffles and Binx curled up on the bed with me, dispelling some of my loneliness and fear. I tossed and turned for a while, which didn't impress my cats, but eventually my wired mind succumbed to exhaustion and I drifted off to sleep.

IN THE LIGHT OF DAY, IT WAS HARD TO BELIEVE THAT the events of the previous night had happened. In some ways, the whole thing seemed like a dream, until I stepped out my front door. Seeing the path that led north over the bridge, the path I'd followed home, stripped away the dream-like quality from my memories, leaving them clear and stark.

I sat down on the front step, cradling a cup of chai tea in my hands. Anger flickered in my chest. I didn't like the fact that someone had made me feel unsafe in my beloved hometown. I silently berated myself for not calling 9-1-1 as soon as I reached the safety of my cottage the night before. Maybe if I'd done so, the police would have caught the person who followed me. Even if that person hadn't actually committed a crime, getting caught by the police might have deterred them from trying anything similar in the future.

As I continued to think things over, I decided not to be quite so hard on myself. Unless a patrolling officer had been close by when I placed the call, whoever had followed me would have had plenty of time to get out of the area once I'd locked myself in my cottage. The important thing was that I was safe and unharmed, even if the incident had left me a bit shaken.

With absolutely no clue as to the hooded figure's identity, I could only speculate as to why they'd followed me. I figured there were a few possibilities. Either someone had simply wanted to scare me for fun, Archie's killer had targeted me, the mystery man in the sunglasses had come after me for some reason, or a random person had intended to harm me. Those possibilities didn't exactly narrow down the pool of potential suspects.

Unfortunately, the mystery of who had followed me was likely to remain unsolved. I desperately hoped that wasn't true for Archie's murder. I felt better about Pops's situation, but my stress and worry hadn't been erased entirely. If the police investigation into other suspects didn't result in any evidence or solid leads, would the cops turn their attention back to Pops?

That unsettling thought got me to my feet. I needed to get to True Confections. The sooner I started work, the sooner I would finish. I loved my job, but I was hoping that later in the day I could do something to improve Pops's situation further. What, exactly, that might entail, I didn't know. I wanted more information about Tammy Doyle, but I wasn't sure how to get it. I also needed to find out more about Oliver.

When Angela arrived at the shop later that morning, I wondered if I'd overlooked a possible source of information all this time. Angela had left Larch Haven for college, but aside from those four years, she'd lived her entire life here. She'd always been social and chatty, and had probably talked to every local resident at some point. She was older than Jolene and a lot younger than Tammy, but that didn't mean she wouldn't know anything about them. In a small town like Larch Haven, everyone tended to know everyone else's business. Even though Tammy now lived in Maine, I didn't think it had been more than a few years since she'd moved away, and she'd resided here for a long time.

"Hey, Ange," I said as I restocked the display case with bonbons and truffles, "do you know Tammy Doyle?"

Angie stacked boxes of salted caramels and assorted bonbons on a shelf. "I know who she is." She glanced my way. "Why? Does this have something to do with the murder? Archie was Jolene Doyle-Brodsky's biological father."

"So I've heard. And, yes, it does have to do with the murder. I was wondering if Tammy could have killed Archie."

"Because she lied about when she arrived in town?"

"Marco filled you in?" I guessed.

"Yes. The police took a copy of the video footage after your discovery."

"That's good to know."

Angie straightened a stack of boxes. "As for whether Tammy could have killed Archie, I don't know. It's weird that she lied, but maybe she was simply hoping to avoid becoming a suspect once she heard about the murder. She does have a temper, though."

"Really?" I asked with interest.

"Well, she used to, anyway. I heard once that she used

to get into fights. Even got suspended from school a couple of times because of it. That all happened in her teens. She was more mellow when Lolly used to babysit her."

"Lolly used to babysit Tammy? I didn't even realize she'd grown up here. I thought maybe she'd moved here as an adult."

"I'm pretty sure she wasn't born here, but I guess she was quite young when her family moved to town. Anyway, most of my knowledge about her comes from gossip and rumors over the years, so I wouldn't rely too heavily on any of that."

"Did any of it come from the Gossip Grannies?"

Angie rolled her eyes. "Not that I'm aware of, but you never know in this town." She looked at me with sympathy. "I heard that you've fallen victim to the Grannies."

"Ugh. Probably everyone has heard their crazy story by now."

"Probably," Angie agreed. "But don't worry. People will forget about it soon enough."

She opened the store then, and customers came inside almost right away, so I returned to the kitchen. As I worked, I thought over what my cousin had told me. If there was any truth to what she'd said about Tammy having a temper, that made her an even more likely suspect in my mind. I wondered if I could find out if she'd mellowed at all over the years. If she still had a tendency to let her anger get the best of her, perhaps she'd struck out at Archie in a heated moment.

I wished I'd thought to ask Sawyer if the police had confronted her about her lie yet. Not that he would have answered the question.

In the early afternoon, Pops arrived at the shop and paid me a visit in the kitchen.

"Hello, my starlet," he said, greeting me with a kiss on the top of my head. "I wanted to tell you that the chocolates you sent home with your grandmother were delicious."

I smiled. "Thanks, Pops. I made an adjustment to the

recipe for the pumpkin cheesecake truffles today. Do you want to try one?"

"Only one?" he asked, feigning disappointment.

"Or two or three." I held the tray of truffles out to him and he selected one to taste.

"Even better than before," he declared as he reached for a second chocolate.

"I'm happy with it now." I'd already sampled a couple myself. The flavor was more intense without being overwhelming, and the blend of spices was just right.

I grabbed a small paper bag. "Will you take some with you? We won't be selling any until the fall, so someone needs to eat these ones."

"I'm willing to sacrifice myself to the cause," Pops said, happily accepting the bag of truffles. "I'm off to the police station now."

My eyes widened and my heart stuttered. "They're questioning you again?"

"No, no," Pops said quickly. "Nothing like that. They're releasing my scooter. I can take it home now."

I put a hand to the edge of the counter as relief left me feeling shaky. "Does that mean they know now that there isn't any incriminating evidence on it?"

"That's what my lawyer says."

I hugged my grandfather. "That's great news. Surely this is a step in the direction of clearing your name."

Pops shrugged. "At least it doesn't make me seem any guiltier."

I untied my apron. "Is it all right if I come with you? I could use some fresh air."

"I would never turn down the chance to go for a walk with my lovely granddaughter."

I did some quick tidying-up and then accompanied Pops out of the store. Maybe it was a long shot, but if I could have a chat with Sawyer, maybe I could learn something that would help me narrow down my suspect list.

Chapter Thirty-One

LOLLY MET US OUT FRONT OF THE POLICE STATION, A helmet in her hand.

"I knew you'd want to drive that scooter home," she said to Pops, handing him the helmet. "You can't do that without this."

Pops kissed her on the cheek. "Always a step ahead of me."

"For sixty years," Lolly said with a smile.

The only motorized scooters allowed on the town's walkways were those for people with mobility issues. Pops could still ride his scooter most of the way home, though, if he took the long way, along the outskirts of town. That probably suited him just fine. He rarely took the scooter out anymore, but he still enjoyed riding on it every so often and would appreciate the extra mile or two.

The three of us entered the police station together. Pops walked straight to the front desk, but Lolly and I hung back. A quiet sob caught my attention.

Tammy Doyle sat in one of the chairs to my left, crying softly, a crumpled tissue in one hand.

I touched my grandmother's arm to direct her attention that way. "Lolly, is it true you used to babysit Tammy?"

"When she was just a wee little thing." Her eyes filled with sympathy when she realized Tammy was crying. "The poor woman."

Lolly hurried over to her. She sat down and put an arm around Tammy, speaking quietly. I couldn't help but wonder if Tammy was crying because she was in trouble with the police. Or maybe she was scared because she knew she was about to get questioned and she thought there was a good chance that the cops knew she had killed Archie.

I wished I could overhear what she and Lolly were saying to each other, but the conversation was too quiet. I'd have to hover right next to them, and I wasn't about to do that. Instead, I joined Pops by the front desk. He was told that an officer would bring his scooter out the side door of the station, so he headed back outside to wait. I asked if Sawyer was in, but I was out of luck. He was on duty but not presently at the station.

I didn't want to appear suspicious by loitering in the lobby, waiting for Lolly, so I followed Pops outside and sat down on a low stone wall that surrounded a raised flower bed. The sun warmed my skin, and I closed my eyes as I listened to the chirping of a bird in a maple tree.

When I opened my eyes again, I spotted Jolene at the nearby dock, tying up her whisper boat. Once the craft was secure, she jogged toward the police station, not slowing until she reached the door. Another minute or two passed, and then Jolene emerged with her arm around her mother, who was no longer crying. She still looked upset, though.

Lolly exited the police station behind them. She said a few words to Tammy, then squeezed her hand and parted ways with the two women. Jolene led Tammy to the dock, while Lolly came to join me by the flower bed.

I stood up as she approached. "Is Tammy all right?"

"She got herself into some trouble. Now she's scared and upset."

"Because she lied about when she arrived in town?"

"How did you know about that?" Lolly asked.

"It's a bit of a long story," I said, not wanting to let on that I'd been doing some sleuthing. "But one of her friends mentioned seeing her here before Archie died. Tammy denied it, but I suspected she was lying."

"And now the police know about it." Lolly shook her head. "I told her to get herself a lawyer."

"Do you think Tammy could have killed Archie?" I asked as we started walking.

I expected Lolly to jump to Tammy's defense, but that wasn't what happened.

"I'm not sure," she said, and I could tell that it pained her to admit that. "I wish I could say absolutely not, but she changed so much after she became a teenager. Her parents divorced, and she didn't handle it well. She started lying a lot, got into fights. Even as an adult, she got into some scuffles when she'd had too much to drink." Lolly sighed, her expression growing sad. "I really hope it wasn't her."

I tucked my arm through Lolly's. "She might have lied simply to avoid becoming a suspect. She could be completely innocent."

"That's the reason she gave me for lying," Lolly said. "The problem is that *somebody* killed Archie, and there's a good chance that it was someone from our town. It's terrible to even think about."

"It is," I agreed wholeheartedly. "The one good bit of news is that I don't think Pops is the prime suspect anymore."

"That's the sense I got from his lawyer too. It's a relief,

but not as much of a relief as it will be when the police have the right person behind bars."

I couldn't have said it better myself.

I walked with Lolly as far as her cottage, then returned to True Confections to finish up the last batch of chocolates for the day. As I left the shop later, I glanced up at the sky. Gray clouds had rolled in again, blotting out the sun. According to my phone's weather app, the next couple of days would likely be stormy. If I wanted to spend any time out on the lake in my kayak, this was the time to do it.

I headed home, planning to briefly play with Binx and Truffles before heading out on the water. When my cottage came into sight, I slowed my pace. Carmen Vasquez stood on my lawn, facing away from me. She looked toward the dock, and then down at the grass. I picked up my pace again.

"Hello? Carmen?" I called out.

She spun around, startled. "Oh, hi, Becca."

"Can I help you with something?" I asked.

She gave me a sheepish smile. "I lost an earring this morning when I was out for a jog. I'm retracing my steps, hoping I can find it. No luck yet, though."

"What does it look like?"

"It's a small silver hoop with a star dangling from it."

I scanned the green grass at the edge of the walking path, but I didn't spot any silver.

"I'll keep my eye out for it," I said as I fished my keys from my pocket.

"Thanks. Oh, you live here?" She glanced toward my cottage. "Nice place. Anyway," she continued without giving me a chance to say anything, "I'll keep looking. Have a nice afternoon."

"You too," I said, although I ended up speaking to her back because she was already walking away.

I crossed the lawn to the front door of my cottage, checking the grass for anything that looked out of place. I didn't see anything of the kind.

I stayed home for a few minutes, and then set out in my kayak, paddling around Shadow Lake. The first drops of rain sent ripples across the surface of the water as I steered back into the canal, but I managed to make it home before the sprinkling of rain turned into a real shower.

Binx, Truffles, and I spent the rest of the day cozied up in the cottage, and the cats curled up on the bed with me when I went to sleep.

In the middle of the night, I woke with a start. I sat up, wondering what had disturbed my sleep. I thought I'd heard something, but I didn't know what.

I listened carefully, but the only sound that reached my ears was the pelting of the rain against the roof of my cottage. The steady rhythm of it soon lulled me back to sleep.

I DIDN'T HAVE A CHANCE FOR ANY SLEUTHING THE next morning. I was too busy in the kitchen at True Confections, whipping up more batches of bonbons and replenishing our supply of chocolate gondolas. The rain came and went with intermittent showers. Although the weather caused the shop to be less busy than usual, we still had plenty of customers, and the rain hadn't diminished their appetite for chocolate, fortunately.

I was in the midst of assembling a chocolate gondola when Angie poked her head into the kitchen.

"Becca, there's a man here to see you."

I touched one half of the gondola to a warm pan for a couple of seconds and then removed it. "What man?" I did the same to the second half, and then gently pressed the two pieces together, making sure they were properly aligned.

"He didn't give a name. I don't think he's local, though. I've never seen him before. Maybe he's a fan." With that suggestion, Angie disappeared from sight.

It didn't happen all that often, but on occasion fans of *Twilight Hills* came to the shop and asked to see me. In case Angie was right, I stopped in the washroom across the hall to check my appearance in the mirror. If someone wanted to take a selfie with me, I didn't want to look too unkempt. I tugged the elastic out of my ponytail and patted down a few strands of hair. Deeming that good enough, I made my way out to the front.

I stopped short when I reached the shop area. Aside from two elderly women pointing out their display case selections to Angie, the only other person in the store was the mystery man in the baseball cap. He was without his sunglasses today, allowing me to see that he had brown eyes. Now that he was only a few feet away from me, I could also see that he had short, dark hair poking out from beneath his cap. He wasn't anyone I recognized.

"Rebecca Ransom?" The man stepped forward and extended a hand to me. "Phil Chalupnik from Ever After Films. Cooper Graystone told me you lived here in Larch Haven, so I thought I'd introduce myself."

I shook his offered hand, relaxing. I didn't recognize Chalupnik's name, but I was familiar with Ever After Films. The company produced popular television romance movies. Cooper Graystone was one of my former co-stars from *Twilight Hills*.

"Nice to meet you," I said. "What brings you to Larch Haven?"

"I'm partly here on holiday, and partly scouting possible future shooting locations. I was having a beer with Cooper a couple weeks ago and mentioned that I was looking for some unique and charming locations for future films. He said that you'd shown him photos of your hometown and he thought it might fit the bill. When he showed me some of the pictures, I knew I had to come see the place for myself."

"Larch Haven is definitely unique, compared to other

North American towns, anyway," I said. "And we've got plenty of charm."

He grinned. "I can see that. I'd never seen a gondola race before this week, and the place looks like it's out of a fairy tale."

"Does that mean you're thinking of filming a movie here?" I asked, excitement stirring in my chest.

A movie production would inject money into the town, and I certainly didn't mind the thought of my two favorite worlds brushing up against each other, if only briefly.

"Nothing's set in stone, but I've been taking a lot of pictures and I'm going to be sharing them around when I get back to work. I think Larch Haven really fits our brand."

"I couldn't agree more."

"Anyway," Phil said, adjusting his baseball cap, "I won't keep you from your work. I just wanted to make sure I said hello before I head home tomorrow. I almost talked to you the other day but didn't want to intrude while you were congratulating one of the race winners."

I smiled. "That was my brother. I'm glad you stopped by today." Especially because I now didn't have to worry about who he was and what he was up to.

"I don't think I can leave without buying some of these chocolates, though." He examined the bonbons in the display case. "They're way too tempting."

The two elderly customers exited the shop, leaving Phil as the only person present other than myself and Angie.

"Point out what you'd like, and I'll fill a box for you," I offered. "On the house."

"You don't have to do that," he protested.

"I want to. Please." I grabbed a box that would hold a dozen bonbons.

Phil pointed out the ones he wanted to try, and I packaged them up for him. After I'd introduced him to Angie, he shook my hand again and thanked me before leaving the shop.

"Did I hear him say that he might bring a movie production here to Larch Haven?" Angie asked with excitement.

"Sounds like he's going to consider it."

Angie squealed and gave me a hug. "Maybe you'll star in it!"

"I doubt it," I said. "I'm a chocolatier now. My acting life is behind me."

"That doesn't mean you couldn't dip your toe back in those waters."

Maybe not, but I didn't have any plans to do so, at least not anytime soon.

A group of customers entered the shop, and I returned to the kitchen while Angie tended to the patrons.

I left True Confections a short while later. Earlier, on a whim, I'd called the local hair salon and booked an appointment. Reminiscing with Sawyer a few days earlier had reminded me of how I'd always wanted purple hair. Except for going blond for a movie role, I'd never actually dyed my hair. I figured it was time to do something about that. I no longer wanted a complete dye job, but I decided I wanted purple at the ends of my hair.

The results turned out better than I'd envisioned. The stylist had trimmed my hair and then added the purple so that it was vibrant at the ends and then blended into my natural dark brown higher up. She'd also styled my hair in loose waves, which was my favorite way to wear it.

When I left the salon in the middle the afternoon, dark clouds still filled the sky, but only a few raindrops were falling. Instead of heading home, I decided to walk around town. Some people were wearing rain gear, and I wanted to keep an eye out for a black rain jacket with a tear in the back. If I could figure out who owned the jacket, I'd know who'd fled from Archie's cabin the other day and, quite possibly, who had committed the murder.

I strolled up and down the canals, passing shops, restaurants, cottages, and town houses. I saw plenty of people, and even spotted a couple of black rain jackets, but none of them were the right style, and none of them were torn in the back.

Eventually, I gave up and headed home to fetch my Jon boat. My search for the jacket had been fruitless, and I didn't want to waste the entire afternoon. The rain had stopped, but the clouds were growing more ominous with every passing minute. I figured I should go and buy some groceries before the next downpour hit.

In the dim light of the boathouse, I climbed carefully into my boat. With the rope untied, I turned on the engine and maneuvered out of the shelter.

Right away, I knew something was wrong.

I heard a rushing sound and water lapped at my flip-flops, tickling the bare skin of my feet.

I cut the engine and grabbed a handful of grass on the bank of the canal to stop the boat's momentum. Desperately, I tried to propel myself backward, pushing along the bank.

Water rushed into the craft through several holes and pooled around my ankles. I grabbed the edge of the boat-house entrance, hoping I could get back inside. It wasn't going to work. The water was pouring in too fast.

My boat was sinking.

I grabbed the mooring line and clambered up onto the bank.

I sat there on the grass, gripping the rope, watching as more water filled the boat.

Now that I was safely on land, my mind had a chance to process what I was seeing.

The water wasn't getting into my boat through random holes.

Someone had drilled a series of them, very intentionally.

And the holes spelled out the word STOP.

Chapter Thirty-Two

MY HEART POUNDED AND MY FINGERS TREMBLED, but I tried to look on the bright side.

At least my phone was dry.

I used it to call Sawyer. I didn't think there was any point in calling 9-1-1 instead. I was safely on the bank now, and whoever had drilled the holes in my boat was long gone.

Luckily, Sawyer answered the call. I gave him a quick rundown of what had happened, and he told me he'd be right there. He arrived on his bike five minutes later, hopping off before he'd even come to a stop. He wasn't working, so he wore jeans and a T-shirt. I wished I hadn't interrupted his day off.

Sawyer leaned his bike against a tree and joined me on the bank.

"You're okay?" he asked as I got to my feet.

"I'm fine," I assured him. "I managed to climb out onto the bank without getting anything other than my feet wet."

We both stared at my whisper boat, which was now

mostly submerged except for the bow. I still held on to the rope, not wanting to let the boat sink completely.

A few tourists had glided past in whisper boats while I was waiting for Sawyer to arrive. They'd sent me curious glances, and a couple of people had asked if I needed help, but I'd assured them that I was okay and that help was on the way. At least my submerged boat was in my little offshoot from the canal, so it wasn't causing any obstruction for other boating traffic.

Sawyer rested a reassuring hand on my shoulder. "Let's see if we can get that rope secured. Then I'll call for some help to get the boat out of the water."

He skirted around the boathouse and disappeared inside. He reappeared, standing at the boat entrance. I tossed him the rope, and he managed to tow the submerged craft close enough to the structure to allow him to secure the line.

He made a phone call, and then joined me on the bank again to wait for reinforcements to arrive.

"You're sure the holes formed letters?" he asked.

The holes were now underwater, but I'd briefly told him about the unnerving message over the phone.

"Positive," I said. "It was hard to miss, once I wasn't worried about sinking along with the boat."

Under different circumstances, Sawyer probably would have teased me about my fear of ending up in the water, but his expression held no humor.

"Have you noticed anybody near your boathouse lately?" he asked.

I considered the question. "Not really. Carmen Vasquez was looking for an earring over by my cottage yesterday afternoon, but otherwise I've only seen people passing on the path."

"What about any unusual noises?"

I started to answer in the negative, but then I stopped myself and reconsidered. "I'm not sure. Something woke me up last night, but I thought maybe it was just the rain."

I wondered if in fact the sound of drilling had woken me instead. I knew Sawyer was wondering the same thing.

He turned his dark eyes my way, his jaw tense. "What have you been up to since we last talked?"

"I'm guessing you don't mean workwise." I sighed in the face of his serious gaze. "I've been thinking about the murder case, but the only people I've talked to about it are Angie and Lolly."

I didn't bother to mention that I'd walked around town looking for the torn raincoat. Nobody knew that I was doing anything other than simply going for a stroll, so that couldn't have spurred someone to leave the warning for me.

"Then I guess you had them worried enough already," Sawyer said.

"You mean the killer, right?"

He didn't answer with words, but he didn't have to. It was written across his face.

Archie's killer was worried I was getting too close to identifying them. Too bad I didn't feel any closer to the truth.

"I need to know everybody you questioned or talked to about Archie's murder," Sawyer said.

"I'll make you a list."

As I said that, a boat turned our way from the main canal. One of the two men on board cut the engine, and the boat coasted toward us. The men disembarked at my boathouse and got to work with Sawyer, trying to get my whisper boat out of the water. There wasn't room for me to help, so I retreated to my cottage and found a notebook so I could make that list for Sawyer.

I put Dizzy, Lolly, and Angie at the top of the list. I knew Sawyer could immediately discount them, but I wanted to make the list as thorough as possible. Then I added the name of every other person I could think of whom I'd talked to about the murder.

When I took the list outside, a uniformed police officer

had joined Sawyer and the other men. They'd managed to pull my whisper boat up on the bank of the canal. There was no missing the fact that the holes spelled out the word STOP.

Seeing the message again brought on a sudden case of jumpiness. I glanced around, wondering if anyone—like the culprit who'd vandalized my boat—might be watching us. Across the canal from us, a woman pushed a stroller, and off in the distance two teenagers zipped along on bicycles. Otherwise, I didn't see anybody.

I spent a few minutes talking to the uniformed officer, who was going to make a report about the vandalism. Then he and the other two men left after I thanked them all for their help.

Sawyer stayed behind, and I handed him my list as we stood next to my damaged boat. "That's everyone I can think of."

He took a look at the names, but didn't comment on any of them. "Thanks. I'll look into it." He folded the list and tucked it into his back pocket.

I rubbed my arms as a damp breeze tickled my skin. "I'm sorry for interrupting your day off."

"Don't be. Like I said before, I want you to call when something happens." He fixed his gaze on me. "But let's try and make sure nothing else does happen."

"I'm good with that," I said.

"Until we've caught who's responsible for this, don't go anywhere alone at night."

"I won't," I promised. I'd already decided to avoid doing that before the latest incident. Now I wasn't even sure if I wanted to go out alone during the day.

My anger from that morning rekindled. Whoever was making me feel unsafe wasn't going to get away with it.

By unspoken agreement, Sawyer and I turned our backs on the whisper boat and walked toward my cottage.

"Have you seen your mystery man again since we last talked?" Sawyer asked.

"Yes, but he's no longer a mystery, and I'm pretty sure he's got nothing to do with my boat getting vandalized."

I told him about the visit Phil Chalupnik had paid to True Confections.

"So there might be a movie filmed in Larch Haven?" he asked when I'd finished the brief story.

I shrugged. "Maybe. It's not a done deal or anything. Do the Derendorfs know about Lexi's pendant yet?"

"Detective Ishimoto informed them yesterday."

"Are they suspects in Archie's murder now?" I asked as we came to a stop on my front step.

"We haven't discounted them entirely, but I don't think they had anything to do with it."

"Really?" Although I wanted that to be the case, I also wanted to know why Sawyer had that opinion. "Do they have alibis?"

"They're each other's alibi, so that doesn't rule them out. My gut tells me it wasn't them, though. They seemed genuinely shocked to find out that Archie had Lexi's pendant. They both broke down when Detective Ishimoto showed it to them."

"I feel so bad for them," I said, my heart aching.

Sawyer stared off into the distance. "Hopefully we can at least find them some closure."

One look at his face told me how much he wanted that to happen.

I touched his arm briefly. "You will."

His gaze met mine and one corner of his mouth quirked up. He slipped two fingers under a lock of my hair and held it. "I like the purple."

"Thanks. I figured it was about time."

"Whatever you paid, I'm sure I could have done it cheaper."

I fought against a smile. "Um, no thanks."

"What?" he said, a mischievous glint in his eyes. "You don't trust me?"

"With my life, yes. Just not with my hair."

He released the lock of hair, letting it slide slowly through his fingers. Something like electricity danced over my skin. My breath hitched at the intensity in Sawyer's eyes as he kept his gaze fixed on mine.

I glanced away from him and gathered my thoughts.

"Dizzy is on her way over," I said. I'd texted her while working on my list of names. "Do you want to come in for a while?"

Sawyer looked up at the sky. "I'll hang around until Dizzy arrives, but then I'll try to get home before the sky opens up again."

Judging by the darkening clouds, that could happen at any moment.

I was about to open the door when I spotted Dizzy heading our way along the canal path. Sawyer stayed long enough to warn us off any further sleuthing, but then he hopped on his bike and headed for home.

Despite Sawyer's warning, and the more frightening one drilled into my boat, I wanted to take action. I didn't like feeling scared and helpless. At the same time, I knew I needed to be careful. Whoever was behind the vandalism and the murder—whether it was one person or two—I wanted them caught, but I didn't want to come to any harm in the process.

I shared all those feelings with Dizzy—after she'd admired the purple in my hair—and together we came up with a plan to track down the owner of the torn raincoat. It seemed to be the only tangible clue we had to work with. Dizzy left for home before it got dark outside, but we agreed to meet up the next afternoon to put our plan into action.

Hopefully, it would get us closer to solving the mystery of Archie's murder.

Chapter Thirty-Three

SLEEP DIDN'T COME EASILY THAT NIGHT. I GOT UP twice to check out the window for any prowlers, unable to forget what had happened to my boat. Eventually, I drifted off into an uneasy sleep, but dark shadows and an undertone of danger filled my dreams. I gladly got up early in the morning, wanting to leave the dreams behind me, and also wanting to get on with the day.

I kept checking over my shoulder as I walked to True Confections, but I arrived at the shop without incident. After putting in a couple hours of work in the kitchen, I took a break and walked to Estelle's town house, hoping to find her at home.

I knocked on the front door and waited, admiring the pretty petunias in the flowerpots flanking her front steps. She also had a window box bursting with bright blooms. Gardening was one of the hobbies that she and my mom had in common.

When Estelle opened the door, she appeared surprised

to see me. I couldn't blame her. I'd never come by her place before and I'd had to look up her address online.

"Hi, Estelle," I greeted. "I was wondering if you needed any help getting donations for the silent auction."

Her face brightened. "That would be wonderful!"

"Have you visited all the businesses on Venice Avenue?"

"I haven't had the chance yet. The only business owners I've talked to so far are you and Tassie Johnson."

Tassie owned Hooked on Books, the store located below Dizzy's apartment. I didn't mind at all that Estelle had already talked to her, since she wasn't on my suspect list.

"I could check with the businesses on Venice Avenue, if you'd like," I offered. "I've got some time this afternoon."

"That would be such a great help, Becca. I'm volunteering at the seniors' center today, so I won't be able to do any work on the auction until late in the afternoon."

"I'm happy to take this task off your hands," I assured her. That was the truth, though she didn't need to know why I was so willing.

"If you hold on one moment, I'll grab the sign-up sheet I printed out." She disappeared down the hall and out of sight. Within seconds, she was on her way back to the door, a clipboard in hand. "You can take the whole clipboard as well. It'll give you something to write on."

The papers attached to the clipboard had one column for the name of the donor, another for noting the type of donation, and a third column for the donor's contact information.

"Great." I tucked the clipboard under my arm. "I'll get this back to you soon."

"Thanks again, Becca!" she called after me as I jogged down the steps.

I waved over my shoulder and had to stop myself from skipping with triumph. The first step of the plan had gone off without a hitch. Dizzy and I now had the perfect excuse to visit the homes or businesses of our suspects. Or some of them, anyway. Maria was a business owner and a natural person to approach about the auction. If possible, Dizzy and I would approach Jolene Doyle-Brodsky as well. She and her husband didn't have a shop on Venice Avenue, and I didn't know what property developers could donate to an auction, but that didn't matter. The auction gave us a reason to talk to them, and hopefully get into their home, and that was what Dizzy and I were really after. If we could help out the hiking club in the process, so much the better.

Getting into Oliver's cottage wouldn't be quite so straightforward. As the president of the hiking club, he already knew all about the auction, so I figured we'd have to come up with another reason to visit him. Maybe we could pretend that we wanted his advice on who to approach for donations.

Back at True Confections, I texted Dizzy to let her know that we could implement the next phase of our plan. I had to wait until she was finished work at the library, so I focused on making chocolates for the next few hours. I was itching to get on with our search for answers, but I knew I'd be far safer visiting the suspects with Dizzy there with me. Besides, I knew she didn't want to be left out.

Time seemed to crawl, but eventually Dizzy texted to let me know that she was on her way to the shop. I cleaned up and was ready to go when she showed up at the kitchen door.

"All right, J. B. Fletcher," she said. "Let's get this show on the road."

"What does the B stand for, anyway?" I asked as I grabbed the clipboard Estelle had given me. "I've always wondered."

Dizzy led the way out of the shop, waving at Angie as she opened the door. "Beatrice."

"Your librarian brain always knows the answer."

"That doesn't really count as librarian knowledge," she said as we stopped on the cobblestone walkway. "That one comes from many hours spent watching *Murder, She Wrote* reruns on TV."

"Clearly, I missed a few episodes."

"It hasn't hurt your sleuthing abilities."

"I'm not so sure," I said. "If anyone here is Jessica Fletcher or Nancy Drew, it's you. You're the one who solved the mystery of why people were making such strange comments about my breakup with Justin. Other than finding Archie's secret stash, I haven't accomplished anything."

"I don't think you should underestimate the importance of that discovery. As for the other mystery, all I had to do was track down some gossip. That wasn't exactly hard to do. But maybe this mission will help us add to our list of accomplishments."

"I sure hope so." I surveyed the line of shops along the canal. "All right, where should we start?"

"With Oliver." Dizzy set off in the direction of Oliver's café, and I followed.

I told her about my idea of pretending we wanted his advice, and she readily agreed to go with that plan.

"I really think Oliver could be the killer," Dizzy said as we walked. "He doesn't have an alibi, and he's so passionate about his hiking club and the local trails. He really hated Archie for trying to prevent the trail restoration project."

"But if he's at work and didn't wear a jacket on his way there, we'll have no chance of finding the torn raincoat, even if it belongs to him."

Dizzy glanced up at the sky. "It's been drizzling on and off today, so there's a chance that he wore a jacket to work, but you're right. If we visit him at his café and don't find anything, we won't have a chance to visit his cottage."

A solution popped into my head. "If we don't find anything at the café, then we can visit him at home tomorrow and say we still want to add to our list of donors but don't know where to go next."

"Perfect," Dizzy declared. "Problem-solving. A great quality in a detective."

Despite my problem-solving, we hit a bump in the road almost right away. Oliver, it turned out, wasn't at the café.

"Do you know if we can find him at home?" Dizzy asked the waitress, who was busy cleaning tables.

"You can try, but I don't know that you'll have any luck. He was heading to Burlington for some sort of appointment. If he were back already, he'd probably be here."

Disappointed, we thanked her for the information and let her get back to work.

We weren't ready to give up on our investigation of Oliver, so we headed for his cottage. Unfortunately, nobody answered when we knocked on his door.

"Okay, that's annoying," Dizzy said as we walked away from the cottage in defeat. "We're getting nowhere."

"Let's try Maria next," I suggested, trying to remain optimistic. Maybe we could still locate the torn raincoat before the end of the day.

At Pure Bliss, we found Carmen in charge of the shop. When we told her we were collecting donations for the silent auction, she told us that Maria wasn't there.

I couldn't believe our bad luck, until Carmen mentioned that her sister was at home.

"She sprained her ankle yesterday," Carmen explained. "She'll be all right, but she's supposed to rest for a couple of days. She won't mind you dropping by. If her frequent text messages are anything to go by, she's bored out of her mind."

We thanked Carmen and hurried out of the shop.

"Maybe this is for the best," Dizzy said. "We'll probably have a better chance of finding her raincoat at her cottage."

"Speaking of raincoats," I said, glancing up at the clouds as a few drops pattered down from the sky, "maybe we should have brought our own."

"Hopefully it's just a brief shower."

The words were barely out of Dizzy's mouth when the rain started pouring down.

We broke into a jog, hoping to get to Maria's cottage as quickly as possible. It took us only a couple of minutes to get there, but we were well and truly damp by the time we arrived.

As Dizzy knocked on the door, I tried my best to tidy my wet hair.

I heard a thumping noise on the other side of the door, and it opened a moment later. Maria stood there, propped up on crutches.

"Hey, come on in," she said, shifting out of the way so we could step into the foyer. "Carmen texted to let me know you'd be stopping by. Something about an auction?"

Dizzy rattled off our cover story while I shut the door behind us.

"I'd love to donate a gift basket," Maria said. "Why don't we sit down for a minute. Do you want anything to drink?"

"That would be great," Dizzy replied. "I'm feeling kind of parched." She took in the sight of Maria's swollen ankle. "Why don't you sit down in the kitchen and I'll fetch the drinks."

I silently cheered Dizzy on. She'd found a way to get Maria out of sight of the foyer closet. If we'd taken seats in the living room, it would have been impossible for me to search the closet without Maria knowing what I was up to.

Maria slowly made her way through the living room and dining room to the kitchen at the back of the cottage. She eased herself down onto a chair by the table. "There's a jug of sweet tea in the fridge. And the glasses are in the cupboard to the right of the sink."

Dizzy opened the cupboard and I sat down on a chair across the table from Maria.

"Nothing for me, thanks," I said as Dizzy set glasses on the counter. I jumped back to my feet. "Maria, would it be all right if I used your washroom?"

"Sure," she said as she propped her swollen ankle up on a chair. "It's down the hall. Second door to your left."

I thanked her and shared a brief glance with Dizzy as I left the room. On my way out, I heard her begin chatting about the auction and its purpose.

I followed the hallway toward the front of the cottage. After noting the location of the washroom, I crept quietly onward. When I reached the foyer, I stopped and listened. I could hear Dizzy's and Maria's muffled voices coming from the kitchen. Carefully, I opened the bifold door of the foyer closet, desperately hoping it wouldn't squeak or creak.

I froze when it groaned. Dizzy's and Maria's voices continued uninterrupted. I held my breath and eased the door open the rest of the way. It didn't let out any further sounds of protest.

Knowing I didn't have long before my absence would become suspicious, I searched through the closet quickly. Maria had about a dozen coats and jackets hanging in the closet, in a variety of colors and styles. Only one of them was a rain jacket, and it was bright red. Definitely not what I was looking for. I shifted through all the jackets one more time, wanting to be sure I didn't miss anything. The second search didn't turn up anything more than the first.

There were a few empty hangers, but I figured those were probably for guests. I took a quick look around the rest of the closet, but nothing stood out to me. Time was ticking by, so I eased the closet door shut and tiptoed to the washroom. I shut the door quietly and ran the water for a few seconds before returning to the hallway.

When I entered the kitchen, Dizzy bounced out of her seat, clutching the clipboard I'd left with her. "I think we've got everything we need." She gave me a pointed look. "Do you need a drink or anything before we leave, Becca?"

"No, I'm good." I addressed Maria. "Thanks so much for donating to the cause."

She made a move to grab her crutches.

"You don't need to get up," Dizzy told her as she set her empty glass by the sink. "We'll show ourselves out. Thank you so much for the donation and the drink."

"You're welcome," Maria said. "Just let me know when I should have the gift basket ready."

"Of course," I said. "Someone will be in touch."

Dizzy and I headed for the front of the cottage. As soon as we were out of Maria's line of sight, Dizzy tucked her arm through mine and practically hauled me to the door. When we had it shut behind us, she turned to me, looking like she was ready to burst from anticipation.

"So?" she asked. "Is Maria the owner of the torn jacket?"

"Nope," I replied, disappointment weighing heavily upon me. "It seems our plan is a total bust."

Chapter Thirty-Four

WE TRIED TO TRACK DOWN JOLENE OR HER HUSBAND, but had no luck there either. They weren't at home or at the portable office by the town house development. Despite our distinct lack of success, Dizzy was determined to remain optimistic, and that helped to revive my spirits. We'd struck out for today, but we would try Oliver and Jolene again the next day. Since we had only one donation listed on our sheet so far, we spent the next couple of hours doing what I'd told Estelle we would do—visiting the other businesses on Venice Avenue. Everyone we talked to was willing to donate something to the auction, and by the time we wrapped up our last visit, we'd filled an entire sign-up sheet.

Dizzy needed to make a trip to the bank before it closed, so we parted ways and I set off for Estelle's town house. I'd hand over the sheet we'd filled up, and keep one of the blank ones to take while visiting Oliver and Jolene the next day.

Dizzy and I had managed to make our rounds of the shops and businesses during a break in the rain, but as I walked toward Estelle's neighborhood, lightning flashed over the mountains. A rumble of thunder followed soon after and big raindrops pelted down from the dark and ominous clouds. I picked up my pace, hugging the clipboard to my chest so the papers wouldn't get wet.

When I reached the shelter of Estelle's small porch, I wiped raindrops from my face. As thunder boomed overhead, I spotted Jolene driving along the street in a covered golf cart. For a split second, I considered trying to flag her down, but then lightning lit up the darkening sky and I thought better of it. There was no point in talking to her now, I realized as she trundled past. She wasn't wearing a jacket, and I couldn't get a look at her closet if I didn't visit her at home.

I knocked on Estelle's door, realizing as I did so that she might not yet be home from her volunteer shift at the seniors' center. I cast an uneasy glance at the sky, wishing I'd gone straight home after saying goodbye to Dizzy.

Estelle opened the door and quickly ushered me inside. "You poor thing. You're drenched! Come on in out of the storm."

I handed over the clipboard and papers before I had a chance to drip all over them. "I still have a couple of business owners to talk to, but we did pretty well, I think. Dizzy helped me out."

Estelle ran her gaze down the list and beamed. "Becca, this is fantastic! Thank you so much!"

She tore her attention away from the list and took a good look at me. "Let me get you a towel. And how about a hot drink?"

"Thank you, but that's all right. I should probably get home before the storm gets any worse."

"Then at least let me lend you an umbrella."

"It's probably best not to use one with all the lightning."

"Of course. How silly of me. Then how about you borrow a jacket?" She opened the closet door. "I've got a couple I never use."

"Thank you," I said, as she riffled through a collection of jackets. "That would be . . ."

My voice died in my throat as I stared at the closet. Amid several other garments hung a black rain jacket with a four-inch tear by the bottom hem.

Terror washed over me. I forced myself to finish my sentence.

"That would be great."

I didn't know if it was another round of lightning or if Estelle's eyes really flashed.

"Well, that was stupid of me," she said, her voice taking on a chilling edge. "I never should have let you see that jacket. I was worried you'd recognized me at Archie's place, but then when nobody said anything about it, I figured I was fine."

"Archie's place?" Even though my throat had gone as dry as a desert, I forced myself to speak normally, falling into the role of someone completely out of the loop. "What do you mean?"

"Nice try, Becca. I know you're an actress, and you might have fooled me under different circumstances, but I saw you there, and I know you ran after me. And you recognized my jacket just now and put all the pieces together. Even an Oscar-worthy performance won't convince me otherwise."

Fear gripped me, making my chest tight.

I lunged for the front door. I tried to yank it open, but it didn't budge.

I fumbled with the lock.

Pain exploded in the back of my head.

Silver stars glittered in front of my eyes.

Then darkness took over.

Chapter Thirty-Five

MY HEAD THROBBED WITH PAIN. I DIDN'T WANT TO open my eyes, but a sense of urgency nudged at my fuzzy mind. I forced my eyelids open and blinked in confusion. It took me several seconds to realize I was staring at an unfamiliar ceiling.

Footsteps sounded nearby. I tried to move, but something was wrong, aside from the pounding at the back of my skull. Some of the haziness cleared from my mind. I bit back a cry of pain as I raised my head enough to get a look at myself. I was in a hallway with hardwood floors. My hands were bound together, resting on my stomach. My ankles had also been tied together.

I rested my aching head on the floor again as memories came rushing back.

Estelle.

She must have killed Archie. And now she was probably going to kill me.

Alarm shot through my body. I sat up, wincing against the pain in my head. I moved my hands to my left pocket, where I'd left my phone. I patted the fabric of my shorts, but the pocket was empty.

I reached for the thin rope binding my ankles together.

"Stop it!" Estelle appeared at the end of the hall.

My pulse pounded in my ears. She had a gun, and it was pointed right at me.

I slowly pulled my bound hands away from my ankles.

"It didn't have to be this way, you know." She moved closer, keeping the gun trained on me. "You should have minded your own business. I tried to warn you. I tried to scare you off."

"I don't know anything." I sounded calm even though I was anything but.

"Yes, you do." Estelle grabbed me by the arm and hauled me to my feet with surprising strength. She shoved me against the wall, holding me there with her forearm while pointing the gun at my chest.

I made myself look at Estelle's face rather than the weapon. "You've known my mom forever." I hoped the reminder would appeal to some part of her that wouldn't want to hurt me.

"You're right. I have. And I can't believe you're making me do this to another friend."

"Another . . . ?" My confusion disappeared in a flash of clarity. Susan Derendorf was her best friend. "You killed Lexi?"

Estelle's eyes grew misty. A tear escaped, and she released her hold on me to wipe it away with the back of her hand. The barrel of the gun drifted off to the side.

I shoved her away from me as hard as I could. She slammed into the opposite wall.

I grabbed the wrist of the hand holding the gun, trying to wrestle the weapon away from her, all the time screaming at the top of my lungs for help.

Estelle kicked my shin so hard that I lost my grip on her. She knocked me to the floor.

I rolled onto my back. Estelle was breathing heavily and her hair was a wild mess, but she had the gun pointed at me again. She pulled two bandannas from her pocket.

"I was hoping you wouldn't regain consciousness," she said. "It would have made everything easier."

She grabbed my shoulder and forced me to sit up. Then she stuffed one of the bandanas in my mouth. I tried to spit it out, to grab at it with my bound hands, but she yanked at my hair right where my head hurt the most. I nearly blacked out from the pain.

When my mind and vision cleared, Estelle had already finished gagging me. She climbed to her feet, still holding the gun.

"Lexi was an accident. I never would have hurt her on purpose. It was so dark on the highway that night, and she was dressed all in black. By the time I saw her in the headlights, it was too late. I was devastated when I realized she was dead. I couldn't tell anyone. I'd had a couple of drinks that night. I would have been sent to jail, even though it was an accident. It wasn't my fault. None of this was my fault."

Now that I was gagged, I couldn't contradict her. Maybe I wouldn't have bothered even if I could talk. I didn't want to do anything to cause her to kill me sooner than she planned.

Fear threatened to send my thoughts into a panicked spin. I tried to breathe evenly through my nose. I needed to stay calm and find a way to save myself.

Estelle yanked me to my feet again. She kept hold of one of my arms and poked the barrel of the gun into my back.

"Walk," she ordered.

A shiver ran through my body at the ice in her voice. I did as I was told. I barely recognized her as my mom's friend, as the woman who had volunteered for so many community events and causes.

"You're as nosy as Archie was," Estelle said as she marched me through a door and down a narrow set of stairs. "He wondered what I was doing in the woods, off the trails. He went poking around and saw that I'd been digging. I thought I'd moved all of Lexi's remains, but I dropped that darned pendant. Archie found it. I never thought he was very smart, but he recognized the pendant when he saw the poster for the vigil. He thought he could blackmail me. That definitely *wasn't* smart."

Why had she moved Lexi's remains in the first place?

If I didn't get myself out of this situation, I'd never find out.

The stairs led down to a damp, shadowy cellar. A single lightbulb dangled from a string overhead. When we reached the foot of the stairs, we stood facing a heavy wooden door. Even though it was shut tight, I knew where it led.

The door creaked as Estelle shoved it open. Damp air rushed at me, along with a smattering of raindrops. The storm was still raging, and it was nearly dark out now, even though I didn't think it was nighttime yet.

Rain poured down in sheets. We stood at the top of wide cement steps, which disappeared down into the water of the canal.

A small, aluminum, V-hull boat was tied up by the steps, bobbing slightly as the wind rippled the water.

I tried to scream, but the gag did its job. The pathetic noise I was able to get out was quickly swallowed up by the swirling wind.

Estelle pressed the gun between my shoulder blades and put her mouth next to my ear. "Get in the boat!"

I looked around frantically, searching for help, but I couldn't see another soul.

Not knowing what else to do, I climbed into the boat. I lost my balance and fell to my knees. The boat rocked as Estelle climbed in after me. I considered throwing myself overboard, despite my fear of the dark water.

I didn't have a chance.

I glanced Estelle's way just in time to see the gun coming at my face. It smacked into my head and I fell onto my side. Pain blurred my thoughts and left my limbs stunned and useless.

Rain pelted against my face and ran down my cheeks. Maybe there were tears mixed in; I couldn't tell for sure.

I felt the boat begin to move. Despair wrapped tightly around me, blotting out everything except pain and fear. But then something else crept through the fog in my head: a desire to survive.

I breathed carefully, in and out. The pain in my head dulled to an ache, and I wrestled my growing panic into submission. I raised myself up on one elbow and took in my current situation.

Estelle sat in the stern of the boat, steering it with one hand while keeping the gun trained on me with the other. The rain had plastered her hair to her head and her clothes to her skin.

Lightning flashed, lighting up the world around us. I hoped someone would see us, would see the gun and call the police, but I couldn't count on that. I was running out of time. Already, Estelle had reached the mouth of the canal. She increased the speed of the boat and we rushed out onto Shadow Lake.

"No one will hear the shot over the thunder," Estelle yelled at me through the wind.

I fought against another surge of panic. We were well out on the lake now, the dark water choppy in the storm. I thought of what might be lurking beneath the surface. Then I took in the sight of the monster sitting in the boat with me.

Lightning flashed across the sky.

Estelle cocked the gun.

As thunder boomed overhead, I threw all my weight to the side.

The boat flipped, throwing me into the lake.

Chapter Thirty-Six

THE WATER SWALLOWED ME UP.

I kicked my bound feet and broke through the surface. I gasped and struggled. The gag in my mouth was saturated with water, choking me. I drew air in through my nose and silently screamed at myself to calm down.

I wasn't choking. I wasn't drowning.

I treaded water as best I could with my ankles and wrists bound. Fortunately, Estelle had tied my hands in front of me rather than behind my back, otherwise I would have had more trouble staying afloat. I yanked the gag from my mouth and immediately found it easier to breathe.

A wave splashed me in the face. I shook off the water and surveyed my surroundings.

The capsized boat bobbed in the water about ten feet away. At first, I couldn't see Estelle, but then a hand appeared over the keel of the boat. Her head popped up next as she clung to the craft, trying to right it. I couldn't tell if she still had the gun, and I didn't want to wait around to find out.

Mad Hatter Island was over my left shoulder, closer than the mainland, but if Estelle followed me to the island, I'd be trapped, with no way to get help. I wasn't even sure if I'd be able to untie my ankles to give myself a better chance of evading her.

I looked at the dark water around me. I couldn't see what might be swimming below me, but Estelle and her gun were far more frightening than the thought of any lake monster, no matter how large.

I made a swift decision.

I turned onto my side and began swimming as best I could, kicking with my bound feet and pushing at the water with my hands. I coughed and sputtered when water hit me in the face, but I didn't stop swimming.

At any moment Estelle could come after me, either in the righted boat or by swimming. If she tried to drown me, I wouldn't stand a chance in the struggle, thanks to my bindings. So I kicked and swam, never slowing, never pausing, even as exhaustion worked its way into every muscle fiber.

A man's voice shouted in the distance. Or was it just thunder?

A wave of water seemed to come up behind me from beneath the surface. It gave me an extra push forward. I kicked harder, making the most of the extra momentum.

Something splashed nearby, and I swallowed a mouthful of water in surprise. Coughing, I raised my head.

Somebody grabbed me.

I nearly screamed, but then I heard a voice. Not Estelle's voice.

Sawyer's voice.

"You're okay, Becca. I've got you."

I nearly sobbed with relief, but I kept kicking at the water, helping to propel myself closer to shore as Sawyer towed me along, standing waist-deep in the water.

Mike Kwan splashed his way into the shallows. Together, he and Sawyer hauled me up onto the beach. They eased me down onto the sand and pebbles.

"I'll get a knife," Mike said before running off toward the Boat Barn.

Sawyer crouched down next to me and touched two fingers to my forehead. "You're bleeding. Are you hurt anywhere else?"

I shook my head, still trying to catch my breath. "Estelle," I managed to say. "She killed Archie. She's getting away."

"No, she's not." Sawyer looked out toward the middle of the lake.

I followed his gaze. As lightning flashed, I saw a police boat swiftly closing in on Estelle, who was still in the water, clinging to the overturned craft.

"How did you know I needed help?" I asked.

"Mike spotted the boat on the lake. He was worried about someone being out there in this weather, so he took a look with his binoculars to see if they were in trouble. When he saw Estelle pointing a gun at you, he called 9-1-1. I wasn't far away at the time."

Thank goodness for that.

Sirens wailed behind me. I turned my head, wincing at the pain that caused. A police cruiser and an ambulance slowly navigated along Venice Avenue to the top of the beach, where they both parked, lights flashing in the growing darkness. A crowd of curious onlookers gathered near the emergency vehicles, despite the stormy weather. I quickly faced the lake again. I didn't want anyone recognizing me and alarming my family with news that I was in some sort of trouble without any solid facts to reassure them that I was okay.

Mike returned with a large knife. Sawyer took it from him and carefully sliced through the rope binding my hands and feet. I rubbed my freed wrists with relief. It felt so good to be safe and free of my bindings that I didn't care about the pouring rain, even though I was shivering in my drenched clothes.

I grabbed Sawyer's arm before he stood up. "Estelle killed Lexi Derendorf too. I think she went to Archie's cabin to look for Lexi's pendant."

His forehead furrowed. "We'll talk about everything later. For now, let's get you to the hospital."

I wanted to protest, because the only place I wanted to go was home, but two paramedics had already converged on me, and Sawyer stepped back to give them room to work.

They wrapped a silver emergency blanket around me and checked me out while I answered their questions. They agreed with Sawyer that I should go to the hospital because of the two blows to my head, one of which had left me with a gash in need of stitches.

By then, I could see that the police had pulled Estelle from the water and had her in custody, so I agreed to do what the paramedics thought was best. They helped me onto a stretcher and loaded me into the back of the ambulance.

While the doors remained open, Sawyer climbed in to check on me.

I grabbed his hand as soon as he got close. "I need to let Lolly and Pops know that I'm okay. And Dizzy too." I patted the pocket of my wet shorts. "I don't have my phone. Estelle took it, and I don't know what she did with it."

Sawyer gave my hand a reassuring squeeze. "It's all right, Becca. I'll make sure they know you're okay."

"Thank you. Maybe Gareth and Blake too? Or Lolly could call them." I knew I was babbling, but I couldn't help myself.

"Hey." Sawyer tucked a lock of wet hair behind my ear and cupped my cheek with his palm, gently directing my gaze to his. "Try to relax. You're safe now."

I drew in a breath and let it out slowly. Some of my anxious tension drained away. "Thank you, Sawyer."

He backed away as one of the paramedics climbed on board, but he didn't break his gaze from mine until he was out of the ambulance.

I closed my eyes as the doors shut and the engine started.

I tried my best to relax.

Exhaustion hit me like a tidal wave, and the trip to the hospital passed in a blur.

Chapter Thirty-Seven

I BLINKED IN THE FACE OF BRIGHT SUNLIGHT WHEN I emerged from the police station the next day. It wasn't yet noon, but the day was already plenty warm. I slid sunglasses over my eyes, and the pain in my head dulled from a roar to an ache.

Dizzy rushed up the steps toward me and tucked a protective arm through mine. "How are you feeling? Do you need to sit down?"

"Other than a headache and sore muscles, I'm fine. And I wouldn't mind stretching my legs. I've been sitting for the past two hours."

"Do you want to head home?" she asked as we made our way down the steps.

"Actually, what I really want is a nice cold bubble tea."

"Then that's what we'll get."

We set off in the direction of Venice Avenue. By the time we got close, I'd grown weary and didn't feel up to walking much farther. I had a mild concussion and had been released from the hospital after just a few hours, but even though I'd spent the night in my own bed, with Lolly watching over me, I hadn't slept all that well. Every time I drifted off to sleep, a bad dream jerked me awake again. Now, having spent two hours at the police station, I didn't have much energy left.

That didn't go unnoticed by Dizzy. She parked me on a shady bench with stern instructions to wait there. She zipped off to buy two bubble teas and returned a few minutes later, passing me a slushy mango tea with pearls.

I took a careful sip—not wanting a brain freeze on top of my headache—and savored the sweet, cold drink.

"So, you got your statement over with?" Dizzy said after sitting down next to me.

"Yes, thank goodness." I'd already gone over the details of what had occurred the day before several times, to Sawyer, various family members, Dizzy, and most recently to Detective Naomi Ishimoto. I looked forward to hopefully not having to repeat the story again anytime soon. The whole town was curious, of course, but I hoped that their curiosity would be satisfied through the local grapevine. If anyone wanted to make sure they had an accurate version of what had transpired, they could always check with one of my family members.

I wanted Dizzy to know everything I'd learned from the police, though. The information helped to fill in some blanks.

"Remember the conversation we overheard between Jolene and Alex?" I asked.

"They sounded guilty of something."

"Sawyer talked to Jolene about it. She broke down and told him that Archie had threatened to spread ugly rumors about her and Alex if they didn't stop the town house development. Rumors that they were doing something fraudulent. Apparently, Alex was arrested for fraud years ago when he was in college. The charges were dropped, but Archie knew about it somehow, and Jolene was afraid that he might use that kernel of truth to give the rumors of present-day fraud more clout. Jolene never did make peace with Archie like she told me. She was actually seething mad at him at the time of the murder. She just didn't want to be a suspect, and she thought if word got out that Archie had threatened her and Alex, the police would think she'd killed him."

Dizzy shook her head. "Archie really knew how to make enemies."

"Seriously."

"Has Estelle confessed?"

"Yes, thank goodness. I guess she figured there wasn't any point in keeping quiet since she'd already told me what she'd done. It sounds like she really didn't mean to hit Lexi with her car ten years ago."

"But she covered it up and left Lexi's parents without closure."

"Exactly," I said. "She's far from innocent. She buried Lexi's body in the woods, not far from the washed-out trail to Whisper Mountain. But then the hiking club started talking about restoring the trail and Estelle got really worried that someone might stumble upon the burial site. So she decided to dig up Lexi's remains and move them elsewhere."

"And Archie caught her in the act?" Dizzy guessed.

"Not quite. He saw her coming out of the woods one day, off the trails and covered in mud. Estelle figures he went sniffing around to see what she'd been up to. When she moved Lexi's remains, she dropped the pendant Lexi had been wearing when she disappeared. Archie found it, as well as signs of recent digging. Then he put two and two together. I guess he must have felt bad for the Derendorfs, at least a little bit, since he gave up on fighting with them about their shed. Too bad he didn't feel bad enough to take the information straight to the police. If he'd done that, he'd still be alive today."

"That's sad," Dizzy said. "Did he try to blackmail Estelle instead?"

I nodded. "And that sealed his fate." Sadness tugged at me. "Estelle hit him from behind with a tree branch and dragged his body into the lake, where he drowned. She's stronger than she looks." As I'd learned through my physical struggle with her at her town house.

Dizzy shuddered. "I can't believe she almost killed you too. It's horrifying. I was awake most of the night thinking about it. I wish I'd gone with you to Estelle's house. Then you might never have been hurt."

I put an arm around her and gave her a squeeze. "Or she might have hurt both of us. Once I saw the torn raincoat in her closet, she wasn't about to let me leave freely."

Dizzy rested her head on my shoulder. "I'm so glad you're okay, and I think you're really brave."

"I don't think I was brave," I said. "I just acted out of self-preservation."

"You escaped a killer, and you overcame your fear of swimming in the lake to do it," Dizzy pointed out. "To me, that definitely counts as brave."

"Estelle and her gun were far more terrifying than anything that might be swimming in the lake."

Suddenly chilled by all too vivid memories from the day before, I stood up and moved into the sun, soaking in its warmth. I closed my eyes as Dizzy joined me.

"You're really okay, right?" she asked with concern.

I smiled and opened my eyes. "Absolutely."

TEN DAYS AFTER MY HARROWING ENCOUNTER WITH Estelle, I was nearly rid of the physical reminders of the incident. My stitches wouldn't come out for another couple of days, but my headaches had cleared and my muscles were no longer sore. I got up extra early in the morning, dressed in shorts and a T-shirt, and took a stroll to the main dock.

Sawyer was there waiting for me.

"How are you feeling today?" he asked.

"Good," I said, glad that was the truth. "Ready to take on a challenge."

"You're not going to try backing out?"

I eyed the murky water of the canal. Nervousness skittered through my stomach, but then I reminded myself of what I'd survived recently. If I could get through that, I could learn how to row a gondola.

"I'm not backing out," I said. "But please don't push me in the water."

"Would I do that?" he asked with a mischievous glint in his eyes.

"You pushed me into the pool at Carly Holt's birthday party," I reminded him.

"I was twelve."

I crossed my arms and waited.

He relented. "I promise I won't push you in." He held out a hand to me.

I took it and he closed his fingers around mine. I stepped carefully from the dock onto the stern of the gondola. After a brief hesitation, I released Sawyer's hand and grabbed on to the oar to help steady myself.

Sawyer stepped on board and stood close behind me, one hand resting on my shoulder and the other on the oar just below my right hand.

"Ready?" he asked, speaking close to my ear.

"As I'll ever be."

He gently shifted my right hand a couple of inches farther down the oar. "You want the space between your hands to be about equal to the width between your shoulders."

"Okay. I know there's a wrist movement you need to get going."

"You move your wrists like this." He maneuvered the oar, and the gondola slowly glided away from the dock.

I tensed but then tried to focus on rowing and not on the murky water below us.

"But you're also going to use your whole body." He

shifted his hand from my shoulder to the oar, guiding it in the correct movement.

I knew the proper rowing motion helped to counteract the fact that we rowed on just one side. The asymmetrical design of the gondola also helped with that.

"There," Sawyer said, letting me do most of the work now. "You've got it." He returned his left hand to my shoulder, leaving his right hand on the oar.

I was glad we were out so early. We had the canal to ourselves, and there was no one to witness if I made a fool of myself by doing a terrible job of rowing a gondola despite the fact that I was born and raised in Larch Haven. I also appreciated having privacy for this moment with Sawyer. It felt like something I didn't want to share with anyone else.

"You know," I said, "I think I've changed my view on the lake monster."

"You've finally accepted that it's not real?"

"Oh, I still believe it's real. But when I swam to shore the other day, and all those times I swam in the lake before I knew about it, the creature never bothered me. Plus, nobody's ever been killed or harmed by it."

"Because it doesn't exist."

"We'll have to agree to disagree on that," I said. "I'm sure there's something down there, but I don't think it means us any harm. It probably just wants to be left alone."

"Does this mean you'll start swimming beyond the shallows again?"

"Probably."

"So you'll race me out to Mad Hatter Island?"

When I didn't respond right away, Sawyer laughed. I felt the rumble of it where my back pressed against his chest. It sent a rush of warmth and happiness through me.

"Maybe next summer," I said eventually. "I need a chance to get back in form."

I leaned a bit too far forward and let out a yelp as I lurched off balance.

Sawyer snaked an arm around my waist, steadying me. "You're all right."

I let out a breath of relief as I regained my balance with his help. Even if I'd never feared the dark water, I wouldn't have wanted to embarrass myself by falling in.

After recovering from that wobble, I gained some confidence and settled into the rhythm of rowing with Sawyer's guidance. I appreciated his help, and also his solid and reassuring presence behind me.

"Thank you for this," I said as he helped me navigate a bend in the canal.

"It's practically my duty as a fellow resident of Larch Haven," Sawyer said as we slid beneath a bridge and back out into the sunshine. "But even if it wasn't, I would have done it."

I smiled at that.

"Are you still planning to stay here?" he asked.

I thought I heard a note of hesitation in his voice. I wished I could see his eyes, but I wasn't about to risk turning around. I wasn't that confident on the gondola yet.

"I'm not going anywhere," I replied.

I thought his stance relaxed with my answer, but the change was too subtle to be sure it was real.

What I was sure of was my response to his question. Growing up, my dream was to work in Hollywood and be a successful actor. I'd done that. I could have taken things further if I'd stayed in LA, but my dreams had changed over time. I'd done enough acting to make myself happy, and while I sometimes missed that life, I'd miss my life in Larch Haven far more if I left again.

This town was where I was meant to be, and after recent events, I appreciated my friends, family, and neighbors all the more.

Here on the canal, in the company of a lifelong friend, I was safe and I was happy.

I was home.

RECIPES

Mint Melty Truffles

- 4 oz milk chocolate
- 4 oz whipping cream
- 2 tablespoons roughly chopped fresh mint leaves
- 8 oz dark chocolate

Finely chop the milk chocolate and place it in a heatproof bowl. In the top of a double boiler, heat the cream over medium-low heat until it's just starting to bubble. Remove the cream from the heat, add the chopped mint, and let the mixture steep for approximately 12 minutes. Then return the cream to the stove and heat again until it's just starting to bubble. Using a strainer, pour the cream into the bowl of milk chocolate, and discard the mint. Mix the cream and chocolate together until all the chocolate has melted and the ganache is smooth. Leave the ganache to cool to room temperature. Then put the ganache in the fridge until it is chilled and completely set. Remove the ganache from the fridge and use a teaspoon or small ice cream scoop to spoon up approximately half an ounce of ganache at a time. With your hands, quickly roll each scoop of ganache into a ball and set it on a baking tray lined with parchment paper. Place the tray in the fridge and chill the ganache balls. Leave them in the fridge until you're ready to dip them.

Roughly chop the dark chocolate and set approximately one-third of it aside (this is the seed chocolate). Put the remainder of the chopped chocolate in the top of a double boiler set over simmering water. Melt the chocolate and heat it until it reaches 113–118°F (45–48°C). Remove the bowl from the double boiler. Add the seed chocolate and stir until the chocolate cools to 90°F (32°C). At this point, the chocolate should be in temper.

Line another baking tray with parchment paper. Using a truffle fork or regular fork, dip each ganache ball into the tempered chocolate, making sure it is completely coated, and then set it on the prepared tray. Leave the truffles to set at room temperature or, if necessary, chill the truffles just long enough to set the chocolate.

MAKES APPROXIMATELY 24 TRUFFLES.

Peanut Butter Pretzel Truffles

- 8 oz peanut butter
- 2 tablespoons salted butter
- 2 tablespoons confectioners' sugar
- 2 teaspoons light brown sugar
- 4 oz crushed salted pretzels
- 2 tablespoons toffee bits
- 8 oz dark chocolate

In a medium bowl, mix together the peanut butter, butter, confectioners' sugar, and brown sugar. Add the crushed pretzels and toffee bits and combine.

Cover and refrigerate the peanut butter mixture for 1 hour. Roll the mixture into 1-inch balls and place in the freezer for at least 1 hour.

Roughly chop the dark chocolate and set approximately one-third of it aside (this is the seed chocolate). Put the remainder of the chopped chocolate in the top of a double boiler, over simmering water. Melt the chocolate and heat it until it reaches 113–118°F (45–48°C). Remove the bowl from the double boiler. Add the seed chocolate and stir until all the chocolate has melted and it has cooled to 90°F (32°C). At this point, the chocolate should be in temper.

Line a baking tray with parchment paper. Dip the frozen peanut butter balls in the tempered chocolate, making sure they are completely coated. Place the truffles on the prepared tray to set at room temperature or, if necessary, chill the truffles just long enough to set the chocolate.

MAKES APPROXIMATELY 22 TRUFFLES.

ACKNOWLEDGMENTS

I'm truly grateful to everyone involved in taking this book from idea to publication. Special thanks to my agent, Jessica Faust, and my editor, Leis Pederson, for believing in this series and helping me bring it to life. Thanks also to the art department at Berkley for creating such a gorgeous, eye-catching cover that fits the story perfectly. A special shout-out to Jody Holford for being such a good cheerleader and an even better friend. A big thank-you to Carina Chao for answering my questions about chocolate and the process of making bonbons and truffles. Any mistakes in that regard are mine alone. Last but not least, thank you to my review crew; my friends in the writing community; and all the librarians, Bookstagrammers, BookTubers, BookTokers, and bloggers who help to spread the word about cozy mysteries.

Keep reading for an excerpt
from the next True Confections mystery

BAKING SPIRITS BRIGHT

Chapter One

THERE WAS NO PLACE MORE MAGICAL THAN LARCH Haven, Vermont, in wintertime. The canals that wound their way through the small town had frozen solid, providing a network of skating trails, and a thick layer of snow covered the cute cottages and the timber-frame buildings. With Christmas approaching, the postcard-perfect town had become even more magical, with twinkle lights strung along the main cobblestone walkways and all of the old-fashioned lampposts wrapped with red and white ribbons so they looked like peppermint sticks.

I loved my adorable stone cottage at all times of the year, but with snow on the roof, multicolored lights lining the windows, and a wreath on the front door, it looked like it belonged in the middle of a snow globe. Every time I arrived home to my cottage and my two cats, a warm glow lit up inside me. I felt the same way whenever I entered my family's chocolate shop, True Confections. Moving back to my hometown in Vermont after living in Los Angeles for several years had definitely been a good decision.

"Ready?" my best friend, Dizzy Bautista, asked.

I finished tying up my skates. "Ready."

We left our snow boots in the shelter of my small boathouse and took our first strokes along the ice. The wind swirled around us, carrying the occasional snowflake with it and stinging my cheeks, but I didn't mind. We were on our way to get hot chocolate.

"There's something I want to show you," Dizzy said as we skated along the curving canal.

We glided beneath a stone bridge and then out into full daylight again.

Dizzy pulled a piece of paper from the pocket of her jacket. "A stack of these were dropped off at the library. I grabbed this one for you."

I accepted the slightly crumpled paper and unfolded it with my gloved hands. It was a black-and-white flyer.

While keeping one eye on the path ahead of us, I read the bold print at the top of the flyer. "Third annual Baking Spirits Bright competition."

"Haven't you always wanted to take part?" Dizzy asked, almost brimming with excitement.

"Not exactly," I said. "I've never even heard of it before."

At this time last year I'd been in Florida, visiting my parents. In the years before that, I'd been in Los Angeles.

"Okay, but now that you have, you should definitely enter."

"I'm a chocolatier, not a baker," I reminded her.

After moving home, I'd trained as a chocolatier so I could work in my family's shop. Now I spent my days making bonbons, truffles, and chocolate versions of the gondolas that were always on the canals whenever the water wasn't frozen. Although I sometimes missed my first career as an actor, I loved working at True Confections.

"But you're a good baker, too," Dizzy said. "And you can showcase your chocolate skills during the competition."

"Okay, but this would be baking with an audience. Do

you remember what happened in tenth grade cooking class?" I almost shuddered at the memory.

Dizzy and I had been partners for a project where we had to do a cooking demonstration for the class. Somehow, I'd managed to set the ends of my hair on fire. If not for Dizzy dousing me with a pot of water, I probably would have lost more than the three inches of hair that I'd had to have trimmed off.

"That was fifteen years ago," Dizzy pointed out.

"And I can still smell my hair burning like it was yesterday."

She rolled her eyes. "Becca, you've cooked and baked eleventy billion times since then without incident."

"But not with an audience."

Dizzy nudged my arm with her elbow. "You've acted on shows watched by millions of people."

"That's different. Give me a script, and I'm fine."

"Then your recipes will be your script." Dizzy twirled on the ice. "You should enter. And you should make your candy cane bonbons. The judges will love them."

"I'll think about it," I promised.

We skated around a group of giggling and gossiping teenage girls. Then the way ahead of us was clear again.

"Well, while you think about it . . ." Dizzy tore off ahead of me. "Race you to the hot chocolate stand! Loser's buying!"

I stuffed the flyer in my pocket and chased after her.

GINGERBREAD AND CANDY CANES SMELLED LIKE Christmas, and that meant the kitchen at my family's chocolate shop did too. I had a batch of gingerbread baking in the oven, making my stomach grumble with anticipation, and I was in the midst of unwrapping a candy cane. Once I had it free of the plastic wrapper, I took an appreciative sniff of the peppermint candy before setting it aside. I loved working at True Confections all year round, but Christmas was my absolute favorite time to be in the shop and in the kitchen. Although this was my first Christmas as a professional chocolatier, I'd worked in the shop part-time while growing up and had often helped my grandmother in the kitchen. Now the familiar holiday scents brought back fond memories of childhood Christmases, and there always seemed to be extra cheer and bustle these days as customers filled their shopping baskets with gifts for others and treats for themselves.

Adding to my buoyed spirits were the fluffy white flakes of snow currently falling thickly from the sky. I didn't have a great view from the kitchen window, which looked out over the narrow alley behind the shop, but maybe that was for the best. If I could see the most beautiful parts of the town, I might not get much work done. Whenever I popped out to the front of the shop, I had a difficult time tearing my gaze away from the large window and the fairy tale–like scene beyond it.

For that very reason, I'd made sure to stay put in the kitchen for the past two hours. In that time, I'd made the dough for the gingerbread and had rolled it out and cut it into the shapes of gingerbread people and Christmas trees. I'd also made a batch of eggnog truffles, as well as several Santa Clauses and snowmen from both milk chocolate and dark chocolate. Now, while the gingerbread baked, I was busy making the ganache filling for my candy cane bonbons, the ones Dizzy wanted me to make for the Baking Spirits Bright competition.

I'd thought about the possibility of entering the competition several times since she'd suggested it the day before, but I still hadn't come to a decision. I enjoyed taking part in town events, but there were far better bakers in Larch Haven than me. Chocolates were my specialty. Everything else was just an occasional hobby. Besides, the shop kept me busy, especially at this time of year.

I turned on one of the stove's gas burners and warmed up the cream in the top of a double boiler until it was just about to simmer. Then I removed it from the heat, dropped the candy cane into the pot, and left the cream to steep for several minutes. Once the cream was infused with the candy cane's flavor, I would heat it again before pouring it over a bowl full of chopped chocolate to make the ganache.

The oven timer dinged, so I grabbed a potholder and removed the trays of gingerbread from the oven, quickly replacing them with two more trays of unbaked cookies. Once the gingerbread people had cooled completely, I would give them chocolate faces and buttons. For the Christmas trees, I would pipe on chocolate baubles and garlands. The gingerbread recipe was a family one, passed down from my great-grandmother, and the cookies were popular with the shop's customers as well as with my relatives.

I set the oven timer and checked on my steeping cream. It wasn't quite ready. I gave it a couple more minutes and tasted it again. The heavenly candy cane flavor was just right.

As I reheated the cream, my cousin Angela came into the kitchen. Our grandparents had started the family chocolate business decades ago, but they had finally retired—for the most part—and Angela had taken over the business side of things while I now filled the role of chocolatier.

"Becca, it smells amazing in here," Angie said as she eyed the baked gingerbread. "Let it be noted that I'm first in line for quality control testing."

I grinned and turned off the heat under the cream. "You mean first in line after me."

"I guess that's fair, since you're the one who baked them." She held up a familiar-looking flyer. "And speaking of baking . . ."

"Dizzy told me about the competition." I poured the cream over the chopped chocolate and stirred. "Are you entering?"

"Me? No way. I can cook, but I don't bake much. There's no need when Lolly's always got something delicious to share. I was thinking *you* should enter."

"That's what Dizzy said too, but the shop is crazy at this

time of year. I don't think I'll have time for the competition." I gave the ganache a final stir and left it to cool and thicken.

"I bet Lolly would step in for you here for a couple of days. That's all you'd need, really."

She was probably right about that. Lolly—our grandmother—still enjoyed helping out at True Confections every now and then, even though she had plenty of other activities to keep her busy during her well-earned retirement. Still, I wasn't sure that I wanted to enter the competition. While I felt confident that I could wow the judges with my chocolates, I'd likely need more than that to do well overall.

"It would be a great opportunity for True Confections," Angie pressed. "Especially since *Bake It Right* is covering the competition this year."

My eyes widened. "I didn't know about that."

Bake It Right was a popular New England magazine. Pretty much everyone had at least heard of it, and its social media posts always garnered plenty of attention and engagement.

Angie had a big smile on her face. "I heard that from Jaspreet Joshi, one of the event's organizers. Isn't it amazing? It would be free advertising for True Confections. You don't even have to win to get in the magazine. They're going to profile all four of the finalists."

"Even making the finals could be a real challenge," I said, not quite ready to fully embrace the idea.

"Give yourself some credit. You're a good baker, an excellent chocolatier, and you've got great imagination and creativity."

I checked on the ganache. "Now you're buttering me up."

"Maybe, but it's all true. So, what do you say?"

I considered the idea for another moment. I enjoyed a challenge, and I always wanted to do what was best for True Confections, so maybe it wasn't a difficult decision after all.

"Where do I sign up?" I asked.

Chapter Two

AFTER I FINISHED WORK IN THE MIDDLE OF THE AFTER-noon, I stopped by the town hall to enter my name in the Baking Spirits Bright competition. Then I set off to meet up with Dizzy at the local library, where she worked. Snow still drifted down from the gray clouds overhead, but the flakes had grown smaller and fell less thickly. The town's employees had been out on their quads with snowplow attachments, clearing the cobblestone walkways that lined the canals.

Aside from golf carts and maintenance and emergency vehicles, cars and trucks weren't allowed in the downtown core of Larch Haven. When the canals weren't frozen, gondolas and whisper boats allowed for passage along the waterways. Otherwise, people mostly got around on foot or bicycle. That was one of the many things I loved about my hometown. It was so peaceful, and the pace of life was so much more relaxed than what I'd experienced while living in Los Angeles.

When I reached the library's front steps, Dizzy was on

her way out the door, pulling a knitted hat down over her dark hair. She waved when she saw me, and hurried down the steps, tugging on a pair of gloves. We'd arranged to do some Christmas shopping together that afternoon, so we headed in the direction of Venice Avenue, where True Confections and many other shops were located.

"I'm so excited you're going to be in the competition!" Dizzy said after I told her about tossing my name in the hat. "You're going to do great!"

"I'm worried I might embarrass myself."

"You definitely won't do that. You're going to make the finals and get into that magazine."

I hoped she was right.

"What are you making for the first round of competition?" she asked.

"Candy cane bonbons, like you suggested, and mandelhörnchen."

"Oh, yum. Let me know if you need a taste tester while practicing."

I laughed. "I will."

We had almost made it to Venice Avenue when Dizzy drew to a stop outside Larch Haven's only art gallery.

"We should go in here," she said. "You need some artwork to put over your fireplace."

That was true. My cottage was mostly furnished now, but some of the walls were still too bare for my liking.

"I'm supposed to be shopping for other people today," I reminded her.

"No reason why you can't do both."

I didn't resist when she tucked her arm through mine and tugged me toward the gallery.

A woman in a gray coat and gray hat stood outside the shop, facing the artwork displayed in the large front window. It wasn't until Dizzy and I reached the door that I got a look at the woman's face. She glared at the paintings in the window, as if they'd somehow insulted her. I might have thought she found the artwork distasteful if I didn't know that an expression of displeasure was typical for her.

"Hi, Irma," I said in greeting, and Dizzy added a hello of her own.

Irma turned her glare on us. Even though she was shorter than me, she managed to look down her nose at us as she strode off, never bothering to return our greetings.

"A bright ray of sunshine, as always," Dizzy said with a shake of her head.

"How can a woman who makes such delicious sweets and treats be so sour?" I asked as Dizzy opened the gallery door.

"I have no idea."

We stomped the snow off our boots and entered the gallery. Irma Jones owned the bakery situated a few doors down from True Confections. She always seemed to be in a sour mood, but I made a habit of letting her grumpiness roll right off my back. I did that now, forgetting about her almost as soon as Dizzy and I stepped inside the art gallery.

As the door drifted shut behind us, blocking the cold air, I tugged off my hat and did my best to pat down the staticky strands of my dark brown hair. There were two other customers in the gallery: a tall man in an expensive-looking dark blue suit and wool coat, and a young blond woman who currently had her back to us.

In unspoken agreement, Dizzy and I turned to the left and focused our attention on the paintings and photographs displayed on the wall.

"Afternoon, ladies." The gallery's owner, Victor Barnabas, approached Dizzy and me. His thinning dark hair was slicked back and he wore a gray three-piece suit and shiny black shoes. "Is there anything I can help you with?"

"We're just browsing at the moment, thanks," I said.

"Let me know if I can be of assistance."

He was about to leave us when Dizzy stepped closer to an autumn landscape practically bursting with fall colors.

"This is nice," she said.

Victor smiled. "You've got a good eye. Oil on canvas by Gregor Marriott."

"*The* Gregor Marriott?" I asked with surprise.

"The one and only," he confirmed.

Gregor Marriott was one of Vermont's most revered artists. He'd died a few decades ago, and I'd never seen one of his originals.

"I thought it was hard to find his work these days," Dizzy said as she continued to admire the painting. "Isn't most of his art owned by his descendants, private collectors, and museums?"

"That is the case," Victor confirmed. "But one such private collector passed away recently and his heirs want to sell off some of his collection."

I stepped closer to the card posted next to the painting so I could read the small print. My eyes widened when I saw the price of the landscape. It was definitely way out of my budget.

"I'm going to keep browsing," I said.

As I turned around, I noticed the man in the expensive suit watching us out of the corner of his eye. He quickly turned his attention to a photograph on the far wall when he realized I was looking his way.

The young blond woman I'd noticed upon first entering the gallery now stood at the sales counter. She glanced our way, catching Victor's eye, and I recognized her as a local. Her name was Paisley and she was in her midtwenties, a few years younger than me, but that was pretty much all I knew about her. She had a small watercolor painting in her hand, and Victor hurried over to help her with her purchase.

Dizzy and I moved along the wall, checking out all the paintings and photographs. I spotted several that I liked, but it wasn't until I'd almost made my way around the entire gallery that a piece of art tugged at my heart and took my breath away. The oil painting was a Larch Haven landscape, depicting one of the residential parts of the town in the springtime, with green grass growing along the canals and a gondola with a gondolier on board making its way along the water. The trees bore bright green foliage and vivid flowers bloomed in well-tended gardens. But what really caught my eye was the fact that my very own cottage was showcased in the painting.

"Oh my gosh!" Dizzy exclaimed when she reached my side. "It's like it was painted just for you!"

"My heart skipped a beat when I saw it."

Reluctantly, I tore my gaze from the painting so I could look at the card with its details. I recognized the name of the local artist, Abigail Tierney. I'd admired her paintings in the past, but none had captured my heart quite like this one. I didn't want to check the price, because I was afraid I couldn't afford it, but I made myself look anyway. Unsurprisingly, the painting would cost me a good chunk of change, but it was far more affordable than the Gregor Marriott landscape across the gallery.

"You have to get it," Dizzy whispered.

I stared at the painting with longing. "It's more than I was planning to spend."

"But the price isn't outrageous."

"I think it's pretty fair, really," I agreed. "And I can afford it. It's just a matter of *should* I spend that much money?"

"For the absolute right piece of artwork? Yes."

I thought she had a point, but I wasn't good at making big purchases on a whim.

"I need to think about it."

"Don't wait too long," Dizzy advised. "You don't want anyone else to buy it."

An idea popped into my head and I looked around the gallery, spotting Victor behind the sales counter. Paisley had already gone on her way, leaving the man in the expensive suit and Dizzy and me as the only remaining customers. I approached Victor.

"Would it be possible to hold the Abigail Tierney landscape for me for twenty-four hours?" I asked. "I'm pretty sure I want to buy it, but I need a bit of time to think about it."

"I can hold it until tomorrow at noon," he offered.

That was about twenty hours, and close enough to what I'd asked for, so I agreed and thanked him.

I spent another minute or so gazing at the painting before Dizzy and I decided to leave and get on with our Christmas shopping. As we headed for the door, the well-dressed man pointed to the Gregor Marriott autumn landscape and said to Victor, "I'll take this one."

The man had good taste. Clearly, he also had plenty of money.

Chapter Three

THE DAY OF THE FIRST ROUND OF THE BAKING SPIRITS Bright competition arrived with a clear sky and a cold, biting wind from the north. As much as I loved winter, I wasn't keen to leave my cottage, not once I saw the temperature on the weather app on my phone.

"I'm going to need extra cuddles to keep me warm," I told my two cats, Truffles and Binx.

Truffles, my gray tabby, sat at my feet in the kitchen and looked up at me with a meow, as if to say she was happy to oblige. I scooped her up into my arms as her brother, my green-eyed black cat, pounced on his catnip banana and somersaulted with the toy clutched in his two front paws. He then zoomed around the cottage. I laughed as Truffles purred against my chest. It took a couple of minutes, but I was finally able to scoop Binx into my arms when he stopped for a breath. Only once I'd given him a hug was I ready to head out into the dark, cold morning.

Outside, the crescent moon glowed bright over the mountains and the biting wind wiped away the last vestiges of my sleepiness. Most of the shops and homes were still dark. The only light I could see on Venice Avenue—aside from that of the streetlamps—was a faint glow in the bakery. I was an early riser, but Irma was always earlier than me. She, like many bakers, probably started work in the middle of the night.

By the time I reached True Confections, my fingers and toes were almost numb. I quickly warmed up once inside and I spent the next couple of hours making chocolates to replenish the shop's supply. Lolly would come in later to relieve me, so I could take time away for the competition, but I wanted to get as much done as possible before then. Working also helped to distract me and keep the worst of my nerves at bay.

After unmolding the last batch of chocolates I planned to make that morning—aside from the ones I'd make for the competition—I washed my hands, drawing in a deep, shaky breath as the warm water ran over my skin. Now that I'd stopped focusing on work, my nerves were taking over.

I heard footsteps out in the hall as I dried my hands. Seconds later, my friend Sawyer Maguire appeared in the kitchen doorway, wearing his police jacket over his uniform.

"Hey," he greeted. "I wanted to stop by to wish you luck. All set for the competition?"

"I think so?" I sounded as uncertain as I felt.

"You'll do great, Becca," Sawyer assured me.

"Thanks." I managed to smile. "I guess I should head on over to the town hall." That was the venue for the competition. Temporary baking stations had been set up in the hall's largest room, along with several rows of chairs for those who wanted to watch the competition unfold.

"What do you need to take with you?" Sawyer asked.

"Just what's in this box." I tapped the cardboard box sitting on the edge of the counter. We'd be provided with basic baking dishes and utensils at the competition, but I'd packed a few of my own favorite tools in the box along with my chocolate molds and all the ingredients I would need.

"Are you walking?"

"Yes." I was hoping the cold air and exercise would help to settle my nerves.

I passed Sawyer and crossed the hall to the office, where I'd stashed my outerwear. He followed me and then leaned against the office doorframe. "I'll carry the box for you."

"You're on duty," I reminded him.

"I'm heading in that direction anyway."

"In that case, I won't say no to the help or the company."

I quickly stepped into my boots and pulled on my coat and hat. I stowed my shoes in a bag to take with me so I wouldn't have to wear my snow boots while baking. We crossed the hall and had just returned to the kitchen when my grandmother appeared in the doorway.

"Oh, good," she said when she saw me. "I was hoping I wasn't too late to wish you good luck."

I accepted a hug from her. "Thank you, Lolly. I hope I won't disappoint everyone."

Lolly patted my cheek. "That wouldn't even be possible."

I smiled at that, and then quickly brought her up to speed on what chocolates I'd made that morning and what still needed to be done. After that, she shooed me out of the kitchen, so Sawyer grabbed the box and we headed out the front door of the shop.

"Are you okay?" Sawyer asked after we'd walked along in silence for a couple of minutes.

"I'm nervous," I confessed. "Way more than I should be. I know it's not a huge deal if I don't make it into the finals, but I want to do well. If I let my nerves get the best of me, that might not happen."

"Maybe pretend that you're playing the role of a baker in a movie," Sawyer suggested. "Would that help?"

I turned the idea over in my mind, remembering Dizzy's tip about viewing my recipes as my scripts. "Actually, it might." The sharpest edge of my nervousness dulled and I smiled. "Thanks. That's a great idea."

My first career as an actor had given me plenty of experience with playing characters. I felt far more comfortable acting than baking in front of an audience, that was for sure. Sawyer's suggestion gave me a way to draw from that comfort.

When we reached the town hall, we stopped outside the front door. The first snowflakes of the day drifted lazily down around us.

"I wish I could stay to cheer you on," Sawyer said as he passed me the box.

"I appreciate you walking with me. And helping me with my anxiety."

Sawyer's radio squawked. He listened to whatever was coming through his earpiece for a second. "I need to get going," he said when he was done listening. "Text me to let me know how it goes?"

"I will," I promised.

After Sawyer left, I made my way into the town hall. I stopped inside the door, trying to do as Sawyer suggested and approach the competition like an acting role. When I felt like I had the right frame of mind, I moved toward the open door on the far side of the foyer.

I'd only made it two steps when the front door opened behind me, letting in a rush of icy air. I turned around to find Stephanie Kang entering the town hall, an overstuffed tote bag in each hand. Snowflakes dotted her long black hair and she wore a knee-length down coat.

She smiled brightly when she saw me. "Hey, Becca. You're in the competition too?"

"And hoping not to make a fool of myself." My nerves had made a sudden comeback. Stephanie owned a cake shop in Larch Haven and made the most divine cupcakes I'd ever tasted. I'd also caught a glimpse of Irma Jones through the open door to the next room. She might not win any personality contests, but as a professional baker she'd be hard to beat. I was up against some stiff competition.

"That's not going to happen," Stephanie said, sounding certain. "You make the best chocolates I've ever tasted."

That brought a smile to my face. "Thank you. I can say the same about your cupcakes."

She beamed at the compliment, and her cheery disposition gave my spirits a boost. We entered the town hall's main room together, where approximately a dozen people had already gathered. Four baking stations stood at the far end of the room. Stephanie and I followed the aisle between the rows of folding chairs to reach a petite woman who stood by the baking stations with a clipboard in her hand. She had black hair in a thick braid that nearly reached down to her waist.

"You must both be competitors," she said when she saw Stephanie and me approaching. "I'm Jaspreet, one of the organizers. If you have any questions, you can bring them to me. But first, can I get your names, please?"

We provided her with the requested information and she ticked off our names on her list.

"We have sixteen people entered in the competition, so we'll have four rounds of four competitors," she explained. "Becca, you're in the first group, and Stephanie, you're in the third."

I'd already received that information by email the day before, and I was glad to be among the first up. Waiting until later in the day would have given me more time to stress about the caliber of my competition. Jaspreet directed me to one of the farthest baking stations and told me I could get myself organized. I was relieved to see that Irma wasn't getting ready to bake in the first round. Instead, she sat in the front row of chairs, arms crossed and eyes closed. I would have found it intimidating to have Stephanie or Irma in my group. Even though I was still technically competing against both women, I wouldn't be constantly comparing myself to them as I worked.

My relief was short-lived, however. Within minutes of my arrival, Roman Kafka strode into the town hall, carrying a clear plastic tub with a black lid. He paused to talk to Jaspreet, who sent him to the baking station next to mine.

"Morning," I said with a smile as he set his tub on the counter.

He nodded in acknowledgment, his expression serious and intense.

I'm just playing the part of a baker, I told myself. *The part of a very competent, calm baker.*

Roman Kafka worked as a pastry chef at the Gondolier, one of Larch Haven's most popular restaurants, owned by my brother, Gareth, and his husband, Blake. I'd eaten several of Roman's desserts and knew he was highly skilled. I was starting to feel like I was in over my head, but after another minute of convincing myself that I was a competent baker, I got control of my nerves and began organizing my station.

Over the next five minutes, the remaining two bakers in my group arrived. One was a nervous-looking young woman who couldn't have been more than twenty years old. Her gray eyes darted left and right and she fidgeted almost constantly. Watching her made me feel nervous again, so I quickly shifted my focus elsewhere. The fourth member of our group was a gray-haired woman who looked to be in her seventies. I'd seen both women around town, but I didn't know either of them.

By the time I had my baking station all organized, about half of the seats in the audience had been filled. Three chairs had been set apart from all the rest, with a sign on each declaring that it was reserved for a judge. Jaspreet was in conversation with three people, who soon broke away from her and settled in the reserved chairs. One of the judges was Victor Barnabas, the owner of the art gallery where I'd bought my new painting. I'd decided to bite the bullet and had made the purchase the day after I'd first seen the piece of art. Now it hung over my fireplace.

The second judge, Natalia Mehta, was the head chef at the Larch Haven Hotel, and the third, Consuela Diaz, owned a small café. I decided to ignore the three of them as best I could. I wanted to focus on baking rather than what the judges might be thinking at any given time.

As I waited for the competition to begin, my gaze traveled around the room and came to an abrupt halt on the well-dressed man I'd seen at the art gallery several days ago. Once again, he wore an expensive-looking suit. With his wool coat draped over his arm, he paused just inside the main room before heading toward the rows of folding chairs.

At some point, Irma had stirred from her nap and left her chair. She intercepted the well-dressed man before he could sit down. I watched as she spoke quietly with him, a smug expression on her face. The man shook his head when she finished speaking and said something to her before calmly walking to the nearest vacant chair and sitting down.

Irma no longer appeared smug. She glared at the man's back before storming to the front row and dropping into the same seat as before. I didn't know how anyone could be in such a foul mood all the time. I felt sorry for her. She obviously wasn't a happy woman. I doubted she'd think much of my pity, though.

I took in the sight of the rest of the small audience that had gathered in the room. Dizzy was at work, but she'd texted me earlier in the day, wishing me luck and telling me I was going to do a great job. A smile broke out across my face when I spotted my brother-in-law, Blake, seated in the back row. When I caught his eye, he grinned and gave me a thumbs-up. Having him there for moral support made me feel much calmer. Whatever the outcome, I was determined to have fun as I baked.

Jaspreet took the floor in front of the audience and gave a quick spiel about how the competition would work. Then she introduced my fellow bakers and me, as well as the judges.

"Bakers, you will have ninety minutes to complete your bakes," she said. "Starting . . . now!"

Tuning out everything around me, I grabbed some ingredients and got to work.